LAST
NIGHT

Also by Karen Ellis

A Map of the Dark

*

Karen Ellis is the author of *A Map of the Dark* (book
one in The Searchers series) as well as numerous other
novels. She lives in Brooklyn, New York. Learn more at
karenellisbooks.com

KAREN ELLIS

LAST NIGHT

MULHOLLAND
BOOKS
HODDER

First published in Great Britain in 2019 by Mulholland Books
An imprint of Hodder & Stoughton
An Hachette UK company

1

A CIP catalogue record for this title is available from the British Library

Trade Paperback ISBN 978 1 473 66281 0
eBook ISBN 978 1 473 66283 4

Printed and bound by CPI Group (UK) Ltd, Croydon, CR0 4YY

Hodder & Stoughton policy is to use papers that are natural, renewable
and recyclable products and made from wood grown in sustainable forests.
The logging and manufacturing processes are expected to conform to the
environmental regulations of the country of origin.

Hodder & Stoughton Ltd
Carmelite House
50 Victoria Embankment
London EC4Y 0DZ

www.hodder.co.uk

For my children, Eli and Karenna,
beloved inspirations.

PART ONE

Tell It to the Judge

1

For the real event they'll be starched versions of themselves, in blue gowns and tasseled mortarboards, but Crisp likes this better: the sea of kids in ripped jeans with rings and tats in full flare; teachers scattered in the back rows of the vast auditorium, casually enjoying the fruits of their labor. A party mood, with mostly just the elders paying attention to his rehearsal of the valedictory, The Speech he practiced at home, over and over, for his mother and grandparents.

Center stage, he finishes: "…and that is why my years at Stuyvesant have been not just formative, but inspiring. *Aut viam inveniam aut faciam*—I shall either find a way or make one."

An explosion of applause tells him that he was wrong—people *were* listening. Adrenaline nearly lifts him off the stage, and there he is, floating over everyone, smiling, laughing, reaching down to feel a thousand fingertips graze the palms of his hands. Feeling like the

3

new balloon at next year's Thanksgiving Day Parade, representing...what? A brown-skinned, fro-headed hybrid of a young man with high-tops clean and white, the way he likes them, and—here's the kicker—*something to say*.

He levitates through the rest of rehearsal and then the 687 other seniors are dismissed until morning, when the official ceremony will take place.

Outside in the buttery June afternoon, Crisp unlocks his bike and flies along Chambers Street and onto the Brooklyn Bridge. Dodging pedestrians with pinball precision, the lightweight bike so attuned to him that it feels like part of his body. Ignoring dirty looks and riding fast, faster across the wingspan suspended between two urban shores. Energized by the fact that a lifetime of New York City public schools is behind him. Wondering how, *if*, he'll fit in next year at Princeton. The sharp tip of that thought bursts his bubble and he feels the air begin to seep out of him. Of course, it won't be easy. He slows along the bridge's off-ramp, merges into traffic, and comes to a stop at the intersection of Tillary and Adams.

"You." A short, burly cop standing in front of the corner diner waves him over. "Come here."

"Me?" Crisp points to himself, his mind whirring.

"You deaf?"

"No, sir." Crisp pedals onto the sidewalk, comes to a stop near the officer, and hops off his bike. "Did I do something wrong?"

The cop rips a curled printout off his ticketing device and hands it to Crisp with a dead-eyed stare.

"What's this for?"

"Can't you read?"

Crisp looks at the ticket and there it is: a hundred-dollar fine and a court summons for riding his bicycle on the sidewalk. He swallows the bitter foretaste of a percolating anger.

"Officer Russo," getting the name off the lopsided tag beneath the badge, "I rode over because you told me to."

"It's against the law to ride your bike on the sidewalk. You oughta know that, kid."

"But you *told* me to come over. When I was riding in the *street*."

"You saying you didn't ride on the sidewalk just now?"

"No, but—"

"You think I'm blind?"

"No."

"Don't do it again." Russo begins to move away.

Color flushes out of Crisp's fingers, he's gripping his handlebars so hard. He shouts, "Who do you think you are? Franz fucking Kafka?" He inches his bike closer to Russo and jerks it to a stop.

"What'd you call me?"

"Franz Kafka is a *who,* not a what. *Sir*. But you wouldn't know that—fucking idiot." He'd meant to think that last part, but somehow the words hissed out.

Forehead sweaty, jowls shaking, Russo whips out a set of handcuffs.

"You've got to be fucking kidding me!"

"Oh, I am not kidding you, son." He snaps open one bracelet and latches it to Crisp's left wrist.

"'Son'? You think you're my father now?"

Muttering the standard Miranda warnings, Russo yanks Crisp's right hand off the handlebar and clinches the second bracelet. The bike crashes to the sidewalk.

"I didn't do anything wrong!"

"Assaulting an officer. Resisting arrest. And now—" Russo glances at the fallen bike. "—littering."

"*Assault?* How?"

"Verbal assault with threat of physical violence."

"What? This is insane!"

"Trying to mow me down with that bike."

"I did not!"

"Tell it to the judge."

2

A rhythmic snapping echoes onto the Dreyfus family rooftop. Lying in the sun, Glynnie opens her eyes and something Ms. Abrams said in class last week returns with a jolt. She said, "It used to be that identity was internalized *before* it was externalized. These days it's the reverse, it seems to me."

It seems to me. Glynnie lops off that final clause in her mind, as a favor to Ms. Abrams, who all year tormented everyone by denuding bold statements with self-doubt. Making these big, interesting statements and then, *wham,* killing them with a weak finish. It was the last English class Glynnie would ever, *ever* take in her life—hallelujah. Another week of freedom before being packed off to *fucking Outward Bound*.

She closes her eyes and conjures Ms. Abrams's face: oval, freckly, a face that never managed to carry authority all through senior year. It isn't that Ms. Abrams is too young or isn't smart; it's that she's unsure of herself.

Glynnie brings the roach to her lips and nearly burns her fingers lighting it. Waves out the match. Breathes deeply, holds in the smoke, lets it out in a wandering cloud. Feels the shiver pass into her brain, loosening her thoughts. The lift. The expansion.

Yes, that's it. That's Ms. Abrams's problem: *She's insecure.*

Snap snap snap.

Ms. Abrams's face fragments like cracked glass. Glynnie opens her eyes again. She lets one bare foot drop off the chaise onto the wood deck, thinking she might investigate the sound, but then she sees what it is, where it's coming from, and lies back down to continue letting the rays soak unfiltered into her skin. The air just a bit chilly on her nipples, puckered in little salutes to the sun. So good to be out here, topless, alone, on a warm blue day after the long winter and meandering spring.

Snap snap snap.

Sitting up, she can make out, in the near distance, several figures milling around inside the caged recreation area on top of the Brooklyn House of Detention, though she can't see any detail. Just a bunch of guys shooting hoops. Exercise hour. Happens every day. But something about the sound of the ball seems different today— sharper, angrier, with every bounce crackling through her nerves.

"Identity was internalized *before* it was externalized," Ms. Abrams said.

Glynnie suddenly understands, really gets what the teacher meant. She reaches her arms out to the sides, flexes her fingers. Yup. It used to be that people had time and space to think, but not anymore. You'd have a chance to know who you are before you wondered who you should be. That's what Ms. Abrams was talking about last week. Finally, at the bitter end, the woman teaches her something that might be worthwhile. Chaucer never penetrated, that's for sure.

Internalized identity. What, she wonders, is *hers*? She knows what it looks like from the outside—her demographics, her family—but from the inside?

The other night she overheard her father on the phone talking to whoever, a Scotch in his hand: "Seven million—that's what our brownstone's at now. Give it a year to reach eight." His voice oozy with intoxication equals booze plus self-satisfaction.

Fucking bourgeoisie. Worse: one percenter. Not *her* fault she's his kid.

Between the Dreyfus manse and the House of Detention two blocks north, a patchwork of windows reveals the lives of condo tenants—million a unit, Glynnie's dad once guessed, maybe two. Seven floors in all, possibly a dozen units per floor—half a full block of "gold coast real estate" was how her dad described it to whoever he was talking to that time. Whoever the Scotch was talking to. Sober, Nik Dreyfus didn't brag about money things; compared to his fancy clients, he was practically poor.

Glynnie hates it, really hates it, all this…this greed…hypocrisy. It doesn't represent *her*. It's not how she *feels*. She feels agitated, restless, bored. But what does any of that *mean*?

She takes another toke and extinguishes the blunt on the side of the chaise.

A window shade in one of the condos across the street blinks shut. Towering behind it, an entire universe away, that *snap snap snap* atop the House announces something less serene. Glynnie stares past a woman watering a condo roof garden and at the shadows milling inside the basketball cage that looms higher than the nearer building by at least three stories. Dark figures whom she imagines darkly (there you go, Ms. Abrams: finally, a poetic turn of phrase from the class fuckup), distinguishable only by slight variations in height.

And then: "I see you!" A voice sails out of the cage. A real voice. Male, plump with intent.

She holds a hand above her eyes to block the sun.

He's standing up against the fence, facing her direction. The basketball is no longer dribbling, she realizes, and in the unanticipated silence the shadow turns into a young faceless brown man with a six-inch fralo (*fro* meets *halo*— her own word; *I'm a poet, don't you know it*). The bulge of basketball pinned between arm and hip. The sky above him a springtime cerulean she wishes she could lick clean of its wispy clouds.

She shouts, "I see you, too!" Testing her instinct that this is a direct communication traversing worlds, that she isn't nuts and he's actually talking to *her*.

"Save some for me!" His voice is bold, edged with what she reads as humor, but she isn't quite sure. She doesn't like not being sure; she wants to know. Save some what? Weed? Or is he referring to her breasts? She suddenly feels as naked as she is but refuses to cover herself up. This is the body she was given at birth; it's a gift that belongs to *her,* and she's proud of it, and *Shut the fuck up* if you think it means anything else.

Bracketing her mouth with both hands to direct all her voice at the cage, she yells, "Come over, why don't you?" Knowing he can't, because he's locked up for some crime he committed...*allegedly*.

A lull, a pocket of surprise. Another man joins him at the fence. And then laughter. But what kind of laughter? At themselves and their predicaments, being caged in— though she imagines they don't find that very funny—or at her? She isn't ready to finish this; she *needs* to know.

"What?" Standing up, spreading her wings. "Can't you fly?" Half naked, open armed, she twirls across her rooftop. Sun queen, temptress, high-school graduate *at long last*. Then, just for the hell of it, she leans over her mother's Italian planter, where a bush of English roses is about to bloom, and spits.

3

Crisp presses the hard curve of the basketball into his ribs, and looks at the half-naked girl on the roof across the way getting stoned in full view of everyone. There's something about her that reminds him of someone, but he can't think who. What, he wonders, would happen to *her* if *she* was locked up and missed the last arraignment roster of the day?

Bullshit.

He knows exactly what would happen; half the kids at his school are just like her. Her parents or somebody would make *sure* she got onto that roster so she wouldn't have to wait her turn to get her charges read out, the judge's decision on bail or no bail, release or more detention. *No way* would anyone with a roof-deck like that (out of the pages of a magazine, with its cushions and sun umbrella and flowerpots and trees—yes, even trees) let their lily-white princess spend a night in jail, which is exactly what happens when you're not on the afternoon's last roster. *No way* would anyone let *her* stand in this cage if she was in his shoes.

Double bullshit.

No way would she even get arrested to begin with. Because she's white. And a girl. And rich—he can see that just by looking at her right now *in the context of her environment,* his sociology teacher Alan might say.

"Huh," Crisp mutters. He palms the ball and triple dribbles it hard.

That's exactly where he is now too: *in the context of his environment as seen through the lens of race and socioeconomics.* And that lens doesn't read anyone as half black, as he is, or half poor, as he is. He *knows* who he is and where he is: stranded in jail with a bunch of other boys and men trapped in their dark skins, missing out, watching that girl dancing around on her rooftop, flapping her arm-wings, feeling the sun and the air on her skin, without any reason in the world to think she'd ever get her liberty taken away.

He wants to shout back at the roof girl, "Sure I can fly! Yes I can!" But what's the point? He's here, she's there. He turns his back and throws the ball to the first man-boy he sees across the cage.

And then he realizes what he recognized about her. It was a certain singsong in her voice when she said that last thing—"What, can't you fly?"—that was familiar, and suddenly he remembers. She's a friend of his friend from school. Over the winter break a bunch of Stuyvesant kids hung out with a bunch of Brooklyn Friends kids, and yeah, right, *her.* She was cool. She did a rap on his name, made him smile.

He claws his fingers through the chain-link fence and shouts across the roofscape, "Glynnie? Yo, Sarah Bernhardt!," which is what he called her that night because of the nutty expressions she made when she sang. She had an unusually flexible face.

She stops dancing and wraps her arms around herself to cover her breasts and her jaw drops open, and he knows she remembers him too.

She yells, *"Crisp Crespo, the Crisco King of Coney? What the fuck!"* She jumps around and shakes her ass at him and cracks up laughing, and he can't help it. He laughs right along with her.

PART TWO

Rumors and Time

4

Friday

The phone won't ring but Detective Lex Cole stares at it anyway, then hates himself for waiting for Adam's call and looks away, then turns back to the silent screen clenched in his hand: that cruel rectangular void.

He switches the phone to vibrate, puts it facedown on his desk, and checks the new case log on his monitor— nothing in since he last looked. After an initial flurry of activity at the start of the night shift, it's as if the whole southern end of Brooklyn went to sleep all at once. Now it's just him and Toby Rios left in the 6-0 squad room. His colleague must have opened a window because suddenly a brisk salty breeze and the rhythm of nearby waves fill the room.

"Think I'll step outside a minute," Lex tells Toby.

When Toby lifts his head from whatever file he's reading, a sheen of light from the overhead bounces off his pate. "Sure thing."

As soon as Lex stands, his right calf muscle cramps,

followed by a note of craving he immediately silences—
that old song of pain wanting relief and the slippery slope
of getting it. Out on the surf that afternoon, he felt the
vibration of a wave coming up behind him and turned to
carve his board into it: flashes of silver light, an exhila-
rating lift out of time. He rode the swell as it chased him
back to shore. As the wave shrank, he felt, irrationally,
as if his mastery had subdued it. Right away another one
crept up, powerful, ready to teach him a lesson. Turning
to meet it, he thought he glimpsed Adam standing on the
beach, watching him—handsome Adam, pale with his
thatch of black hair, light and dark like a two-tone cat. It
wasn't Adam, though: it was another man who vaguely
resembled him. In that single, hapless moment, Lex's calf
seized and he nearly lost his balance. A moment of injury
in its full innocence; the treachery always came later.

He bends to push a hand into his boot and massage the
muscle. Slides his phone into the back pocket of his jeans
and heads for the stairwell down to the first floor.

Out on West Eighth Street in the moonlit darkness he listens to the roar of the ocean. Coney Island
is uncharacteristically quiet, the Wonder Wheel at rest,
Luna Park's dazzle switched off. The solitude grips and
terrifies him. He reaches for his phone and almost calls
Adam, but resists the urge. Let Adam be the one to break
the silence.

Toby clips past, jangling a set of keys to one of the
precinct cars. "Caught one. I told Minnick you're out here
if someone else comes in."

"Thanks," Lex says. Whatever lands next will be his.

After that, new cases will have to wait in line for whoever gets back first.

Just as he's about to head inside, his phone vibrates and he stops breathing. The screen comes alive in his hand, but not with Adam's name.

A text from his brother, David:

> Sorry to ask but any chance you could bring Ethan to school tomorrow morning? Babysitter's sick and I've got an early meeting with the AG.

David's been angling since late winter for that meeting with the New York State attorney general, wanting to discuss a judgeship that's about to open. Justice David Cole. Smiling, Lex taps out his response.

> Short answer-yes. Long answer-if I don't get derailed by a case. Better arrange a backup. Otherwise see u @7, that work?

> Yes and will do and I owe you one.

> Another one u mean.

> ☺

Second time this month. David should consider finding either a new babysitter or a second wife. But in truth, Lex enjoys his rare one-on-one time with his nine-year-old nephew. Once Ethan is old enough to get himself back and forth to school and spend a few hours alone in the apartment, there won't be any more calls for standby parenting on David's custody days. Lex doesn't look forward to the moment he'll stop being the cool cop uncle and become just another asshole authority figure.

On his way through the lobby he nods at Minnick, the front-desk officer, mealy in his uniform, with a fringe of thinning hair poking out from beneath his cap. Minnick nods back in acknowledgment of the detective's return.

A small woman clutching her purse to her side blasts through the precinct entrance and announces to Minnick, "My son is missing!" Her shoulder-length brown hair is frizzed from the moist night air, defying an apparent effort to straighten it. Lex pauses in the stairwell door. This is unusual, someone coming on foot to report a missing person; typically they panic and pick up the phone.

He turns and watches Minnick suck in his cheeks as he faces the monitor on his desk and clicks through to open a new case report. The officer asks, "How old is your son?"

"Nineteen."

"Oh. Okay." Minnick clicks through to a different page, presumably having opened a report for a missing minor, based on the mother's relative youth and her level of agitation. As he takes down the basics, Lex backtracks to the front desk; the case is just going to find its way upstairs to him anyway. Glad for something to think about not-Adam, he takes the printout that Minnick hands him.

"I'm Detective Lex Cole." He gives the mother his card. "How can I help?"

Her forehead ruts. "My son never came home tonight. He was arrested yesterday and then—"

He glances at the report—her name is Katya Spielman—and interrupts, "Mrs. Spielman, let's go talk somewhere quieter."

"It's quiet right here." Impatience spikes her tone. "And it isn't *Mrs.* I'm divorced."

"My mistake." He says it gently, in the hope of knitting a strand of calm into her worry. He leads her to one of the first-floor interrogation rooms, windowless gray walls that might have been white once, the metal table etched with someone's initials.

She looks at his card, then at him. "Your full name is Alexei."

"Yes, but everyone calls me Lex." He sits, and gestures toward the opposite chair. "You were starting to tell me that your son," he looks at the report, "Titus—"

"He also doesn't use his given name. He goes by Crisp."

"Crisp. That's unique, but then so is Titus."

"I'm so worried."

"You were saying that Crisp was arrested yesterday, meaning Wednesday, right? Technically today's already Friday. Just to be clear."

"Yes, Wednesday. On his way home from school."

Lex listens carefully, taking notes as she unspools the story: her son's ticket for riding his bicycle on the sidewalk, followed by a "wrongful arrest" for assaulting an officer, "which he would never, ever do." He spent a night in the Brooklyn House of Detention before finally appearing on the arraignment roster at around noon.

She explains, "When he got home this afternoon—no, that would be yesterday afternoon now, Thursday—he wasn't good. He looked exhausted, obviously, but it was more than jail. It was missing his graduation yesterday morning—*speaking* at his graduation—the honor of being valedictorian gone because some cop was trying to meet his quota. The principal himself tried pulling strings, but it was too late."

"If the arrest was wrongful," Lex assures her, "the charge will be thrown out."

"It *was* wrongful. But then..." She lowers her face into her hands to stifle a groan of frustration. "I *never* should have told him that the Princeton dean's office left a message. That was a mistake."

"It upset him?"

"They gave him a full scholarship—everything, even housing. He must be worried they found out about the arrest, but who knows why they called? He said he'd return the call later, but I pressed the issue, and then he stormed out—and that was that."

"He's nineteen."

"Yes."

"An adult."

"Only technically."

"Yeah, I get that, I do. But usually we give it a little time when it's an adult, especially when it's an older teenager."

"This is a good boy. An *unusual* boy."

"You said you're divorced—could he have spent the night with his father?"

"My ex-husband isn't in the picture, not since Crisp was a baby."

"Does he have a girlfriend? Buddies he stays over with sometimes?"

"No girlfriend, no friends close enough to stay over. He's more of an...an...*intellectual*. He spends time with the family, me and his grandparents, and he reads. A lot. He has never gone out and not come home. Crisp would call, absolutely, unless something prevented it. This is a good boy—valedictorian of his class."

Lex realizes that she's started to repeat herself; it's not unusual for worried family members to lose themselves in a loop. The wall clock tells him that it's coming on three a.m. Pushing back his chair, he makes a promise. "Katya, I'll do everything I can to find your son as soon as humanly possible."

"Thank you." She picks up her purse as if about to stand, but pauses. "Detective, if you don't mind—do I hear an accent? Russian, maybe?"

"You've got a good ear. Most people don't hear it."

"I grew up with Russian parents. I still live with them; they helped me raise my son."

Lex smiles. "That's nice."

"I'm curious: How long have you been here?"

"Twenty-two years, since I was a kid."

"You came with your parents?"

"No. Long story." He stands. "I'm curious about something too: Why did you come all the way here instead of calling?"

"We live nearby, in Brighton Beach." The runnels

deepen across her forehead. "Also, our apartment is small and I didn't want my parents to hear me talking. My mother had a massive heart attack last year. I can't worry her unless it's absolutely necessary."

"I'd probably do the same thing," he reassures her, though in fact he has no idea what it's like to be an adult child with aging parents. His didn't stick around long enough to sprout gray hair. "I'll get in touch the minute I know something."

"Thank you, Detective Cole."

"Lex."

"Thank you, Lex."

Back in the squad room, the pluck of classical guitar tells Lex that Gaston Fulton got back sometime while he was downstairs with Katya Spielman. Some of the guys did that when they found themselves alone: playing their own music right in the common space. If it was Toby, it would have been jazz. Jason Kahn, rap. Tag Riordan, salsa. Lex never plays music here, even when he has the chance—a habit, he realizes only now, from home, where Adam is the resident DJ.

The trill of notes cuts off abruptly as soon as Lex walks in. "No need," he tells Gaston. "I like it."

"You sure?"

"Yeah."

The music resumes.

At his desk, Lex can't help wondering if Katya Spielman overreacted by reporting her son missing so soon. It's not unusual for nineteen-year-olds to stay out all night, regardless of how angelic their mothers think they are.

He starts by opening the arrest record. Just as his mother described, Crisp was stopped for riding his bicycle on the sidewalk, and then the incident escalated. The report details an arrest for "disorderly conduct after the subject verbally berated the arresting officer." Lex shakes his head, seeing that; it's perfectly legal to curse out a cop. What exactly did the kid say? Or is PO Mario Russo especially thin-skinned?

From there, everything Lex learns using the information and log-ins that Ms. Spielman gave him only confirms her glowing assessment of her son. In his college recommendations, his high-school principal calls him "one of the best students we've ever had here, and that's saying something." His history and literature teachers call him "exemplary" and "brilliant." His math teacher says that Crisp is "really impressive for a humanities kid." His French, Latin, Spanish, and Italian teachers all cite an "extraordinary gift" for languages. Lex learns that Princeton isn't the only fancy school to offer him a full ride: so did Stanford, and Columbia, Harvard, Yale, and Brown all came close.

Lex sits back, stares at the ceiling, listens to a tricky onslaught of guitar notes. Maybe the mother was right to worry. But at nineteen, it's too soon to raise an alarm.

His calf twinges and he hoists his boot onto the desk and digs in to massage the muscle and silence the cry. In a gap of thought, he recalls the last things he and Adam said to each other the night before. Their argument— no, *fight;* that's how nasty it got, their words flying at each other like precision weapons only people who know each other well can deploy with real damage. He accused

Adam of keeping secrets. Adam accused him of being paranoid. They both said things they shouldn't have said and could never take back. "Devious." "Monster."

"Just tell me what you're doing every night," Lex demanded. Again. Adam was a doctoral student in psychology who, if he wasn't at the library, spent a lot of time at home. There was no obvious reason for him to slip out so often, so late and for so long. It had been going on for over a week.

Again Adam answered, "Nothing."

"You never lied to me before. I've always trusted you."

"You can still trust me, Lex."

"Where do you go?"

"I told you: I'm doing something to help a friend."

"Who?"

"Please stop asking."

But Lex knew: Adam was seeing someone else. And then he would leave Lex, because that's what Adam did. He'd lived with his last boyfriend, William, for nearly three years before their breakup just over a year ago— a breakup triggered by what started as a fling with Lex. He remembers seeing Adam for the first time, at a party thrown by their mutual friend Diana; he was holding a beer on her light-strung roof-deck. Remembers how good Adam looked in his dark jeans and purple shirt. How drunk and disorderly William became before he was dragged home by his long-suffering partner. Soon after, Lex and Adam met for coffee, then kept meeting. Adam admitted that he'd had enough of his valiant efforts to keep his alcoholic boyfriend afloat. That was when Lex put out his hand and his heart, and Adam took them both. At the time, Lex saw Adam's leaving William as an act of strength, not a foretaste of the weakness that would not only destroy them too, but lead Lex back to his own worst place.

"You know what?" Lex blurted. "I've had enough. Don't come back. Stay with him, whoever he is this time." Why should he wait to be left? He'd never said anything like that to Adam before and it startled them both. And Adam, compassionate Adam, had never looked at him so blankly, as if something inside him had snapped. Lex felt suspended in middle space—that moment after you've broken something delicate and beloved, when you wish you could rewind time but you can't.

"You got it," Adam said. "I'm out." The door slammed and the apartment shook and Lex was alone.

Adam wasn't home when Lex got back from work in the morning. He darkened the bedroom and tried to sleep but, despite exhaustion, couldn't. Eventually he gave up and took his surfboard to the beach, desperate to free his mind of suspicion, but the questions followed him and the moment he thought he saw Adam on shore…well. That was pretty much how it had happened in college with his baseball injury: a moment of distraction, a misplacement of form, the backward snap of his wrist in service to a home run, followed quickly by blackout, hospital, opioid haze, and, within a year, that single treacherous taste of heroin. The opening of a hole, an abyss, of perpetual craving. A person-size hole now, with the prospect of Adam leaving.

Through the raised window he sees a plane buzz across the sky.

Moving his sore leg off the desk, Lex promises himself, as he did last night, that if Adam *isn't* leaving him, if he *does* come home, he'll follow his boyfriend next time he gets the chance. Then, just as forcefully, he promises himself that he would never sink so low. Things between them were so easy, so good, for so long. When did that change?

He awakens his monitor and there again is the problem of Crisp Crespo. Lex makes a decision: if the teenager still doesn't turn up soon, he'll head over to Brighton Beach and canvass the area for anyone who might have seen him after he left his family's apartment. If he does turn up, Lex will head to Brooklyn Heights and take Ethan to school. Work. Plans. *That* is how to fill the hole.

5

Detective Saki Finley pretends not to notice her colleague Jack Dinardo's low thrum of laughter as she arrives for her early-morning shift. The sound of the squishy soles of her Wallabees squeaking across the tiled floor of the 8-4 squad room has never failed to amuse the old fart.

Maybe, she thinks, eyes anchored to the goal of her neatly organized desk at the far end of the unit, maybe if Dinardo ever did any real work he wouldn't have so much attention to spare for her sartorial preferences. Once, he came right out and asked why she always dressed in black—if it was an emo thing, or if she was trying to be cool—and she told him, without a glint of humor, "Because it's practical." Rarely any jewelry, because it gets in the way, and never her engagement ring, because it attracts attention she doesn't want. By the time she reaches her desk, Dinardo is focused back on his movie or whatever it is he's looking at to tick out overtime on top of his regular shift.

Saki leans down to open the bottom drawer of her

desk, removes her lumbar support cushion, and stows her black fanny pack in its place. At first, it wasn't just Dinardo: nearly all the other investigators needled her for her various comfort accommodations given that she's only thirty-two and in excellent condition. It was a relief when the jokes mostly stopped coming; she didn't really understand them, and it took time to explain herself, and she hated the distraction from more important business.

She pulls her ginger hair into a ponytail and secures it with the band from around her wrist. Removes her dark aviators and folds them into her shirt pocket. Turns on her monitor, refreshes her screen, and clicks open the log.

The most recent case, entered by Dinardo fifty-seven minutes earlier, was instigated by a call from a Margaret O'Leary-Dreyfus. The mother reported that her eighteen-year-old daughter failed to come home last night. Dinardo's notes read, *Teenager with problems, wait and see.* A flash of irritation and Saki glances across the unit at her colleague, yawning now, stretching, turning off his monitor, standing up. She dials the number on the report.

A woman answers, high voice strung tight: "Hello?"

"This is Detective Saki Finley, Eighty-Fourth Precinct, following up on your daughter. Am I speaking with Ms. O'Leary-Dreyfus?"

"Yes." The voice higher now, tighter.

"Any word yet from—" Saki checks the report for the girl's name.

The mother jumps into Saki's brief pause. "Glynnie. *Her name is Glynnie.*"

6

Last Night

Crisp pulls the buds out of his ears when Glynnie appears on the Dreyfus stoop across the street, and he taps his phone to silence the Strokes (noticing that his mother has now tried calling him three times). One-of-a-kind Glynnie in orange flip-flops, ripped jeans, and a striped T-shirt, her thin blonde hair tucked behind her ears. Just like last time they met, she has this perpetual look of messiness about her. No makeup on her face, green polish on her toenails. Wireless Beats hanging off her neck like a broken choker. He's wanted to set the record straight with her, make sure she understands why he was up there in that cage yesterday, and after a terrible homecoming this afternoon he decided he might as well tell her in person. He had to go somewhere, see someone, and all his friends were out celebrating with their families. He hopes she doesn't feel he overstepped by showing up.

"There you fucking are, Crisco King!" She bops across

the street, smiling. "Guess they didn't give you life in prison."

"Not yet." He also smiles. Something about this girl is just so funny. He's glad he came.

Simultaneously, they raise hands and high-five.

Back in the winter, Glynnie thought he was handsome, not-her-type kind of handsome, and not because he's African American or a public school kid but because he's too, well, *clean-cut* somehow, despite the fralo. His round face has a shine, his dark eyes a sparkle, his chin a deep dimple, and his hair, his hair is so black it glistens. His jeans look new and his white high-tops are weirdly spotless. He's wholesome, is what he is, in a way that none of her private school friends are. She might call that *ironic* if she were writing a paper about socioeconomic disparities (or something), which she isn't, *thank God*.

She asks, "What's up?"

"Not much. You?"

"Well," she says, "I graduated last week. Miracle of miracles."

"I didn't know you were a senior. Congratulations."

"Thanks. You too."

"Well." He licks his bottom lip, lets his eyes fall away from her face. "I kinda missed my graduation this morning."

"Seriously?"

"Just got released this afternoon."

"You were there *all night*?"

"You want to know what for?"

"Yeah. I do." She parks herself on the nearest stoop and pats the spot next to her.

He sits down but makes sure to leave room between them—he doesn't want her getting the wrong idea. He likes her, a lot, but not *like that,* and it isn't because she's white. His own mother is white. His grandparents are white. His cousins on that side are white. It's because there's so much to her that's, well, *raw,* and it scares him a little bit.

He tells her, "I rode my bike on the sidewalk."

"I don't understand."

"It's why I got arrested."

"You got arrested *for that?*"

"Well, maybe also for calling the cop Franz Kafka."

Her laugh is more a shout, loud and sudden. "I didn't know *that* was illegal either."

"Possibly it was also the tone of my voice." He grins. "And how I dropped a few f-bombs into it. Anyway, I kind of wanted to tell you since you saw me, you know, *up there.*"

"Don't worry, I didn't tell anyone." Did she? She can't remember. "Is that why you're here—so I'd know for sure you're not an ax murderer?"

He laughs. *Ax murderer*—as if. In all his life, it's the last thing anyone would have thought of him, and as soon as it crosses his mind it feels like a...what? A kind of grace. "I had to get out of the apartment. Me and my mom, we had words."

"I bet. So you missed your own graduation. That's epic."

"I was supposed to be valedictorian."

"Valedictorian at *Stuy*. I heard you were going to Princeton."

33

"I was."

"*Was?* Really?" Now she wonders if maybe, just maybe, the real reason he's here is to commiserate with a known fuckup. An *expert* fuckup. A fuckup so good at fucking up that she could draw her parents' disappointed faces from memory. "You mean they already kicked you out and you haven't even gotten there yet?" Impressive.

"I don't know for sure," he explains. "First thing when I walk in the door, my mom's like, 'The Princeton dean's office left you a message on the home phone. They want you to call back as soon as you can.'"

"Did you call?"

Crisp shakes his head. "I couldn't handle it." He breathes back a sharp memory of arriving home. His mother, sitting on the couch (which at night she'd unfold and turn into her bed) as if she was waiting for him, wearing the new dress she'd bought for his graduation and with her hair professionally blow-dried, silky straight instead of the usual frizzy curls. She was even wearing makeup and high heels, as if some small part of her had clung to a hope that he'd make it out in time for graduation.

"I'm sorry I let you down, Mom."

"It's you who should feel let down," she said. "By yourself."

Silence. He couldn't believe this was happening. "Where's Babu and Dedu?"

"Your grandparents aren't feeling well. They're resting."

"I know how much everyone was looking forward to today, Mom."

More silence, like cold rain, from a mother who had only ever been warm sunshine. Was it because he was technically a man now? Because he was starting to resemble his father? Was this how she'd looked at Mo when he turned around and left his teenage wife and baby without once glancing back, ever? The phantom who abandoned his half-white son with the absurd name of Titus Crespo.

He was back in the hall and halfway down the stairs faster than she could stand up and follow him in her heels. He heard her clopping steps and then her voice filled the stairwell: "Come back!"

He still hears it, hours later, sitting beside Glynnie on someone's front stoop with twilight starting to gather around them. He's starkly aware of her family's imposing brownstone across the street, with its window pots sprouting red geraniums and dangling vines with tender heart-shaped leaves, the clean glass winking his reflection back at him as if to say, *You're not meant to see in.*

"So your parents," Glynnie says, "must be pissed at you. Mine would be."

"Parent—mom. My dad's not around. I don't know if she's pissed, but she's definitely disappointed."

"Have any brothers or sisters?"

Crisp shakes his head. "It's just us. Well, and my grandparents."

"Wow, three generations under one roof. That would drive me *crazy.*"

"It doesn't bother me—my grandparents are cool." Just as sunset eases into a darker shade of purple, Crisp

35

notices a sudden shift in the expression of a white guy at the end of the block, walking down the sidewalk in their direction. Suit and tie, briefcase, Whole Foods shopping bag, stiff gait that sends a rod up Crisp's spine.

Glynnie says, "I saw all my grandparents last week at graduation and after for lunch, and, like, it was nice of them to come, but all they wanted to talk to me about was why were my jeans ripped—I mean, I had that gown thingy over them, so who cares?—and, you know, college." She feels a warble of gratification at the memory of how uncomfortable her choice of clothes made her mother: *Mags O'Leary-Dreyfus, casting director,* anorexic stick figure in a bright floral thousand-dollar Dolce & Gabbana dress that screamed *I'm not actually fifty years old!* and a pair of three-inch Ferragamo pumps with a perky bow as if a little bird had landed on her flawlessly manicured toes and the long vertical ridge of her shinbones rising above her skin like the sharp edge of a knife. Glynnie would *never* be like her mother. *Ever.*

"Where *are* you going to college?" Crisp immediately wishes he phrased it differently. "Are you going?" would have been better, more open-ended, for a kid like her.

"Sarah Lawrence, supposedly, eventually. It's where my mom went." She rolls her eyes. "I'm supposed to take some courses at the New School next year—you know, raise my grades—and then I'm supposed to apply."

"Sounds like you're not into the plan," Crisp says.

Glynnie shrugs, her slender collarbone lifting and making what looks like wings under her pale skin. "I'm not."

"What would you rather be doing?"

"I don't really know—that's the problem. But what's the difference? My future is set in stone. *First* I'm going to Outward Bound for the summer, *then* I'm living at home with my asshole parents and taking courses in the fall and filling out the Common App. They obviously think Outward Bound's going to give me a good essay topic, but it won't work. I know it won't."

"You're not eighteen?"

"I am, but so what?"

"You're a legal adult—you can make your own decisions."

"Technically. But without them I've got no place to live, no money, so what am I supposed to do?"

Work, he wants to tell her. *Find a place to live, figure it out on your own.* But he doesn't say it; shouldn't it be obvious? Two shades scroll down simultaneously on the parlor floor of a brownstone next to the Dreyfus house.

"Are *you* eighteen?" she asks him.

"I just turned nineteen." In a year he'll be twenty, then twenty-one, then twenty-two, then twenty-three and either a Princeton graduate or someone's janitor. His hands curl into fists. "Maybe I should head home now."

"Hang out a minute," she says. "So what are you doing this summer?"

"I've got a gig delivering for a restaurant and in my spare time I thought I'd learn German." He cringes as soon as that spills out; he's long realized that his itch for mastering foreign languages comes off as weird to kids his age.

"You mean, *the language?*"

"It's kind of my thing—it's like a freak talent. Totally useless. What about you?" Aching to change the subject. "What've you been doing since graduation?"

"Seriously, how many languages do you know?"

"Six," he admits. "I mean, not including English."

"Which ones?"

"Okay. Well…French, Italian, Spanish, Portuguese, Russian. And Latin. I mean, it's the root of the romance languages, so once you know that it's easy to…never mind."

"No, Crisp, it's *so cool*. I wish I had a brain like that." She raps her knuckles against her skull and asks herself, "Anyone home? Well, no one ever accused me of being smart."

"You're smart, Glynnie." Giving her the benefit of the doubt.

She smiles, grateful for that. "You really want to know what I've been up to since graduation?"

"Yeah, I do."

"Hunting down beads to make a charm bracelet for my mom's birthday this weekend. I've probably been to every bead store in the city, plus online. Sad, right?"

"Not at all," Crisp assures her. "It's really nice of you."

"Well, if you saw the beads, you might not think so."

"Like what?"

"Never mind."

"I told you about my languages. Tell me about your beads."

"Well…skulls and daggers and stuff like that. My

mom's going to hate it." Glynnie grins, because offending the stylish Mags O'Leary-Dreyfus is exactly the idea. Payback for her mother's master plan for her betterment, starting with a survivalist summer in the wild.

"That's kind of…I don't know." *Infantile and harsh,* is what he stops himself from saying.

The white man in the suit pauses in front of them. Crisp regulates his pulse with a deep breath.

"Glynnie, you okay here?" The man's voice thick with misgiving. And the way his gaze slides to Crisp—so hot with bigotry he can almost feel his skin melt off. Crisp leans forward, about to stand; it's *definitely* time to head home now. But Glynnie stops him by throwing an arm around his shoulders.

"Everything's great, *John,*" edging her tone with sarcasm, hoping he feels the cut. "Why do you ask?"

John's face tightens. He keeps walking. At the next house he climbs the stoop and lets himself through the front door.

"Fuck that racist!" Glynnie lets her arm fall away.

"Never mind. I'm used to it."

"Now I feel shitty."

"Don't let it bother you." He's positioning his buds to replant them in his ears, knowing the music will help, when she stops his hand midair.

She says, "Well it's got to bother *you.*"

"Not really. I mean, a little bit, but I get it all the time."

"That sucks."

"Yeah, I guess it does."

"What are you listening to?"

He tells her, "The Strokes."

"What song?"

"'Last Nite.'"

"Cool. I love Julian Casablancas's voice. I'll sync." She positions the soft earpieces, drowning out street noise, and sends the song from her phone to her Beats. Then, to help them float above the asshole neighbor's racist bullshit, she digs into her front pocket for the roach she knows is there. Except it isn't. "Shit!"

"You don't have to shout!" he shouts.

They both free their ears at once, look at each other, and laugh.

"Hey, Crispy Cream, do you get high?" She mimes holding a joint to her lips and sucks in air.

"Sometimes." On weekends, when his work is done. Never during the week. And never within a five-block radius of his apartment building—far enough away that his mother and grandparents would never suspect.

She digs a hand into her other pocket, comes up empty. "I thought I had some on me but as usual I'm wrong. I know where we can get some, though."

"Right now?"

"You have someplace better to be?"

He thinks of his mother and grandparents, waiting for him at home, and asks, "How far?"

"Red Hook. We could walk."

"My dad grew up in Red Hook," Crisp says. He's studied maps of the area, researched its history, written about it for school, but never wanted to visit in person— or, more accurately, never allowed himself to want to. All his life, that slip of land hooking into the bay has been forbidden territory.

"Cool. You in?"

Is he? The depletion of a night in jail is powerful, the look on his mother's face a looming shadow, and the way Glynnie's neighbor's eyes just cut him down to size... well.

Impulsively, he answers, "Sure."

"I'll see if my connect's around." Glynnie thumbs a text to JJ, her dealer, who answers almost instantly. She briefly wonders if she should run inside for her purse, in case she needs something, but doesn't bother. She'll be home in an hour or so.

7

The color of dusk as it slips into night needs its own word. Crisp contemplates what that might be as he walks beside Glynnie up to Court Street, the same song in their ears. They turn left and pass a funeral parlor, a Thai restaurant, and an artisanal soap store pumping the scent of—what?—*honeysuckle* through its open door onto the sidewalk. The word he's looking for will need to capture the rich and gradual melding of lavender and blue and violet and almost black. *Blauvet,* maybe, he thinks, realizing it's clunky and he'll have to tweak it later. You could leave the *t* silent or omit it and add an accent to the *e*, and voilà, it would sound a little bit French. He hopes to take his mother to Paris someday for a visit—*hoped*. It won't happen if he doesn't make it to Princeton first. *He should go home.* Suddenly, an olfactive memory of days-old pee returns him to the crowded jail cell. He snorts out a blast of air to dispel the rank odor memory and breathes in one last note of honeysuckle before exiting its range. *The blauvet (blauvé) night swallows them as side by side they dance to music no one else can hear.*

Now, Glynnie thinks, *finally* it's starting to feel like a celebration. It's pretty cool that Crisp showed up. Ballsy. Sweet, even, how he went out of his way to make sure she knows why he was up there in that cage playing basketball with the other inmates, who, before this, she always assumed were the kind of people she would never cross paths with. See how much she's learned in the last half hour, Mr. Harkavy, sophomore sociology (C minus), just by actually encountering a real person with real problems in the real world, as opposed to reading statistics in a book? Glynnie knows she isn't stupid *or* hopeless (despite the lengthy narrative commentary of nearly every single end semester report), but she also knows that she hasn't stumbled on the locus of her intelligence, not yet. But she will. She feels it. And look: Crisp Crespo, academic wonder, is hanging out with *her* on what was supposed to be his graduation night.

She taps his arm and holds up her phone.

"Sure," he says. He doesn't much like selfies but everyone else does and so he goes with the flow. They come to a halt and press their faces together, buggy-eyed and tongues wagging, laughing at nothing. He waits while she posts it somewhere.

The song ends. Without discussing it, they both tune in to whatever they feel like.

Walking again, darker, cooler, she feels bad that he missed his graduation when it sounds like for him school has been okay. If *she* missed *her* graduation, no one would have been surprised—a little annoyed, maybe, but not broken. They would have all just gone to lunch anyway. She glances at him. *Valedictorian, and he wasn't there.* His moves are jazzy, with the occasional pop of an elbow or knee. What's he listening to? For her the groove now is Beyoncé.

Crisp wonders what she's got on her Beats now that their song is over. She's swaggering like it's hip-hop, white kid hip-hop, which he hates because he's half white kid himself, though never acknowledged as such. He pushes that thought away and lets Thelonious flow through his mind.

At Union Street, they dance their way across the bridge that spans the expressway, a traffic-roaring separation that feels like leaving one town behind, entering another. Just ahead, loading docks and the East River. The bright puzzle of Manhattan's skyline recedes as they turn onto Van Brunt Street and follow the luminous black seam of water as it edges them deeper into Red Hook.

Glynnie leads the way along Van Brunt Street, the commercial strip, until stores, people, even Fairway Market and its night shoppers vanish into the background. Moonglow brightens the way to an old warehouse that fills a slip of land between Beard Street and the Buttermilk Channel, where it siphons into the bay. The first time she came here she was scared shitless, scared but excited, and then she met the dealer, JJ, and her fear evaporated. Now she likes coming here. She notices that except for walking, Crisp has gone still, his hands are jammed in his pockets, and there's that zipped-up look on his face again, like when her fuckwad neighbor John stopped to make sure everything was "okay," which is the opposite of what he really meant, the racist asshole.

Crisp's defenses rise to orange alert: alone with a white girl in the dark in what feels like and looks like and smells like and sounds like and *is* a shuttered-for-the-night semirevived industrial jetty. Alone here, their footsteps echo. There are no streetlights in this voracious darkness. The smell of ocean, fishy and dank; the rhythmic splashing against an unseen bearing wall; the feeling of slipping away from solid ground. And all of it, all of it colludes to inform him that he's easy prey. As simple as that. She could be the one with a gun to his head, but he would be the one arrested. He knows this in his bones.

"I dunno," he mumbles.

Glynnie laughs. "It's okay, really. JJ's cool."

"But this place."

Her laugh has the strange effect of both easing his doubts and also alarming him. It's not as if he doesn't know her world; he lives half in it, after all. But ever since the hormones hit, the universe has reacted to him as someone he almost doesn't know himself. "Know your enemy and know yourself," said Sun Tzu, "and you can fight a hundred battles without disaster." (History of Eastern Philosophical Thought, junior-senior advanced placement.) So if he doesn't know himself, which he doesn't, not really, won't his battles inevitably end in disaster? Is that what the Chinese philosopher was telling him? One thing Crisp knows for sure is that life as a young man who is half black and half white is a daily battle. Maybe the real question needs to be: What is the battle *predicated on,* exactly? He knew when he handed in his final paper that he hadn't explored the idea deeply enough, that despite the A plus he'd failed the subject, because *the truth is he doesn't understand any of this shit.* Which is what he's thinking as he denies his intuitive urge to flee and continues to walk with Glynnie alongside the low brick building that hulks beside the open mouth of water.

Glynnie stops at an iron gate, uses her foot to push aside a loose vertical bar, presses herself through the narrow opening. A hundred feet ahead, she comes to a chain-link fence. When she looks around for Crisp she finds him still at the gate, hesitating, and wonders what his problem is, exactly.

Crisp watches as Glynnie slips through a tear in a raggedy fence. Wondering where she gets her confidence and why he feels so powerfully drawn by it—toggling between *She's fun so relax, just go with it* and *She's reckless, just go home*—he squeezes himself through the narrow opening in the broken gate. Then he contorts himself through a rupture in the chain link and, without consciously deciding anything, joins her on the other side. He has just begun to contemplate the mutability of free will when she says, "Come on," and he follows her around to the end of the building.

Here all pretense of restoration vanishes: brick crumbling, paint flaking over rust. Surrounded now on three sides by water, civilization reduced to distant twinkling shorelines. At an arched iron door flecked with age-old residue of black paint, they come to a stop.

Glynnie bends down to pick up a stone and throws it at a second-floor iron shutter, and repeats twice—their prearranged signal. She hardly ever misses anymore and thinks of her (former) gym teacher Mr. C.: *Wish you could see me now*.

The shutter creaks open to reveal a window without glass and the black face of a boy. Crisp does a double take; this dealer, this JJ, is nothing but a child.

"Yo," Glynnie calls up to the window. "Okay if we come up?"

JJ points to the door.

Glynnie moves toward the entrance but Crisp just stands there. She whispers, "Coming?"

"I dunno," he whispers back.

"Seriously?"

The way her dimples pinch reminds him of a girl from ninth grade, the one who gave him a quick flat "No thanks" when he asked her to "hang out some day." But he heard her loud and clear: *No thanks, I don't hang out with nerds*. There it is again on Glynnie's face—the look that tells him, *No matter how smart you are—in fact,* because *you're so smart—I can't stand being near you*. It's enough to make Crisp forget his better judgment and tell himself to *loosen up* and *Don't be so uptight* and *Another thing I can learn this summer is how to have some fun*. And then, the final hammerblow to his wobbly nail of uncertainty: *I'm finally here, in Red Hook, where my father grew up*.

He follows her.

Glynnie wishes he'd chill: Crisp's nervous energy is making *her* nervous. They're just going to score a little weed. She pushes hard on the left half of the double doors and it screams open the way it always does into a dust-caked entryway with a staircase leading to the second floor of some old factory. Not liking the eerie vibe, she picks up her pace.

As soon as they step into the musty entrance hall, Crisp realizes that they're inside an abandoned section of the Beard Street warehouses (he once mapped the entire Red Hook waterfront for an eighth grade social studies project on nineteenth-century urban economies). Originally it was a storehouse for southern cotton working its way north through the exchanges and onward to the upstate and New England mills, Mr. William Beard having built his Red Hook Stores warehouse and his Erie Basin to get to it and *also* having built a false narrative of how an Irish immigrant achieved the American dream when the *real* story is how he got rich off a corrupt economic partnership between American slavery and northern ingenuity.

Trailing Glynnie up the stairs, Crisp recalls some-thing else: the combustibility of cotton and constant fires in the warehouses leading to the next industry Beard's enterprise spawned—women and children picking good cotton from the chars. The fruits of slavery clinging to acceptable cruelty in a march toward the ready-to-wear cotton industry. And here he is, almost two centuries later, following a restless, compelling girl to meet up with another kid doing business in the storehouse, ghostly with cotton fibers that Crisp can practically feel threading themselves into his lungs' bronchi with every breath. Breathing in history—*living history,* a teacher once called it. Which one? He can't remember if it was Amy or Pietr. *Because history dies and lives in the same breath,* he thinks, feels, his lungs filling with spectral cotton in the echo chamber of his and Glynnie's steps along a hallway until they come to a doorless entry that leads into an enormous loftlike room.

In the far right corner of that room, the boy has set up camp. A sleeping bag in disarray. A spate of cast-off furniture: rickety table, single chair, small shelf stacked with textbooks. One of those plaid Chinese bags filled with something soft and bulgy—clothes is what Crisp guesses, interpreting the scene for what it is: a homeless kid running drugs out of his squat. Keeping up, getting by.

A flashlight turns on to encase the visitors in a cone of transparency, and there they stand, being eyed by a boy three whiskers into puberty. Twelve years old, Crisp guesses, maybe thirteen. In the flood of light, a framed photo atop the shelf shows a younger version of the boy sandwiched between smiling parents, everyone in their Sunday best for the portrait—a memory of love that saddens Crisp so abruptly it takes him aback. At home, his own family must be wondering where he is by now.

Glynnie throws up her arms in a victorious embrace of the spotlight, hollers "Janjak of the Jungle, we have arrived!," and bows at the waist.

"Who's *we?*" says a voice that cracks between high and low.

Glynnie says, "This my homey—"

Crisp cringes. Please. No.

"—Crisp Crespo, the Crisco King of Coney, yo."

The boy, JJ, Janjak, blue jeans sagging over tighty-whities that look as though they need a wash, approaches with his light still on them, the beam narrowing until he's so close its source forms a neat bright target on Crisp's stomach. "Your name's *what?*" JJ asks.

"Titus Crespo," he answers. "Everyone calls me Crisp."

Up close, JJ has a long oval head and a pointed chin. Thick arched eyebrows. A broad unfinished nose. Small cockleshell ears. A mouth that dips naturally into a smile. Tight curled lashes. His skin looks moist and babyish, his hair rakish and in need of a trim. The air between them smells funky, and Crisp wonders where the kid brushes his teeth in this hellhole or if he does. What happened to the family in that photo?

JJ looks at Glynnie. "I *told* you don't bring people."

Glynnie inwardly cringes, realizing that he'd meant the directive with more seriousness than she'd received it, that for him this probably—no, *definitely*—isn't a game. She really is an idiot and this only proves it. She regrets her (now) obvious bad judgment, but it's too late.

"Crisp is cool," she assures JJ. "You don't have to worry about him."

The flashlight glares right at Crisp and his eyes burn. "Turn off that light, unless you're *trying* to attract attention from outside."

The boy turns it off.

"Hey JJ, check it out." Hoping to ease the awkward moment, Glynnie hands him her headphones.

"Wireless Beats?" JJ turns them over, inspects them. *"Word."*

"Try 'em."

He puts them on.

She scrolls to an Odd Future song, thinking he'll like it, and taps Play. But he just stands there, unresponsive. Assuming the volume's too low, she raises it.

"Whoa!" JJ yanks off both ears at once. Loud music spills out and echoes in search of a stopping place.

Crisp wishes she'd turn down the noise on that tinny crap. Can't she do better than that for this poor home-less kid? A little Coltrane to ease his soul would be more like it.

"Sorry." Glynnie lowers the volume as JJ puts the headphones back on, realizing that this is how he listens to music, still as a statue, not making a wave in either time or space. And that, she thinks, is just so sad. After a minute he tries to hand back the Beats but she tells him, "They're yours," surprising even herself.

"Nah." JJ holds out the headphones. "I can't work on barter. Just cash."

"I'm giving you cash for the weed. That's a gift."

"No joke?"

"Nope." Proud of herself now. Seeing how much it means to him. Knowing she can buy herself another set exactly the same and her parents will never be the wiser.

"Yeah, well, that's nice. I mean, thanks. But—" He shows them his old flip phone. "—can't exactly use them with this."

"We'll figure that out," she promises.

JJ eyes Crisp. "So, how am I supposed to know this guy isn't a snitch?"

"Trust me: Crisco King just spent the night in jail. He's definitely not a snitch."

"For real?" JJ asks.

Crisp answers, "Unfortunately."

"That's cool."

"Actually it wasn't *at all*," Crisp says. "Going to jail is *not cool*."

JJ hangs the Beats around his neck and looks at Glynnie. "How much you want this time?"

She digs into her front pocket and pulls out a ten-dollar bill. "Dime."

JJ crosses the space away from his living quarters and vanishes into a shadow. Crisp listens to the boy rustling through something, and watches as he materializes to hand Glynnie a tiny baggie containing a little fist of bud in exchange for the bill. She retrieves a crushed pack of rolling papers from her back pocket, plunks cross-legged on the floor, and proceeds to roll a joint.

Only Crisp sees, with a whoop of panic that feels like drowning, when JJ pulls a gun from the back of his sagging waistband.

8

Friday

Saki climbs the stoop of the Dreyfus brownstone and rings the bell. She holds her wallet flapped open so the mother, Mags O'Leary-Dreyfus, will immediately know who she is; given that the daughter is still missing, time could prove crucial. She adjusts her sunglasses and waits.

The door swings open and a blonde woman in a tight designer dress and bare feet looks at the ID and starts talking in the agitated voice from the phone. "You're the detective! Thank God you're here! Please, please, come in."

Saki follows her into a spacious front hall with a strong floral scent, presumably from the fresh bouquet on the entry table. There's an orderliness to the place, a hush that seems to amplify the squeaking of Saki's shoes as she crosses the polished wood floor into the living room.

Ms. O'Leary-Dreyfus gestures for Saki to sit down on one of the matching armchairs, then sits opposite on the couch. A framed family portrait is on the glass side table: a handsome father in a suit jacket and open collar; the stylish mother with hands clasped over pressed-together knees; a boy of about four, wearing khakis and a button-down shirt; and a blonde girl, pressing out a smile glittery with braces, in a dress and patent-leather flats—Glynnie, presumably, at around the age of twelve.

Saki begins. "What time did your daughter leave the house last night?"

"Sometime before seven forty-nine, I guess, because that's when she posted an Instagram photo with her and a…some guy. They were on Court Street; I recognized the store they were in front of."

"Friend of hers? The guy."

"Could be, but I really don't know. He looks young, maybe late teens or early twenties. African American. Long—well, *tall*—hair."

Saki makes a note, and explains to the mother, "We can trace where she was when she posted the photo. She could have taken it another time and posted it while she was at home."

"I thought she *was* home. It's not unusual for her to avoid us, to not come down for dinner, to just stay upstairs in her rooms. We didn't think anything of it."

"I take it you didn't find her to say good night."

"She hates it when we do that. So we don't."

"You're sure she didn't come back in and then go out again early in the morning?"

"Her bed's still made. The housekeeper was here yesterday and Glynnie *never* makes her own bed. And she was definitely out at twelve twenty-three in the morning because the bank shows she withdrew three hundred dollars."

"Bank ATM or store?"

"Chase. The branch on Hamilton Avenue, on the border of Carroll Gardens and Red Hook."

Saki makes another note, then says, "Tell me about your daughter."

"She's a typical teenager, I guess." Mags O'Leary-Dreyfus rolls her eyes to the ceiling and shakes her head briskly as if trying to discharge a demon from her thoughts. Saki makes a mental note of that. "She's not easy, but she's got real potential. She graduated from high school last week, and to answer your next question, no, she was not a good student. And to answer your *next* question, no, she isn't going to college next year. We're working on that."

"Summer plans?"

"Outward Bound."

"She happy about it?"

The way the mother's smile cracks hard on her face, the answer is clearly negative.

"You're sure she's not at a friend's place?" Saki asks. "The unidentified friend's, maybe."

"I called everyone—that I'm aware of, I mean. For all I know…" The mother stops talking. "I guess she *could* be with him or some other friend she never mentioned. I mean that *could* be possible."

Saki explains, "Because your daughter is eighteen, Ms. O'Leary-Dreyfus—"

"Mags, please."

"Mags, your daughter's not a minor," Saki continues. "She has the right to go where and do what she wants, which means—"

"Exactly." Mags sits forward suddenly, her eyes bright with anxiety. "That's the problem."

"Yes, I understand, but legally we're limited because of her major status."

"What?"

"Status as a major, not a minor."

"Oh." Mags delivers a stare that's familiar to Saki—when someone starts to realize that she might be (and in fact is) somewhere on the spectrum. The mother clears her throat. "So what does this mean? Do I just sit here and wait?"

"You don't have to sit here. But we do have to wait a little longer before it's reasonable to determine that Glynnie is missing not of her own volition."

"Will you please take off those sunglasses?"

"I apologize. I forgot I had them on." She folds the glasses and tucks them into her collar. "When it comes to young adults, we often find that they return on their own. The rule of thumb is twenty-four hours."

"You're saying wait until tonight to start worrying?"

"Yes."

"You're telling me not to worry right now?"

"Not actively. Not yet."

"But she's my child. I am worried. How can I not worry?"

"I understand," Saki says in a tone she hopes expresses

sympathy. "Let me worry for you," she tries. "We also find that sometimes an investigator can get farther than parents can with the person's friends."

"The person." Mags throws up her hands. "Fine. I'll make a list of all her friends that I know of. But I'm not going to the office today. I'm canceling all my appointments and waiting here for Glynnie because I *am* worried."

"Of course you're worried." Saki's voice is toneless, probably sounds as if she doesn't mean it, though she means it more than she can express. She hands the mother her card. "I'm going to get started right now finding your daughter. Here's how you can reach me."

Mags proffers her own card. "What should I do now?"

"Wait here in case she comes back. Keep your phone close."

Saki rises and walks a squeaky tempo back to the door. Mags follows. Standing at the top of the stoop, the detective struggles to hold eye contact but the intensity of the mother's gaze makes it difficult.

Averting her eyes, Saki says, "I promise to stay in close touch." Family members always like to hear that, even though to her it seems like stating the obvious. She excuses herself and walks down the stoop. When the Dreyfuses' front door closes, she exhales.

Standing on the sidewalk, Saki takes out her phone and starts the search with two official requests: first, to the Information Technology Bureau for cellular location tracking on her subject, and second, assuming that Chase Bank's Hamilton Avenue location has a security camera in place, as most do, to the magistrate for a warrant for last night's footage around the time of Glynnie's withdrawal.

This early in the morning, sure she'll catch most of the neighbors in, Saki begins her preliminary canvass with the house immediately to the left. With brownstones she makes it her practice to try both the parlor and ground-floor entrances, since sometimes the buildings are split into multiple units.

She climbs the stoop and rings the bell, her credentials at the ready. After a few moments, the door is answered by an older man in a robe and slippers, thick silver hair askew. He asks, "Can I help you...detective?"

Saki launches into a standard query. "Good morning. Sorry to disturb you. I'm asking around about your neighbor Glynnie Dreyfus. Her mother's worried because it appears she didn't come home last night. Have you seen her any time in the last twelve hours?"

The man clears his throat and says, "No, I haven't seen her for at least a few days. Nik and Mags are good people, and I don't think Aidan gives them any trouble, but he's young yet. Glynnie, though? Well, she'll come around, I'm sure."

In the apartment below: a young woman in a business suit with hair wrapped in a striped towel. "Are you talking about that teenage girl who lives next door and blasts her music in the middle of the night with her windows open?"

Two houses down, a man in shorts and sneakers is locking up his front door. He removes his ear buds long enough to say, "I saw her last week when I thought I smelled a skunk but it was her, sitting on my stoop, smoking weed."

Across the street, a mother escorting twin girls to school whispers so her preteens won't hear, "If my girls talked the way she does I'd ground them for a month."

An older woman returning with her cocker spaniel from a walk says, "Glynnie Dreyfus used to be a nice little girl. That's all I have to say."

A trim fortyish man in a well-fitting suit with a brief-case tucked under his arm is dragging his trash cans from the curb to his house. He turns his attention to Saki. "Are you asking about the Dreyfus girl across the street?"

"I am," Saki answers. "Her mother's worried because it appears she didn't come home last night." She proffers her identification.

"She's missing?" The man's expression tightens.

"Not necessarily. Did you see her last night or this morning?"

"Yes," he says, pointing to the neighboring stoop. "I saw her last night sitting right there with a black man."

She hears the racial emphasis loud and clear, and imagines how he'd describe *her*. *Asian lady. Woman detective.* She asks, "What time was that?"

"Around eight fifteen, eight thirty."

"Did you recognize the man?"

"No, I didn't. I stopped to make sure she was okay. I asked if there was a problem."

"Did she seem like she wasn't okay?"

"I couldn't tell, but—"

"The man—what did he look like?"

"Young. Wearing blue jeans. He had that big puffy hair, the way they do."

"They?"

A pause. "Teenagers."

"Oh. You said *man*."

"Young man. Could have been Glynnie's age or a little older. Did he do something to her?"

"Did they seem like friends?"

"I couldn't tell. I was only trying to help. Her response was…obnoxious. I went inside."

The neighbor, John Phelps, takes Saki's card in case he thinks of anything else. He turns and walks swiftly in the direction of the subway around the corner, leaving Saki alone on the sidewalk with a cold feeling she doesn't like. Across the street, through the vaporous white curtains draping the Dreyfus brownstone's floor-to-ceiling windows, she can make out the shadowy movements of someone pacing: the mother, worrying a trench into the expensive carpet.

Saki's phone vibrates with a call. She answers, "Finley."

"This is Pam at ITB."

Saki glances at the time. Seventeen minutes since she put in her request to Information Technology. Not bad. "What do you have?"

"The Instagram post made at seven forty-nine p.m. points to two twelve Court Street, posted thirteen seconds after the photo was taken. After that the signal traces to Red Hook, where it stays until twelve fifty-one a.m., when it stops at sixty-two Mill Street. There's a big housing project there; it's always hard to get a signal once someone goes in."

"Thanks, Pam."

"One more thing. There were significant still periods when the signal stops moving: first on Beard Street near the coastline, then it blanks out in a dead zone some-where, then on Hamilton Avenue, then at Mill Street."

"That's all between seven forty-nine and twelve fifty-one?"

"Yup."

"Thanks again."

"Hope that helps."

It helps to a point, in that it puts Glynnie in Red Hook for a set period of time. But it doesn't tell Saki if the young African American man was still with the girl at the bank and, better yet, if anyone at the housing project can identify him.

She returns to the silver Ford she signed out of the station house lot, buckles up behind the wheel, opens the windows to let in the soft June air. She's about to start the engine when she thinks to text her fiancé, Russ, to remind him that tonight it's his turn to make dinner, as he often forgets. But before she can tap in the message, the phone rings in her hand. She answers, "Detective Finley."

"DAS here," a woman says. "Just wanted you to know that the bank footage you asked for is up now. Didn't say emergency, but I saw it's a missing persons, so…"

"Thank you."

On her phone, Saki taps the Domain Awareness System app and downloads the bank security footage. A van with music blaring pulls beside her at the end of a line of stalled traffic waiting on a red light. She closes her windows and fixes her attention on the video clip as it reveals four and a half minutes of last night.

Glynnie approaches a pair of ATMs; she looks nothing like the poised preteen girl in the family portrait. Braless in a striped T-shirt, lank hair, orange flip-flops, lime green pedicure and torn jeans—everything about her oozing rebellion. A young man and a boy, both African American, follow but hang back as she dips her card into the machine on the right and makes the withdrawal. The young man, with his round wide fro, fits the general description from the neighbor and also matches the Instagram post the mother mentioned. The other one, the boy, is slim and nervous in sagging jeans showing his underwear. Saki wishes she could reach into the video and pull up the boy's pants. He's too young for this, whatever it is they're up to.

A short stack of fifties spew out. Saki counts along, one, two, three, four, five, six, as the girl checks her money, folds it, and slips it into her pants pocket. Six fifties. The three hundred dollars the mother reported seeing in the bank record online.

What were they planning to do with three hundred dollars? In the projects? In the middle of the night?

9

Last Night

Glynnie glances up from rolling the joint and sees her dealer pointing a pistol at her friend. "What the fuck, JJ?"

"Cool, right?" The boy turns the gun sideways, displaying it. "It's mine, a Ruger twenty-two. Just got it from Big Man's cousin—gave me a break on sticker 'cause, you know." His eyes flick to Crisp, obviously hoping for approval, and Glynnie sees it—*it* being the guy thing, maybe even the race thing—and feels a drainage of situational power.

She gets to her feet, holding the joint between two outstretched fingers (channeling Audrey Hepburn at a cocktail soiree), and asks, "Where can I get one?" She extends her free hand to receive the weapon.

"I dunno if the cousin'd be cool with that," JJ says.

"What," Glynnie argues, "he's the one person in America who doesn't like making a sale?"

"Yeah, he likes it." JJ hesitates, then hands her the gun. "Just sometimes it's hard knowing how he's gonna be."

"This is *absurd*." Crisp's initial shock melts into irritation that this conversation is happening at all. "You're kidding, right, Glynnie?"

She was, a little bit, at first, but the longer she holds the firearm the more she loves the idea of it. And Crisp's knee-jerk reaction against it pisses her off a little, truth be told. She asks, "How much?" Last she looked there was about a thousand dollars in her debit account.

"Mine was two Cs," JJ says. He translates: "Two hundred bucks. But like I said, I got it on the cheap 'cause I work for Big Man."

"An employee discount," Glynnie says. "That's cool. I'd do three Cs. This could be fun."

"No," Crisp argues. "It wouldn't be fun. It would be stupid." He takes the gun out of her hand and uses the bottom of his shirt to wipe off their fingerprints. It's heavier than he thought a gun would be. He asks JJ, "Do you really need this?"

The boy shrugs and looks at his feet—the too-small sneakers with holes cut for his big toes—and something clicks in Crisp. An understanding, or the beginning of one: maybe JJ *could* use a weapon on hand, given his obvious vulnerability. If the world is out for Crisp, only half black and Ivy League–bound, imagine how fast and hard it will come after *this* kid.

He hands the gun to JJ. "You can put it away; you won't need it tonight."

JJ crosses the room into a dark corner. He returns with an abashed "Sorry 'bout that."

"Nah, I get it." There's so much Crisp wants to say right now, but face-to-face with this homeless kid squatting alone in an abandoned warehouse, he doesn't have the heart to argue his principled belief that modern America would be better off with not fewer guns but none at all.

Glynnie decides not to push the gun thing for now, not with Crisp so all up in his attitude about it. She lights the joint, takes the first drag, then hands it to JJ. He sucks hard and then offers it to Crisp.

The smoke coils into Crisp's lungs and in moments his brain starts to unwind.

They pass the joint among them.

Glynnie's stomach grumbles. "Anyone else hungry?"

"I could eat," Crisp says. "What's around here for food?"

"There's pizza on Van Brunt," JJ suggests. "Or sometimes I get those meatballs at IKEA."

The moment he suggests the Swedish specialty, Glynnie's mouth ignites with a craving for the salty sweet mash of cheap ground meat and lingonberry sauce. And those giant milk chocolate bars they have at IKEA—she could get one of those too. "I'm in."

"Me too." Crisp hasn't had IKEA meatballs since he was in sixth grade, when his mother took him to size a new bed because he'd outgrown his old one. A gustatory memory flares from his tongue—that smoky, meaty deliciousness with the bright red sauce that perfectly, *perfectly* counterbalances salty with sweet. Stoned, feeling magnanimous, Crisp insists, "JJ, you're coming with us. My treat."

The boy smiles. He puts on the Beats, Glynnie cues up a song she hopes he'll like, and the three fast friends head into the night.

At the end of Beard Street, the monolithic building looms blue and yellow and uplit.

Inside the superstore's mazelike showrooms they link arms and stumble and sing "I'm off to see the wizard!" as they dance-step along the floor arrows that turn the giant space into a board game of ardent consumerism. Crisp laughs when that passes through his mind and then lets the thought go like a helium balloon. *Good-bye. I don't need you.* On the rare occasions that he's gotten high he has wondered why he doesn't do it more often. (And then the next day, foggy brained, woolly mouthed, he *knows* why he doesn't.)

They follow JJ's lead when he stops to look into a corner bedroom display: burnt-orange walls, mahogany furniture, faux bearskin rug stretched across the floor, round mirrors hung asymmetrically behind a bed plush with a comforter and masses of pillows. Dresser displayed with a glass lamp and a potted cactus. Desk with a short stack of book facsimiles, task light and swivel chair tucked at the ready. Off each item hang orange tags, crowded with umlauted words, measurements, prices.

Enchanted by the sudden thought that she has miniaturized and can now *actually enter a dollhouse room,* Glynnie starts the invasion: skipping into the display, beelining to the dresser, opening every drawer, announcing, "Empty! Empty! Empty!"

Crisp stands at the threshold, watching as JJ tentatively

enters this facsimile of a home before getting comfortable, stretching long atop the bed, closing his eyes. Finally Crisp joins his friends and sits on the desk chair, feeling it crimp beneath his weight; he doesn't dare swivel for fear of crushing one of its plastic parts. Even stoned he knows this isn't for real, that if he breaks it he'll buy it, and he's already burdened by that hundred-dollar ticket he can't pay.

"Don't mess around in there!" A woman has joined them in their secret world, her buzz cut, yellow IKEA shirt tight over a bloated middle, and long paper measuring tape hanging from a belt loop telegraphing an odd but convincing authority.

Back in the maze, they arrive at the searing-bright cafeteria. They get their food (using up Crisp's entire twenty but he's glad to do it) and sit together at the first available table and bend over plates to dig into their heaps of gravy-slathered meatballs and fries and *oh yes* that sweet, sweet sauce.

After a while, Crisp, sated, begins to feel a modicum of brain power return. He looks across at JJ, a gelatinous drop of scarlet glistening in the corner of the boy's mouth, and asks, "How'd you get to be homeless?"

JJ's gaze rises to meet Crisp's, taking the measure of this older teenager, this young man, who wandered into his life out of nowhere on the arm of a customer. Crisp feels the intensity of the boy's process, its importance, and allows himself to be considered. And then, after a long minute, JJ answers, "I'll tell you, but not here."

"Where?"

"Home."

"Home?"

"The place I sleep. My crib. Whatevs."

Glynnie burps and says, "I feel a little sick now." Suddenly the meatballs don't seem as good as they tasted in the moment.

* * *

They sit on the floor facing one another in the dark glass-less window lit by the moon, ocean lapping just outside.

JJ says, "My folks got deported back to Haiti."

"When?" Crisp asks.

"Last year. ICE came when I was at school. Sent my folks back to Port-au-Prince that day." He settles his eyes on the portrait of his family, pressed together, smiling. "Had a couple foster families, but..." He looks away from the photo as if what happened next is something his parents can't hear.

Crisp grows sad as JJ recounts the memory of kissing his mother, Esther, good-bye for the last time. He can practically taste the nooks and crannies, slides and tilts of the mother's Haitian accent as the boy repeats the last words he heard her speak: "I will see you outside school at three o'clock."

And the father, Kervens, advising, "Stop at every light, traffic or no," in a tone lush with discipline and love.

It was the first time JJ was allowed to walk to school alone, and the last time the St. Fleur family would be together.

No one came to meet him after school.

His first foster father sexually abused him.

His next foster family seemed to forget he was there. Then his case worker stopped checking in. He'd fallen through the cracks.

"That's when I moved in here," JJ tells them. "No one bothers me. I get good grades. A lot of food gets tossed in the dumpster by Fairway every night. For pocket money, I do a little selling for Big Man."

"But the last foster family," Crisp says. "Didn't they tell anyone you were gone?"

JJ shrugs. "I showed up at my old school for the first day of seventh grade, signed the mom's name on all the papers, kept on going, and never heard a thing about it. I stay under the radar. Never miss a day of school— can't draw attention or they'll put me back in foster." He grinds his jaw. "I can't have that."

Glynnie pivots to her knees, throws her arms around JJ, slight, bony, skin so soft, and whispers, "It's okay." Why did she never think to ask him that question: "Why are you homeless?" Now she knows that he's not *JJ, her kid dealer* but *Janjak St. Fleur, beloved son of Esther and Kervens*. Homeless, abused, neglected, surviving by his wits.

"What about your parents?" she asks him. "Are they coming back?"

"I hope they trying."

I hope they are *trying,* Crisp thinks, but keeps the correction to himself. Janjak St. Fleur needs an offhand correction like he needs a hole in the head (as Crisp's grandmother, Babu, would say). The boy's story fills the space with a palpable loneliness. Crisp knows well the sensation of abandonment, how it gradually erodes you until you realize that part of you is missing, how you look and look for the one piece that fits. He wouldn't recognize his own father if he passed him on the street, and it isn't as if he hasn't wondered what the man looks like now, *that one man,* a stranger lost among a billion faces. No one can replace JJ's parents, and until Esther and Kervens St. Fleur return (*if* they return), what the boy needs is practical help.

Crisp leans into the tight circle and asks, "You're done with seventh grade, right? Then eighth grade at the same school?"

"Got another week of school, then I'm done. And yeah. Same school next year."

"And then what?"

"High school." An intonation of *duh* is heavy in his tone.

"Does your school go through twelfth?" Crisp clarifies, knowing that few public schools do.

JJ answers, "Eighth."

"Then you're going to have to come up with a list of high schools."

"A list?"

"It works like this." Crisp lays out each thread of the process, carefully weaving them together to create a baroque tapestry of the New York City public-high-school selection process. The endless tours and research. The prioritized list of twelve "regular" schools, due by December. The specialized exam for entry into the

70

exclusive "top" schools. Auditions for the "talent" schools. Essays. Interviews. It was like applying to medical school, but Crisp's mom had made a spreadsheet that kept him organized and on track. Together, they parsed and mastered the complexities of the system and launched Crisp toward a potential future that (if he could just get to Princeton) would be the polar opposite of JJ's, given the odds against him. This boy who is black as night, who dumpster dives for food, who sells drugs for expenses, who is completely alone—he won't stand a chance.

When Crisp is finished talking, JJ looks overwhelmed, Glynnie shocked.

"You've got to be kidding me," she says. "I heard public school was complicated, but that's just insane." For her, the journey from kindergarten through senior year of high school has taken place in the same well-appointed nineteenth-century Victorian pile in downtown Brooklyn, while apparently Crisp fought his way from borough to borough through a vast and fucked-up system, chasing an education that for him, at least, hasn't turned out badly. The thought that he missed out on being valedictorian this morning now makes her burn with anger. She realizes at this moment that the honor *really was* no small thing.

Crisp feels almost guilty for having ripped away their veils of innocence, but given what JJ's up against, he has no choice.

"I'll help you," Crisp tells him. "I'll take you through it step by step." He can accomplish this regardless of whether he ends up staying in New York serving McDonald's or actually makes it to college—Princeton is only a train ride away. "And I'll tutor you for the specialized exam."

"Nah," JJ says. "I mean, that's nice, but I probably can't afford it."

"You don't have to pay me."

"Everything costs," the younger boy says with resolve.

"Sometimes it doesn't."

"Yeah it does. That's something I learned. Like…" JJ softens now, gaze moving to the ceiling, thinking. "Maybe if there's something I could do for you, then we'd have ourselves a deal."

A deal, Crisp thinks, *as if everything boils down to quid pro quo.* It doesn't. But before he can say "No deal, I *want* to help, in fact I *insist* on it." Before he can quote Mahatma Gandhi, who said, "You must not lose faith in humanity. Humanity is an ocean; if a few drops of the ocean are dirty, the ocean doesn't become dirty." Before he can recite the Dalai Lama's words "Love and compassion are necessities, not luxuries. Without them humanity cannot survive." Before he has a chance to open his mouth and really earn that A plus in Compassionate Rebellions of the Twentieth Century by persuading JJ that receiving is just as important as giving and also that sometimes you have to allow others to step in and help *and also and not least* that letting Crisp do something powerfully well-intentioned will help him put a better spin on a truly shitty twenty-four hours *and also and perhaps most importantly* will show his mother that he is who she thought he was, who she raised him to be, that his soul has roots and his mind has wings, that getting arrested was (he hopes) a meaningless blip. Before he can open his mouth with a few choice words to express all that, Glynnie is on her feet.

"I know!" she announces, energized by the sense that two puzzle pieces have just slipped into place, a perfect fit—and she, a witness, has only to spell out the obvious. "JJ, I'm going to buy you a phone you can use with those Beats. In exchange, you'll take me to your gun guy, and you'll also let Crisp help you—that's part of the deal."

Crisp can't believe they're talking about this again. He raises his voice to make sure he's really heard: *"No gun, Glynnie."*

"JJ has his pride," Glynnie argues with quiet authority, a feeling more powerful than shouting. "He doesn't want to take your charity for nothing, Crisp. You've got to be realistic here. JJ does *not* want to be in debt to you—he's got enough problems. You do this for him, he does this for me, *and* he gets a smartphone. Seriously, could you *imagine* your life without music?"

Crisp looks directly at JJ and counters with his own calm explanation: "You'll help me with something in the future, when I know what I need. Or you'll pay it forward later and help someone else. Seriously, 'All comes out even at the end of the day.'" (Voltaire.) "JJ, you've heard of karma, right?"

The boy picks up the Beats, puts them on, and closes his eyes as if listening to a song when they all know there's nothing but silence. He takes them off. "A new phone would be good. But like I said, it's hard to know how Big Man's cousin's gonna be."

"If anything goes wrong," Glynnie tells JJ, "I mean if *anything* feels even a little bit off, we're out of there. I promise."

"Can't draw any cops."

"God no," Glynnie agrees. "You have my solemn promise on that one."

JJ puts the Beats back on and closes his eyes and says, "Snap."

"Good." Glynnie claps her hands and smiles. "That's a done deal."

"Why do you even want a gun?" Crisp pleads.

"Because usually I *can't*. This is an *opportunity*. Plus," thinking on her feet, "I'm going to Outward Bound. What if there's a bear?"

Crisp mutters, "Now I'm starting to understand," *her foolishness*—but he doesn't come right out and say that to her face.

But Glynnie perceives the intent beneath his words and it stings. She has no intention of ever *using* the gun—why would she? (Well, maybe on a bear, and only in self-defense.) But the thought of owning one slides deliciously through her imagination, and now, *especially now* that Crisp has staked himself against it and on top of that is *judging* her (just like everyone else, her parents, her teachers), now more than ever she wants to see this happen. She wants it because she wants it. She *needs* it because no one thinks she's capable of succeeding, but she is. She will succeed at *this*.

"Can we get the gun tonight?" Glynnie asks.

JJ slides his right ear free. "We can try."

"I'll get the phone tomorrow," she promises. "You good with that, JJ?"

"Yeah, I am, I'm good with it."

* * *

Van Brunt Street past midnight is all but abandoned except for bars whose windows showcase late birds enjoying themselves well past bedtime. Walking along with Glynnie and JJ, glimpsing the fact of other people's eager sociability, Crisp feels more separate than ever. Separate and sober and regretful that he ever left Brighton Beach this afternoon. Stormed out on his mother like that. Found himself here, doing *this*.

Walking beside Crisp, Glynnie feels she's not so much walking as *leading* him and JJ through the quiet night, which makes her feel…what? *Coaxed*. By herself. By possibilities. *Prodded,* even, by Crisp's reluctance. Coaxed and prodded into an unknown future, into the unplanned slips of time her parents can't reach or control. An unfolding-now future that is of her own making. Coaxed and prodded and *excited*. The risk and daring of what they're doing thrills her more than she'd be willing to admit out loud. She's *in control,* making *decisions* and *choices,* moving forward *of her own accord*.

Wait until that fucking bear sees her with a gun—no one will expect her to survive, and then she will. It will be her first headline: "Girl Survives Encounter with Bear in the Wild." No, scratch that: "Woman Survives Encounter with Bear in the Wild." Now that she's eighteen and a high-school graduate, no one has the right to call her a girl ever again.

On the corner of Van Brunt and Coffey, she grinds to a halt at the sight of a cash machine built into the wall outside a deli. Dips in her debit card, feeling that curl of anticipation she experiences whenever she's decided to do something she shouldn't. Waits for the stack of bills to slide out of the slot. Instead, a message reads No CASH AVAILABLE AT THIS TIME.

Aggravated, she consults her phone and discovers that Chase has an outpost way over on Hamilton Avenue. She walks and the boys follow. When they finally reach the bank she struggles a little with the door until Crisp supplies the final tug that wrests it open, which she reads as implicit cooperation with her venture.

She steps up to one of the ATMs. The only customer at this hour of the night.

Morning now. A new day.

The slot pumps out a stack of fifty-dollar bills, three hundred dollars in all. She counts the cash and then folds it into the front pocket of her jeans.

"Glynnie," Crisp begs, "will you please reconsider? Can we at least talk about it before—"

"You don't have to come." She's disappointed to realize that he still isn't on board. "Seriously, Crisp, I know this bothers you and I respect that, but why don't you just head home?" She holds back from affectionately calling him Crispy Cream, as she might have a couple of hours ago, because his unwillingness—no, *disapproval*—no longer feels idiosyncratic, interesting, or fun.

"I will," he says. "But first I want to see where you're going, get the lay of the land."

JJ looks at him. "And then you're leaving?"

"Don't worry, I'm still going to help you, JJ. My promise holds. And seriously, you do not have to do any of this to *pay* me. I don't need payment. I—"

Glynnie corrects him: "We have a deal."

"Okay," JJ says. "Cool."

Crisp pulls open the door and the three are back in the quiet night.

A car drives past. Half a block over, rhythmic waves swish against an unseen shore, and above it the dark sky glows reddish from industrial New Jersey on the other side of Manhattan's southern end. Crisp means what he says about going home once they've arrived at Big Man's cousin's building, but not before then. And he means what he says about returning to help JJ figure things out.

"Why *are* you coming with us at this point?" Glynnie asks Crisp. "So you can show them where to find the bodies?"

"Someone should know where you are."

"It isn't like that," JJ says. "He just makes his sale and then we go."

"Like you did," Crisp says, "when she brought in a stranger?"

JJ hesitates before answering; they both saw his alarm bells go off when Glynnie introduced an unknown by bringing Crisp along on her buy. "Yeah, maybe it'll take a minute," JJ admits. "Sure. But I'm gonna explain. If we're cool, he'll be cool. He'll want to make his sale."

Glynnie argues, "Unless he's an idiot he's not going to mess with a customer with three hundred bucks in her pocket. He's a businessman. And if he has half a brain he'll also be thinking about nurturing a *return* customer. I am just so not worried about this, Crisp, so please keep your thoughts to yourself unless they're, you know, *productive*."

Silenced, incensed, humiliated, baffled by her recklessness, he walks along with them. Why did he think it was so important to let her know what he was doing in that cage yesterday? If only he hadn't called out to her and made sure she saw him. If only he had stayed and faced his mother and made that call to Princeton. If only he hadn't jumped on the subway to go somewhere, anywhere, and foolishly decided on Glynnie Dreyfus as a destination, an innocuous destination (he'd thought) that would kill two birds with one stone: rumors and time. As if he was in control of either.

10

Friday

The leather soles of Lex's boots clap up the concrete stairs of the High Street station. Out on the street it's quiet except for a light thrum of traffic ramping off the bridge into Brooklyn Heights.

He's glad it worked out that he can help with Ethan's morning school run, that reprieve landing when Katya Spielman got in touch to report that her son had finally checked in with a text saying he was out with friends— not where, or with whom, but it was enough to allow her to stop worrying. It's more than Lex got from Adam, or offered Adam; they're heading now into a second day of silence.

He wonders (again) if Adam ever went home last night and tries to understand (again) when things began to sour. He fleetingly recalls that first night they spent together without Adam running home to William like Cinderella back to her keeper. They lay in bed as daylight crept into the room, peaceful in each other's arms, and

Adam confessed how good it was to be with someone who wasn't an alcoholic, how much he admired Lex's strength, how surprised he was to discover that he could be this attracted to someone who wasn't a total mess. Lex didn't doubt his sincerity, or his relief, having himself grown up with a raging drunk for the first eight years of his life, and knowing from hard experience that love binds without judgment.

The bright morning sun hurts Lex's eyes after two nights and a day without sleep. He pauses to fish in his backpack for his sunglasses, finds them nested at the bottom, and slips them on. He makes his way up Cranberry Street and turns onto Willow.

David rents the parlor floor of a brownstone, and as Lex comes up the block he sees Ethan perched in one of the front windows, watching for him as he always does. His nephew smiles and waves and disappears. Moments later, father and son emerge at the front door, dressed for their respective days of business and school: David with his short brown hair neatly parted and combed and his dark blue suit and stuffed briefcase, Ethan in crisp jeans, spanking-new sneakers, and green T-shirt emblazoned with a soccer ball dead center over the boy's heart.

David turns to lock the door. "Thanks for this, Lex. I really appreciate it. My timing this morning is ridiculously tight."

"No problem."

As Ethan trots down the stoop his broad smile reveals a surprise: tracks of braces now cover the jigsaw of his teeth. Lex tousles the thick head of red hair the kid inherited from his mother, who still lives in what was the family apartment on the Upper East Side, near the hospital where she's an ER doctor. Ethan used to take a bus back and forth to his Brooklyn Heights private school, but after the divorce, David moved closer to ease the commute. (And, Lex is sure, to be closer to Elsa Myers, who lives nearby.) Now Ethan spends weekdays with his father and weekends with his mother in Manhattan.

They walk together until they reach the Clark Street subway, where David peels off toward the express train.

"Good luck," Lex calls after his brother.

David waves, and is gone.

"Hey buddy, how about some breakfast?" The Clark Street Diner, their favorite, is just across the street.

Ethan answers, "I had some cereal at home."

"Doesn't school start at eight? It's only ten past seven. You can have a second breakfast, or watch me eat."

"I have earth science club at seven fifteen. My mom signed me up." He rolls his eyes.

"That's pretty cool, Ethan."

"Not really."

"Come on, let's get you there on time." Lex breaks into a jog. Laughing, Ethan catches up and stays close, dodging dog walkers and baby strollers all the way to Joralemon Street.

The brick Gothic school building looms over the otherwise residential block. Watching his nephew run up the stairs and disappear into the vaulted entrance, Lex feels grateful for David and Ethan, the only family he has left—a feeling that yanks the scab off a memory he tries not to revisit but sometimes can't avoid.

Himself, eight years old, alone and frightened, entering the jaw of Sheremetyevo Airport while his drunk-in-the-morning father stands there and watches him go.

What did his father think, what did he feel, putting his child on a plane to America to live with his first wife and son, Yelena and David, whom at that point Lex had never met? The memory lands whole with a reminder of forfeiture so painful it encompasses every sense.

The river of Russian language, its sounds and symbols, that was so familiar he never thought about it until it was gone.

The sour taste in his mouth from morning tea but no breakfast.

The chill of overcooled industrial air.

And the stench of his father that lingered as the distance between them grew.

They say that vodka is odorless but Lex knows what it smells like. It smells like the far edge of alcohol and the near edge of abandonment. Like two sharp sensations you know are there because you intuit them but you can never quite describe their most salient qualities. You just know that one stinks and the other hurts and together they represent disaster.

It was the last time he would ever see his father before cirrhosis killed him a year later.

The last time he saw his mother was two months earlier, and the smell she left him with was lilac. Sometimes she couldn't get out of bed, she was so tired, but that day, their last together, she was not only up but wearing a dress, purple with wavy yellow stripes. Her long brown hair fell neatly down her back. Her perfume was strong; she had just put it on. He was sitting cross-legged on the floor, doing homework. She didn't say anything but when she kissed him there were tears in her eyes and one of her cheeks was violently red—he didn't have to ask if his father had hit her again. He would never forget the hard click of the door closing behind her and the soul-sucking quiet that followed. A few years later he was told that she, too, had died, but the way the news was presented, without detail, left him with a fantasy that it wasn't true and a hope that one day he would find her. Searching for clues about what happened to their family and where Nina might have gone, he would study the single photo his father sent him off with: a boy rooted happily into his young mother's lap, her hands clasped around his slender waist, the father standing behind them wearing the creased, humorless mask that was his face. But there were no clues in that frozen image. Eventually Lex grew up, filed away his father's death certificate, stored the photo in the cloud, and consulted it only at his weakest moments.

Standing outside Ethan's school, he abhors this feeling and pushes it away—this toxic memory of abandonment, this certainty that he was born for it, that he's destined to be deserted again and again, that the cycle will never stop and the dread of it will destroy him and anyone he loves.

He could go home now, but he isn't ready to face the quiet.

He could go to the diner and have something before getting on the train, but he doesn't want to eat alone.

Then he thinks of the perfect solution. He takes out his phone and opens a new message to Elsa, his friend and once colleague (before David ever met her).

I'm in the neighborhood. Breakfast?

11

Last Night

At the corner of Verona and Richards Streets they
come to an entrance to the projects. A cream-on-
maroon sign—WELCOME To Red Hook Houses /
Property Of New York City Housing Authority—
stands in front of a mazelike collection of six-story brick
structures pocked with small rectangular windows.

A *thullump* in Crisp's chest makes him pause a moment.
This is where his father grew up. His mother mentioned
it only once but Crisp never forgot: "Mo never could get
past the Red Hook Houses in his head." At the time, he
pictured a block filled with red houses shaped like hooks,
as if that's even possible, but later understood that when
a black person grew up in "the houses" it always meant
the projects.

For all the baggage of half his lineage, Crisp has never
actually been inside a housing project, not the low-income
kind, anyway. He's driven past them, walked beside
them, observed them from a distance, read about them

in the newspaper, watched stories about their dangers. But it has always been so clearly off-limits to step onto the grounds of a project, possibly even suicidal, that he never actually considered doing it. The internalized self-loathing racism inherent in that assumption hits him suddenly and hard.

Glynnie has never stepped foot anywhere near a housing project, and as far as she can tell it isn't so bad. The brick buildings aren't pretty, but they're solid. There's grass, sort of. A playground, outdated, but still. Her blood pumps and she picks up her pace as she follows JJ into what feels like a forbidden zone.

"Bye, Crisp," she calls behind her, trying not to pay too much attention to that look on his face. "Talk soon, okay?"

"Wait—which building are you going to?" Crisp calls after them.

"I don't know the number," JJ answers. "I'll know it on sight."

From Crisp's vantage point at the nexus of these two streets, the complex appears so vast that it's impossible to count the buildings or even the number of blocks involved. And those narrow asphalt paths that seem to intersect and yet lead nowhere. He trails them into the nest of buildings where most of the path lights are out, creating an avid darkness.

He thinks of his mother, how much she loves him, how hard she's worked to raise him, and he feels horrible for his vanishing act today. He pulls out his phone and thumbs her a quick text so at least she'll know he's alive:

I love you. With friends. When he doesn't hear the send *swish* he wonders if, along with the more obvious deficits, housing projects are also bereft of adequate signal and *add it to the list* and *stop thinking*.

Crisp follows, silenced phrases popping inside his mind: *Bad idea, turn around*. And yet his body keeps moving forward. *Get the building number, then go*. The buildings are identical, paths webbing through decimated lawns, rusted benches, no one sitting on them, or at least that's what Crisp thinks and then suddenly he hears a voice, a pair of voices, and his pulse jumps.

Two men materialize on a deeply shadowed bench.

No, not two men. Three.

He pauses behind JJ at a fork in the path as the boy decides between Building 8 on the left and Building 7 on the right. Almost there.

One of the men speaks: "Yo, kid, what you doin' out so late?"

"That you, Dante?" JJ asks the man who spoke, the largest of the three.

"Yeah, man. Whazzup?"

"I got you a cus—"

"Shut the fuck up. I know what you got, I ain't blind. Who are they? White chick *my ass*." A thicket of gold chains and filigreed pendants glimmer around his neck. In the dark, it looks to Crisp as though there's something sitting on his head.

Glynnie's stomach flip-flops. The man's tone, his words, the way he and his friends are hunkered into the darkness, sends a flourish of delicious warning through her.

She lifts her chin: she has every right to be here even if she's white and rich.

"I'm—" she begins, but JJ cuts her off.

"They cash be good," JJ says. "You in or ain't?"

Crisp notices JJ's full slide into the Ebonics he only dipped into before, and feels reassured by the boy's intuitive understanding of the power of language as a survival tactic. He fleetingly wonders if, along with prep for the specialized high-school test, he might be able to start him in the basics of Latin.

The man stands and so do the other two, and together they ease out of the shadow—two black and one white. The first man, Dante, looms over the others. He says, "Let's take this inside to my *office*."

At the word *office,* the underlings—at least that's what Crisp thinks they are—titter, amused. The white one tilts his Nets cap. The other one, in a heavy leather jacket, grins with lips so taut they almost disappear into his broad face.

Crisp holds back as Dante and his friends veer left at the fork toward Building 8. And then he whispers to JJ, "Guess I'll go now. I'll get back in touch with you tomorrow."

"You said what?" The large man, Dante, addresses Crisp directly.

"Um, I'm heading out. That's all."

"No you ain't."

"Yo, Dante," JJ interjects. "*She* the buyer, not him."

"Shut the fuck up. Like I said, we don't talk in the open. Gimme your phones—you'll get 'em back on the way out."

Crisp rejoins the group, a seed of helplessness blossoming in the soil of his best intentions.

"Maybe this isn't such a good idea," Glynnie mutters. Wondering, only now, if it actually *isn't*.

Dante's grin is a ribbon of gold in the moonlight. He nods at Leather Jacket, who holds out his hand.

Onto the weathered palm Glynnie places her iPhone, sparkly in a transparent rubber case. JJ adds his LG flip, and Crisp his black Samsung Galaxy. Nets Cap pulls some kind of silver pouch out of his pocket and Leather Jacket dumps the phones inside. The bag is made out of a signal-blocking material, Crisp realizes with a twist of panic. These men are ready for this—whatever this is.

The first thing that strikes Glynnie when they enter the lobby is a circus smell—hay, popcorn, hot dogs— and it steadies her shaky confidence enough to keep her moving forward. Mustard-tiled walls and cracked linoleum floors. Free-hanging lightbulbs. An elevator that doesn't work. The rank airlessness of the internal stairwell as they follow Dante up four flights. The second thing she notices is Dante's crisply ironed jeans, pristine black-and-white sneakers with long studded tongues, and white windbreaker decorated with black diamonds and crowns. His hair, she sees in the stairwell's harsh lighting, has been straightened, curled, and set in a kind of bouffant. Sitting on top of the hair, almost planted in it, is a red MAKE AMERICA GREAT AGAIN cap. With every step as he mounts the stairs, silver FENDI tags designed to look like license plates flash on the back of his sneakers.

As Crisp walks up the stairs between Glynnie and JJ,

his mind thrashes, struggles to get hold of the moment, the here and now, the distortions of assumption and challenges of perception. He urges himself not to worry so much. Reminds himself that he's overthinking as he always does. *Just chill, get through this, go home.* The heavy steps of the gun dealer's two cohorts bringing up the rear offer a constant reminder that if he bolts, they'll only stop him.

All the bulbs in the fourth-floor hallway are out, so Dante uses the torch on his phone—a black Galaxy, same as his, Crisp notices—to light the way. Then, at the door marked 4F, he pulls out a large key ring and turns seven bolts.

Building 8, apartment 4F, Crisp memorizes.

Dante flicks on an overhead to light the room, a square with two windows covered with dark green bedsheets, a half-collapsed corduroy couch in the corner, a freestanding stove and padlocked refrigerator near the door, and in the center a card table with four folding chairs. A copy of *Vogue* lies open on the table: a fall fashion preview of men in penny loafers, knee socks, and tartan kilts. On the left wall are two closed doors.

Dante pulls out one of the chairs and sits with his legs spread wide. He puts his phone down on the table beside the magazine. Leather Jacket drops the lumpy silver bag on top.

Dante asks Glynnie, "What you looking for?"

She glances at JJ, wondering when he plans to step in and negotiate, but he looks terrified, frozen, almost, and she realizes that she's on her own. She clears her throat and tells Dante, "A gun."

"A *gun,*" he mocks. "Girl, that's like going into a restaurant and ordering *food.*" He laughs, those golden teeth again. "Kid," to JJ, "you wanna help her out?"

"Something like what I got," the boy's voice stuck on soprano, not cracking at all.

"You think I remember exactly what I sold you?" Dante snaps. "You think you my only customer?"

JJ clears his throat. "Ruger twenty-two."

"She too pretty for a deuce-deuce." Nets Cap's eyes roam Glynnie from head to toe and back again in an edgy, threatening appraisal, and she realizes with a spike of fear that she's *getting eyeballed* in a brand-new way.

She looks at him now, really looks at him for the first time in full light, and sees the deep creases across his forehead, the lines around his mouth that have nothing to do with smiling, the choker of crude dollar signs blue-tattooed above his collarbone, the crevice beneath his Adam's apple that looks like someone tried to kill him by pressing down a thumb. He's got a silver ring on every finger of both hands, even his thumbs, heavily carved symbols and skulls with the Gothic flare of the gargoyles on top of the Manhattan building where she used to see a psychiatrist until she told her parents to go to hell. He licks his lips. She wills herself not to frown or scream or tell him off. She can handle these assholes; she can and she will.

"That sounds good to me," Glynnie tells Dante, a waver in her voice. She steadies herself. "I'll take one. How much?"

"Nah." Dante gets up and goes to the kitchen area.

He keys open the padlock on the refrigerator and swings wide the door onto an unlit interior with no shelves. He pulls out a long case. Leather Jacket moves the magazine and phones to a chair to make room on the table.

Dante opens the case to reveal an *alarming,* Crisp thinks, *ridiculous, outrageous, disturbing* collection of semiautomatic rifles and handguns—a massive collection including military-grade weaponry that anyone could waltz right up and buy. Anyone. Glynnie. Right now. With cash from her pocket.

Reaching in among the firearms, Dante selects an elaborately carved nickel pistol with a pearl grip. He says to Glynnie, "What *you* want is this one, 'cause it pretty, like a toy. This a Baby Browning twenty-five, been sitting here just waiting specially for you."

It isn't what Glynnie pictured—something more utilitarian and modern, like JJ's, was how she imagined herself warding off that bear—but seeing this now makes her reassess.

She asks, "Does it work?"

"'Does it work?'" Dante repeats. He lifts his chin at Leather Jacket, who opens the fridge and from a produce drawer filled with ammunition selects what he wants. Dante takes the gun, cracks open the barrel, slots in the cartridge, and passes it to her. "It work just like it supposed to. So, you buying?"

The Baby Browning smooth and elegant in her hand, she asks, "How much?"

"Eighteen Cs."

"I don't have anywhere near that much on me."

"Well, what you got?"

"Three," she says. "Cs."

Glancing at Nets Cap, Dante mutters, "What you think, Jerome? Not too many customers just right for this baby."

Jerome removes his hat and tilts his head. Grizzly hair going thin at the crown. The skin under his chin sagging enough to show some age. "I can think of a way she can work off the rest."

Every nerve in Glynnie's body lights up.

The hairs prickle on the back of Crisp's neck.

Dante tells Jerome, "Happy early birthday, my man."

"No," Crisp says. "She doesn't have enough money to buy it. I think it's time for us to go." He grabs Glynnie's sweaty hand. "JJ, come on."

Dante steps forward to loom over Crisp, hiding his teeth in a frown. Meanwhile, Jerome eases his way toward Glynnie. He reaches out a hand and touches her, actually touches her, and the entirety of her skin goes cold all at once and seems to shrink. She tries to shake off the hand, causing Dante to laugh and Jerome to slip a finger under the collar of her shirt.

She tells him *"No."* But he doesn't stop.

"Dante—" JJ begins.

"Get outta here, kid," Dante snaps. "This ain't for you."

"Please."

"I said *get*. And keep your mouth shut—you snitch, you dead."

"Go on," Crisp urges the boy, appealing silently with his eyes: *Building 8, apartment 4F. Tell someone.*

Leather Jacket opens all seven locks. JJ rushes out. One by one, the bolts slide back into place.

"Don't do this," Crisp tries to reason. "This is a mistake. You don't have to. Just let us go before anything happens. Let's be smart about this—"

"Smart? Rodrigo, you hear that? This little dude telling us 'Be smart.'"

Rodrigo chuckles, sloughs off his leather jacket, hangs it on the back of a chair, and cracks his knuckles, getting ready.

Jerome slides his hand farther into Glynnie's shirt.

Crisp recalls the self-defense class his mother enrolled him in when he was ten. Thinking stops in a rush of adrenaline. He pinches together the tips of his thumb and forefinger to make a sharp weapon, intending to peck Jerome's right eye first. He inches closer.

Dante pulls out a chair and sits down with a rifle resting on his knee, ready to watch the show. Jerome pressing his body against Glynnie now. Glynnie struggling, saying, "Hey! *Stop it*." Rodrigo approaching as if to help, but not to help *her*.

"You fucking white bitches all the same." Jerome's tongue comes out of his mouth and snakes in the direction of Glynnie's ear.

"You're white," she reminds him, but it doesn't seem to penetrate.

She feels the wet of his tongue in her ear and then his whisper, "I ain't nowhere white as you." She closes her eyes, tries to pretend this isn't happening.

Closer now, Crisp raises his pinched fingertips and

calculates his best shot at Jerome's eye. To his side, he notices Rodrigo starting toward him, raising a hand to block him.

A gun goes off, and the thunderous crack freezes them all.

And Crisp can't think.

And Glynnie can't breathe.

And time—it just stops.

12

Friday

Lex is waiting outside a café on Smith Street, near Elsa's apartment, when she strides up with her striped canvas workbag slung over her shoulder. Wiry, hair tucked behind her ears, she wears her trademark long pants and long sleeves even in summer, hiding her damaged skin.

"You look great," he tells her.

She answers, "You know I don't like bullshit."

"I sure do."

He opens his arms and she walks right into his hug, a gesture of acceptance that pleases him. She's softened a bit since her father died last August. Lex will never forget the night, earlier that summer just after their case ended, when he drove her upstate to see her father in the hospital. It was the kind of case, and the kind of night, that leaves you raw, empty. By the end of it, he learned that she didn't consider herself worthy of friendship, and he learned why. Now, hugging her hello, he realizes that she's actually hugging him back. Not much, just a little, but he feels it.

"It was so nice to see your message this morning," she tells him, standing back, looking at him.

"Spent half the night tracking down a missing kid. Naturally, I thought of you." He grins.

"You said you were in the neighborhood."

"Damn, you're a good investigator!"

She laughs. "How old's the kid?"

"Nineteen. He turned out not to be missing, though— he texted his mother a couple hours ago."

"Well," she says, "nineteen isn't a kid in my book. Not officially. Brain development, well, that's a whole other thing."

He'll never forget that either: the significance of the demarcation line of a child's eighteenth birthday. And he won't forget last summer, looking for a girl about to hit that legal milestone and the time it took for him to decide whether to treat her as a child or an adult until Elsa joined the case and cleared that up. Her work on the FBI's Child Abduction Rapid Deployment team had taught her to be vigilant with details, and technically, at two days shy of her eighteenth birthday, Ruby was still a child at the time of her abduction.

Lex pulls out a chair for her at one of the café's outdoor tables. She ignores his gallant gesture and sits opposite. He takes the seat he meant for her and, while scooting himself closer to the table, his calf muscles seize, and he winces.

"You okay?"

"Got a nasty cramp out on the water yesterday; still hasn't worked itself out."

"Swimming?"

"Didn't you know I surf?"

"You're kidding."

"Took it up after college. I love it."

"Sounds like you're enjoying life in the Rockaways."

"It was a good move. The Six-O, that was a good move too." Not saying what started the bouncing from squad to squad, how a stint in Vice with easy access to serious drugs, the kind he wanted when he wanted them, sent him running. To Forest Hills, where he met Elsa. To downtown Brooklyn, until he realized that the property clerk located there also stored confiscated drugs and it proved too close for comfort. To Coney Island, where he is now. "Trying to get Adam on board, but no luck."

"*On board.*" She cocks her head. "Is that where the saying comes from—surfing?"

"Could be."

"So how's Adam?"

"He's fine. Working on his dissertation. The usual." Lex looks at Elsa and wonders why he's holding back, considering the secrets she allowed him to glimpse last year, the slashes of self-inflicted scarring up and down her arm. He'd show her his own breaking point one day, he would—show by telling because his spell of addiction left no visible scars. But today, he opens up just a little. "Adam and I have hit some bumps lately," he confesses. "He leaves late at night, comes home early in the morning, and won't tell me where he goes. It's been going on for over a week. Maybe I should be more patient, give him space, but..."

The waiter arrives and they both order coffee, eggs, toast, orange juice.

"Think it'll blow over?" she asks.

Lex shakes his head. "A couple nights ago, when he was heading out, I told him not to come back—I didn't say it quite that nicely, though. I haven't seen him since. But if this is it, if it's over, then it's partly my fault too."

"How?" She leans in, as if challenging him to provide a solid rationale for a weak premise.

"Here's something you might not know about me: I'm the green-eyed monster."

"You think he's cheating?"

"That's the big question. I mean, he cheated on his ex with me."

She nods. "Ah—not a great start."

Lex steers the conversation away from Adam, and they chat about politics and the news until their food arrives. After they eat, Elsa checks the time. "I should head out."

"Busy day?"

"Not that I'm aware of, but I'm sure that'll change."

He knows it will.

She asks, "You?"

"I should go home—find out if he really left, talk it out if he didn't. Sleep a little, if I even can."

"I've got to see you surf one of these days." An arch twinkle in her eye.

"Come have drinks with me at the beach club and

maybe I'll let you watch me make a fool of myself on the water."

"Now *that* would be fun."

The check arrives. Elsa lays down a twenty-dollar bill and stands up. "Think I'll hit the ladies' before I go."

Lex puts down his own twenty. While Elsa is in the bathroom, his phone rings—a number he doesn't recognize. Out of curiosity, he answers.

A man's voice, flinty, unfamiliar: "Detective Cole?"

"Yes."

"Sergeant Gordy Boyd, Eight-Four."

Lex's interest perks up at the mention of his former precinct. "What can I do for you, Sergeant?"

"I understand you caught a missing persons last night—Titus Crespo."

"I did. Already closed. He got in touch with his family."

"Sorry to tell you, but it looks like it's not so simple. Just got a call from Detective Finley—you know her?"

Lex thinks back to his brief stint at the downtown Brooklyn precinct. "No."

"Probably came in after you left. She gave me an earful—wants you to meet her as soon as you can." Sergeant Boyd talks and Lex listens as the prospect of his day off is transformed by a trickle of urgency and then flooded out of existence.

13

Last Night

Crisp stares down at the fallen man, sprawled, motionless, blood seeping from his brow, dark pupils growing to fill the whites of his eyes. Jerome looks dead because he *is* dead. He's *dead*. The Baby Browning lies on the floor near Glynnie's feet.

Rodrigo crouches beside his friend, colleague—Crisp doesn't know what they are, were, to each other exactly—and presses two fingers to the dead man's neck.

Crisp holds his breath, waiting for another explosion, a retaliatory rifle shot, a tirade, something from Dante to demonstrate the rage he must be feeling. But all the man says is, "Now this just won't do," without any emotion at all. Crisp looks at Glynnie, whose skin has lost its scant color. He didn't know someone could become that white, so white you can see blue veins crisscrossing underneath.

Glynnie feels hot, then cold. Cold and afraid. She can't believe she just did that. *Killed someone. With a gun.*

She never knew that blood smells like sparks off fresh-cut metal.

"I'm so sorry…" Speaking fast, mind reeling. "I didn't mean to do it, I don't know how it happened, did you see what he was doing to me? It wasn't my fault."

"Shut the fuck up, bitch." Shouldering the rifle, Dante walks over to look down at Jerome. "What do you think happens when you pull the trigger?"

"But—"

"Now I'm down a man."

"I'm *so so* sorry I hurt your friend."

"He's not *hurt,* sister, he's *dead*. You killed him. And he ain't my friend. He was a fucking asshole and I never liked him. But still, I'm down a man—you hear me?"

Crisp meets her gaze. She's never seemed so—what?— sober. All that confidence flickering in her eyes an hour ago, it's gone now.

He glances at the door with its seven locks. The case full of guns. Rodrigo with his arms crossed over a barrel chest and eyes that suddenly look jaundiced, as if someone lowered the lights, as if death has somehow dimmed the room. And Dante, Dante with his rifle and his ironed jeans, exuding control.

"What I'm saying is *I'm down a man,*" the gun dealer repeats.

Crisp asks, "What exactly do you want?"

"Rod," Dante says to his associate, "you know me a long time."

"Yeah, boss, that's right."

"Tell me, what do you think I want?"

Rodrigo doesn't hesitate. He looks at Crisp.

"That's right. Sit down," Dante tells Crisp. "Time to get acquainted, now you're part of my team."

"I don't understand," Crisp says, untruthfully, because he does, he does understand, he understands perfectly well. Dante wants *him*. This cannot be happening, not after the night in jail *because he rode his bicycle on the sidewalk*. Okay, and mouthed off at a cop. And visited a friend. And followed her to what turned out to be *here*—his father's world, not his mother's—not en route to college but hurtling away from it.

"What don't you understand?" Dante asks.

"I can't work with you."

"No one works *with* me. You work *for* me. Got that?"

"I can't."

"You think you got a choice? I'm minus one." Dante tips the rifle butt in Jerome's direction, then looks back at Crisp. "I'm minus Jerome so I add you, and we're back in business."

"I'll do it." Glynnie's voice is choked by fear, barely above a whisper. She summons volume and says, "It's my fault, like you said. I did it. I'll work for you. Take me."

"What're you on?" Dante says. "You look in a mirror lately? You a *white girl*."

"It's a big city. I'll...I'll help broaden your market."

"Glynnie," Crisp hisses. *"Stop."*

Dante says, *"Glynnie*—so that's your name?"

"It's short for Glynneth."

"Glynneth. Sounds like you walked out of a castle from England, and you think you gonna be on my crew?"

"Well *he* can't." She points at Crisp. "He's going to Princeton."

Dante grins his golden grin. "You don't say? Well ain't that fine. Let the schooling start right here and now. You just got yourself a summer job, kid. *Summer job,* Rod, you hear that?"

"I hear it." Rodrigo shakes his head and half smiles, but not with humor.

"What about you, my man?" Dante asks Crisp. "What do you call yourself?"

I'm not your man, Crisp wants to say, but doesn't. Why did Glynnie blurt that out about Princeton? Now they'll never let him go.

He takes a breath and answers, "Crisp."

"Well now I've heard it all. Glynnie and Crisp, Princess and Princeton. Shit." Dante yawns and hands Rodrigo the rifle.

"What now, boss?"

"Keep an eye on them. I'm gonna get some shut-eye."

"What about Jerome?"

"Stick him in the tub. We'll deal with him later."

"You not worried about the kid out there?"

"That runt says a word, he gone. Nah, I ain't worried." Turning to Glynnie, Dante orders, "Clean up the mess."

The dealer picks up his phone from the table, pauses, and, as an afterthought, also takes the silver bag. He retreats through one of the two closed doors and a lock clicks behind him.

Rodrigo leans the rifle against the wall, then opens the second door to reveal a bathroom. As soon as she sees it,

Glynnie realizes how badly she needs to pee. She hears the rough swish of a shower curtain being pulled across a metal bar. Rodrigo returns to lift Jerome and carries him out of sight. The shower curtain swishes closed. A cabinet door opens and slaps shut, and Rodrigo emerges with a roll of paper towels and a garbage bag.

He drapes the bag over the back of a chair, tosses the paper towels to Glynnie, and says, "Who the cleaning lady now?"

Glynnie catches the thick, soft roll and lifts her chin. She can do this, no matter what anyone thinks.

"I'll help you," Crisp offers.

"You sit your ass down over there while she do all the work. *Her* mess." Rodrigo points the nib of the rifle at the far wall.

Crisp crosses the room and sets himself down on the floor and watches as Glynnie, hugging the paper towels like a teddy bear, approaches the bloody linoleum.

Rodrigo drapes himself awkwardly on the lopsided couch, cradles the rifle in his lap, and tells her, "Go on. Get to work."

Glynnie's stomach bucks as she drops to her knees. *She can do this.* She swallows hard, and begins. Covers the blood with ribbons of paper towel until the roll is nearly finished. Pushes the bloody mess together into one central blob until there's enough bulk that she can shove it into the bag. At the sight of her hands stained red she gags again.

"Turn off the light." Rodrigo uses the rifle as a pointer again.

When she touches the light switch by the door, she leaves behind a red fingerprint.

"Clean that fuckin' bullshit up," Rodrigo orders in a tone that channels his slumbering boss. Trying the role on for size, while he can. *Hail, Il Duce,* Crisp manages not to say out loud.

Glynnie uses her bare elbow to wipe away the mark.

Quietly, she says, "Maybe I should wash my hands."

"Maybe you should, but don't touch nothing while you do it."

Using her forearm, she manages to turn on the cold water in the kitchen sink. The water turns icy and her fingers ache, she scrubs so hard and long. She turns off the tap and dries her hands and arms on her shirt. Looks at Rodrigo, then follows the rifle's instructions to cross the room.

Streetlight dribbles past the edges of the green sheets blocking the windows. In the scant light Crisp reads the fear in Glynnie's eyes as she joins him, sliding her back down along the wall, her ass finding the corner of the floor.

She whispers, "What now?" Thinking that even Crisp probably doesn't have the answer. Is she a murderer now? By dragging him here, has she made him an accessory? Has she managed to completely destroy both their lives?

"Shut the fuck up!" Rodrigo says.

Crisp pats his shoulder so she knows she can use it for support. And she does. But he doesn't know what else to do other than offer this meager comfort. How will he ever explain this to his mother and grandparents? He can't even begin to process the depth of their disappointment when they find out where he is...and how will that happen, anyway? Best-case scenario, JJ is out there getting help right now—but that's doubtful: he's afraid of the police, possibly even more afraid of Big Man, and Dante's threat sounded real. Worst case, he and Glynnie will be killed and no one will ever know how they got here.

The shock will probably destroy Babu, his grandmother, who endured one heart attack and probably couldn't survive another, and then Dedu will die of heartbreak, and his mother will be all alone. Alone in the apartment where she grew up and then spent her adulthood, instead of going out and making her own life, so that her parents could help her raise him. Eighteen years old when she had him—a year younger than Crisp is now. Shame blossoms at the thought of his grandparents' pride in him. The way Babu introduces him to her friends on the boardwalk, as if it's an honor: "Titus Crespo, *my grandson*." It's always been clear that now it's up to him, an American with African blood and slave ancestry, to help his Russian Jewish grandparents die in peace when their time comes, knowing their sacrifice has not been in vain.

Crisp rests his face in his hands in an effort to hide his tears from Glynnie.

Still, she knows. She can feel it in the way his body is moving beside her, how he's trying not to make any noise, but he's definitely crying. She forces herself to breathe slowly, the way her father used to when she was little and she'd have one of her meltdowns and he'd slow-breathe to set an example, and it worked, her breath would also slow and she'd calm down. After a few minutes she can feel Crisp's breath relax. Soon he falls asleep leaning against her, and she sits there listening to Rodrigo's ridiculously loud snoring. His head is tipped back on the couch now. The rifle lax across his legs.

Next thing she knows her eyes open in a disoriented fog and she realizes she nodded off. Crisp and Rodrigo are still asleep. Pale early sunlight traces the darkened windows, and with a start she realizes it's morning. She wonders if her parents have even noticed that she's gone.

She stares at the front door and wishes she could just get up and walk over there and open those locks and waltz out. But there's no way anyone could sleep through the racket of all those bolts unlatching. She counts to seven, letting her gaze settle on a lock before counting up to the next one, and then she counts again going down. Before she realizes what she's doing, she's counting to the rhythm of Rodrigo's snoring, her eyes lingering on a lock until he issues his next sawing grunt.

And then it hits her. Why not?

She gently eases Crisp to the floor, jams her flip-flops into her back pocket, and pads quietly across the room, hiding her steps under the snores. She reaches the door. No one has woken.

She holds her breath and waits. Just at the moment the snoring crescendos, she turns the bottom lock.

Repeats.

And again.

On the fifth lock, Rodrigo turns over and she's sure

he's about to open his eyes, but he doesn't. He settles into a new position and the snoring resumes.

She waits. Turns the sixth lock. Looks to make sure Rodrigo is still asleep and he is, *he is*.

Bleary, disoriented, Crisp awakens to see Glynnie turning the seventh lock under cover of Rodrigo's snoring. She *is* crazy. Shocked by her audacity, he catches her eye and opens his hands in a silent *What the fuck are you doing?*

She mouths *Let's go* and waves him over, relieved that now she won't have to risk crossing the room to wake him.

Crisp unlaces his sneakers, holds them in his hand, and pads carefully, quietly, across the floor. When he reaches her, they both hold still to make sure Rodrigo is still asleep.

She waits for a snore, then eases the door open.

Crisp doesn't remember the hinges making any sound when they came in earlier, but there were six of them and their footsteps must have drowned it out. But now, now the opening door emits a hairline squeal.

Rodrigo springs off the couch, knocks into the table, and two chairs crash over. The bedroom door flies open and there is Dante in his T-shirt and boxers with one side of his hair flattened, a circular indentation atop his head where he'd worn the hat.

Standing behind Glynnie, Crisp feels his shoulders pinned under Dante's big hands.

Frozen in the open door, Glynnie jolts into the hall at the sound of her friend's panicked voice: "Run!"

She does: she runs.

Behind her, the crash and hurl of Rodrigo coming after her in the dark.

Dante's face contorts and Crisp braces for whatever's coming next. A portentous quiet hangs in the hallway—invisible residents hovering on the other side of their doors, afraid to find out what their gun-dealing neighbor is up to now. Crisp senses, in the heavy voiceless listening, that no one would dare step forward to help him if he raised his voice. So he doesn't. He wonders what Rodrigo will do with Glynnie when he catches her, and he goes cold at the possibilities.

PART THREE

Think Like a Teenager

14

Friday

Lex looks up from his phone to see Elsa returning from the bathroom. He tells her, "So...that easy case from last night, the one that was closed? It might have just cracked back open."

"Don't you hate it when that happens?"

"Yeah, except it hardly ever does, at least not this fast."

"What changed?"

They vacate their table and stand on the sidewalk, bustling now with morning foot traffic leading mostly in the direction of the subway. Cars, taxis, trucks pile up at a red light on Smith Street. The hectic beginning of a new day.

"Apparently a friend of his, an eighteen-year-old girl who lives near here, just showed up at home after she was reported missing last night too. Says my guy's being held by a gun dealer in Red Hook."

Elsa's eyebrows lift. "Wow."

"Looks like *something* happened last night," he says,

"and according to her they were together, but I'm told she's not always reliable."

"Teenagers are hard to read."

"Hey, Elsa—"

"I can't."

"It's five blocks from here—in Boerum Hill. Come for a few minutes, help me read the situation. We both know you're better at teenagers than I am."

"Well," a sly grin, "that's true." She thinks a moment. "I guess I can be a couple minutes late today."

They start walking.

"Tell Marco you're consulting on a case." Lex knows from experience that Elsa has her supervisory agent, Marco Coutts, pretty much wrapped around her finger.

"Not if the kids are eighteen or over, I'm not."

"Yeah, well, Ruby was two days shy of eighteen when you consulted on that one, and two days older than eighteen when we found her, and the only thing that changed in the interim, besides becoming a legal adult, was that she was—" He stops abruptly. Elsa's knuckles gripping the strap of her bag have gone white. He shouldn't have reminded her.

They walk in silence the rest of the way, a heavy silence, his recollection having thrust them back to Ruby Haverstock and those terrifying days last summer before they found her. He will never forget the tangle of unreliable narratives spun by that group of teenagers, Ruby's friends, whose lies cost more time than the investigation could afford.

They arrive at a wide brownstone with ceiling-to-floor

windows and scrolled iron railings leading up the stoop. Lex rings the bell.

As they wait, Elsa says, "Welcome to *Brownstone Brooklyn*." Her tone is tweaked with sarcasm.

"You live here too," he points out.

"I live seven blocks away and there isn't a single house this fancy on my street."

"Tale of two cities," he agrees, but just to placate her. He's been to her building, and while it isn't fancy, it's pretty nice.

A slim Asian woman dressed all in black opens the door—or part Asian, Lex self-corrects, given her blue eyes and the flame-colored hair swept into a ponytail. She has her ID at the ready so that he can see exactly who she is without having to be told.

"Detective Lex Cole," he greets her. "I got a call from Sergeant Boyd."

"We seem to have an overlap in a couple cases," Detective Saki Finley says.

"I heard. This is Special Agent Myers, FBI CARD unit—child abduction. We happened to be together when I got the call."

"It's not an official consult," Elsa clarifies, "since I understand your subject is eighteen and that's—"

"The cutoff," Saki says. "Yes, I know."

Lex and Elsa follow the detective inside. She leads them into a modern living room, white and brass and dark wood, a penetrating aroma of coffee. A portly gray-haired man and a gaunt blonde woman share a long couch with their daughter. Three full mugs on the low glass table, one black, two milky. The girl looks worn out, and her feet, Lex notices, are filthy despite a perfect pedicure. In contrast to her dirty feet, her white T-shirt is pristine, her tight jeans cuffed neatly at the ankles. The parents sit erect, as if in hypervigilant preparation for another shoe to drop, while the daughter has herself draped partly over both of them. An interesting triad that suggests a volatile, unbalanced dynamic.

Lex smiles, hoping to put the family at ease, and introduces himself and Elsa.

"Nik Dreyfus." The father stands with his hand already extended. "This is my wife, Mags, and our daughter, Glynnie. Glynnie's been through a nightmare, and her friend—" He glances at the girl.

"Crisp," Glynnie says.

Saki interjects, "His full name is Titus Crespo. He goes by Crisp."

Lex nods. "I'm aware."

The girl pitches forward. "He's in *trouble*. He needs *help. You have to help him.*"

"I want to help him," Lex assures her. "But you'll need to tell us everything that happened and everything you know, as calmly and slowly as you can."

"I already told *her*." Glynnie looks at Saki.

Lex says, "Would you mind, please, telling me again?"

He sits opposite the couch in one of two matching leather chairs. Elsa sits in the other one. They put on their patient listening faces, though Lex has a strange feeling he can't quite isolate. This teenage girl has an outsize confidence that's already raising an alarm.

Glynnie talks. She talks and talks, spewing what sound like hyperbolized details of last night's adventure or trauma, depending on which part she's telling. How she and her friend Crisp wandered into Red Hook "for no particular reason." How she withdrew cash to eat at a "restaurant that doesn't do plastic," though they never made it to the restaurant. How they "got lost and ended up in the projects" before they realized where they were. How the rest "happened fast" when "two scary dudes" ambushed them and made them go inside. How "Dante, the head dude, had a shitload of guns, it was so crazy." How she "tried to use my cash to buy a gun just as a way to get out of there and it almost worked but then he changed his mind, I don't know why." How she managed to escape while her captors were sleeping but her friend, Crisp, didn't.

Lex and Elsa both take it in. He notes the way Saki also listens closely, without expression, to a story she's heard once before.

"Thanks," Lex says. "That's helpful. So, the reason I'm here right now is this: Last night I had a visit from Crisp's mother at the station house out in Coney Island. She was worried because she hadn't seen or heard from him since earlier yesterday, and he'd had some problems, which—"

Glynnie interrupts. "He got arrested on Wednesday for, like, riding his bike on the sidewalk after *a cop told him to ride his bike on the sidewalk*. Totally bogus."

"He told you about that?" Lex asks.

"Yeah, when he came over last night."

Mags asks, "To the house?"

"I saw him when he was locked up," Glynnie clarifies. "On Wednesday afternoon. That's the reason he came over. He was in that basketball cage thingy on top of the jail and I was on our roof. He saw me first. We shouted to each other. That's why he came over last night—so I wouldn't think he was some kind of criminal. He wanted to explain."

"Wait a minute." Nik Dreyfus faces his daughter, jowly with concern. "Are you telling me that you had a conversation with someone in that basketball pen on top of the jail?"

"Not someone—Crisp. I already knew him. We hung out last winter with some other friends."

The parents trade a sharp glance, shocked that so few degrees of separation could come between their daughter and a presumed criminal locked up in the House.

Seeing their reaction, Glynnie tells them, "Mom, Dad— *Crisp is a good guy*. He's going to *Princeton*. He was supposed to be valedictorian at *Stuyvesant* before that asshole cop arrested him for bullshit." Then, to the investigators, she offers, "Sorry."

"Don't worry about it." Lex is used to the insults some people hurl at cops just for breathing. He picks up a loose thread of last night's story. "Here's the thing I don't understand: Crisp's mom called me to say she heard from him this morning—he told her not to worry, said he was with friends."

"This morning?" Glynnie seems surprised.

"He texted her—early, about five a.m."

"That's strange," Glynnie says. "They took our phones at, like, one o'clock or something."

Lex makes a mental note of the discrepancy in time, and asks, "Who took your phones? The man you called Dante?"

"No, this other dude, Rodrigo—*he* had our phones, but Dante *told* him to take them. And then he stuck them in this silver bag thing."

"A Faraday bag." Lex glances at Saki. The men sound like professionals.

Glynnie asks, "A what?"

"Did you get your phone back?" Lex asks.

"No. I got out of there the second I had a chance."

"How did you come upon these guys, Dante and Rodrigo, in the first place?"

"I told you."

"Tell me again."

"We were just walking. You know, around Red Hook. And we accidentally kind of just wandered into this place. It was dark. We couldn't really see."

"Her phone last pinged at the Red Hook Houses at twelve fifty-one," Saki confirms. "After that, the signal was lost. I'm wondering if the girl—"

The mother interrupts in a chilly tone: "Her name is Glynnie."

"Excuse me, ma'am." Saki tries again. "I'm wondering if Glynnie can point us at the exact building and apartment. The complex comprises dozens of identical buildings in which there are a total of two thousand, eight hundred and seventy-eight apartments. Interference at the Houses makes it difficult to triangulate a cell signal with any precision. I've found that before."

Lex's jaw nearly drops, listening to that. The Dreyfus parents spent some time with Saki Finley before he and Elsa arrived, so they've presumably already been exposed to what now crystallizes for him: the detective is…unusual. Luckily, he tends to like unusual people: he finds their differences intriguing. He glances at Elsa and wonders what she's thinking, but she's too good at holding her poker face to offer any hints.

Lex asks Glynnie, "Can you remember the building number they took you to?"

"I wasn't really paying attention to that," she says.

"What about the apartment? Would you remember the number or letter?"

"Well, it was the fourth floor. The elevator didn't work so we had to walk up."

"That's something," Lex says to Saki.

"Possibly," she responds, "but elevator failure is common in the projects. The statistics aren't good, un-fortunately."

"In that case," Lex says, "you're right. Glynnie will have to show us. Could you do it if we showed you a picture?"

"Maybe."

Elsa produces her laptop from her bag, opens Google Satellite, and zeroes in on an aerial view of the Red Hook Houses.

After a few minutes of turning the view, of expansions and contractions, Glynnie sighs. "I'm not sure. It was really dark. And I was scared."

Lex asks, "Would you be able to lead us to the building if we took you back in person?"

"I think so."

"I don't know if that's such a—" Mags begins.

Glynnie cuts her off. "I'm eighteen. I say yes."

"If one of you wants to come along," Lex offers.

Mags immediately volunteers. "I'll go."

"Maybe *I* should," Nik counters.

"Why? Because you're the man? If you were such a man—"

"Mom! Dad! Neither of you are coming. I'll be with all of *them*." She gestures sweepingly at the three law enforcement agents.

To stop himself from reacting to the family's histrionics, Lex stands up and walks into the front hall. Elsa and Saki follow.

Keeping his voice low, he asks his colleagues, "What do you think?"

"Hard to tell," Elsa answers. "She's throwing a lot of words at it and she seems sure of herself. But something isn't sitting right."

"I know what you mean," Lex agrees.

Saki tells them, "She left something out of her story both times I've heard it."

"What's that?" Lex asks.

"A boy, a second boy, younger than Crisp Crespo. He appears briefly on the bank footage, but when I asked her about him she maintained she doesn't know who I'm talking about."

"Keep asking her," Elsa advises. She hoists her bag

onto her shoulder. "Listen, I've got to get going, but if you need me later, just shout. I'm happy to consult unofficially. And don't let her off the hook about the other boy. My best piece of advice: When you're looking for a teenager, think like one."

Lex follows her onto the stoop. "Thanks. I'll call you soon, get you over for that drink."

"Looking forward to it." She smiles. "Keep the faith."

Unsure if she means about the case or Adam or both, he says, "I'll try."

Rejoining Saki in the foyer, Lex dials Katya Spielman. She answers quickly and he gives her the news—just the basics about another high-school kid claiming that Crisp could be in a little bit of trouble, but not the whos or wheres.

"How can that be?" Katya asks. "I just got another text from him."

"You did?"

"He said he'll be home later."

"Would you forward that to me, please?"

"Hold on."

It comes through in seconds, time-stamped 8:06 am:

This is Crisp borrowing someone's phone. Home later. I love you.

Lex asks Katya, "Whose phone did he borrow?"

"I don't know."

"Send me that number too." It could be someone else sending the texts on Crisp's behalf, and not necessarily to help him. But he doesn't want to worry the mother with that unless he can confirm it.

Lex immediately forwards the number to a tech at ITB and requests that a source identification be added to Crisp's case files as soon as possible, with the addendum "Possible missing teenager."

He tells Katya, "Listen, this whole thing isn't very clear at the moment, but we're going to follow up on what the girl is saying."

"What if she's making it up?"

"Could be, but we're giving her the benefit of the doubt, for now."

"I've never heard of her. How can she be his friend?"

"Teenagers…" Lex's phone vibrates. He taps open his case management app and a quick read shows him that Crisp's second text to his mother came from a dummy number already associated in the system with one Dante Green, a convicted felon out on parole. Glynnie referred to the gun dealer as Dante. Lex decides not to share this information with Katya. Not yet. Too much is still unclear.

Katya asks, "What do I do now? How can I just go to work? *I can't.*"

"Stay put," Lex urges. "I'll keep in close touch with you. The minute I—" *know something*, he's about to say when she cuts him off.

"Where are you now?"

"At the girl's house. A detective from the local precinct is here and—"

"What precinct?"

"The Eighty-Fourth. But—"

"I'm coming."

"Listen, Katya, please just—"

"Isn't that where he'd be taken if you find him?"

"Yes," Lex says. *If he's lucky and doesn't have to be brought straight to a hospital. Or the morgue.*

She repeats, "I'm coming."

"Fine," he relents. "Check in with the public information officer; every station has one. We'll tell them to take good care of you."

After the call, Lex turns to Saki. "Looks like we might have some trouble—this guy Dante has a record. I want to see if any other texts or calls went out from his number in the last few hours. Which one of us requests the trap and trace warrant? My kid, your precinct."

Her eyes pause in calculation. She tells him, "I'll take care of it. But if I were you, I'd ask for one on the boy's number too—your precinct, this time."

Lex lifts his phone. "Doing it right now."

They drive over to the Red Hook Houses, Glynnie Dreyfus slumped in the backseat like a kid on a field trip.

Think like a teenager, Elsa told him.

Lex remembers back to when he was a teenager and the worst moment, the cruelest of days: when he lost Yelena. Beloved Yelena—his father's first wife, his brother David's mother, the woman who took him in after he landed alone in New York City at the age of eight. Losing her to cancer when he was fourteen staggered him more than anything before or since, with the exception of the news, three years earlier, that his real mother had died. He was a teenager when Yelena, his second mother, died—what did he think? He tries to remember and what comes back to him isn't thoughts but a series of irrational actions he couldn't explain now if he tried.

He ran out of the apartment, ran through traffic on the West Side Highway, ran to the edge of land, and jumped fully clothed into the Hudson River. Not to kill himself— that didn't even occur to him—but because Yelena had always said you couldn't swim in the "filthy Hudson" and now that she was gone he could, so he wanted to test the breach of the first open boundary that sprang to mind.

Then, soaking wet, stinking of something bad from the river, he walked into a gay bar on Eleventh Avenue and ordered a vodka neat, his dead father's drink, which he didn't like and didn't finish and didn't pay for. They hadn't carded him but they wanted their money and the bouncer chased him down the street until he slipped into a dark narrow alley between buildings on Thirty-Second Street.

He climbed the first fire escape he saw, rattling the iron steps up all four stories, and lost himself in an aerie of connected rooftops. He didn't think about anything, not even Yelena. He knocked over a laundry rack, sent socks and boxers and pants and T-shirts onto the tar, picked up the clothes and stuffed them into an uncovered chimney, kicked a hole in an exhaust duct, peed over the edge, and heard someone scream below.

He clattered down a fire escape several buildings east, knocking on windows all the way down, drawing shouts, curses, threats. The cops picked him up as soon as he descended to the sidewalk.

The charges were disorderly conduct, destruction of property, underage drinking, and theft of services and goods.

The booking officer took down his name and address and asked his age.

"Fourteen."

"Fourteen." The officer shook his head. "Why'd you do all that?"

Because I'm all out of mothers now, is what he thought, but not what he said. What he said was, "Because I felt like it." The exact same rationale he used five years later as an older teenager, in college, when he drove a needle into his arm: because his prescription had run out, this was cheaper anyway, and he felt like it.

Think like a teenager, Elsa told him. Translation: *Don't think at all. Act and react. Think later.*

15

W hat the fuck, son?" Dante yanks Crisp back from the door.

Answers ping around Crisp's brain but there isn't one good enough. He almost apologizes for his friend's escape, then stops himself. He stands there, rigid, gaze fixed on the refrigerator, trying not to think about all those guns, that dead body in the tub.

The stairwell door yawns open and falls shut. Footsteps in the dark hallway and Rodrigo is back, breathless—alone.

"Where is she?" Dante's voice is tight, eyes narrowed to slits.

"It was dark all the way down, boss." Rodrigo's neck seems to retreat protectively into his thick torso, waiting for something worse than words. "And she's fast."

"What kind of fool can't catch a skinny white girl?" Dante snaps each of the seven locks. "We got to get the fuck outta here."

"What about Jerome?" Rodrigo asks.

"Well he can't walk by hisself, can he?"

"I'll get him ready, boss."

"Work fast, asshole."

Rodrigo retreats to the bathroom. Dante hangs back, runs his hands through his hair to fluff out the flattened side, considers Crisp in a way that sends a cold chill through the teenager.

"Please," Crisp begs. "Let me go. I won't tell anyone. I swear."

Dante smirks, looking at him. "*Princeton*—guess you're that smart. Guess you think you don't got to pay a price." Dante pulls a gun from the back waistband of his boxers. He studies Crisp from head to toe.

"I'm no different from you," Crisp tries. "I just got lucky. My father, he grew up right here in the Houses."

A light in Dante's eyes and the gun hand relaxes to his side. "Tell me you ain't Mo Crespo's kid. *Crisp*—I figured it was just some messed up name." The thug's demeanor shifts into something avuncular, an old-timer you bump into on the corner. "How's old Yo Po doing these days?"

"Yo Po?"

"S'what we used to call him."

Crisp's mind races. Did his father hang out with the neighborhood thugs? Was he, is he, one of them?

Don't think about that now.

Hoping to play this for survival, Crisp says, "I never knew him," appealing to a different Dante buried under the bling and hair product. "He left when I was a baby."

"No shit?" Dante leans in like the town gossip, so close Crisp picks up the sour of half-digested booze. "I saw that motherfucker just last week. Drives up in my Uber; couldn't believe my eyes. Fucking Mo Crespo, not as young as he used to be, but who the hell is after twenty-plus years? Only the name says my driver supposed to be someone else, not Mo. But I know, I *know* I'm looking at Yo Po's face."

"What was the name?" The question bubbles up before Crisp can stop it. "Never mind. I really don't give a shit." Why should he care about a father who would name you something like Titus Crespo and then not hang around to help you learn to live with it?

Ignoring the disclaimer, Dante says, "Can't think of it. Some crazy-ass name sound like some Wall Street dude. So I get in the backseat and I start to think and I say to him, I say, 'Yo, Po!' He eyes me in the rearview. I mean, he *sees* me. But he don't say nothing. He just drives, pulls into the street cool and easy. So I bide my time. I wait until he stops at a red. Then I ease on up closer, you know, like this." Dante angles forward, folded arms clasped at the elbows hovering in midair (the gun resting on one elbow), and Crisp pictures him leaning into the front seat with those mean eyes and that golden smile and that hat.

Despite himself, Crisp begins to smell the pine air freshener dangling from the rearview mirror containing his father's eyes. He's in the car with them now, paying attention to every move his errant father makes, listening closely while Dante colors in the outline man Crisp has spent years trying to erase from his imagination.

"And I say, 'Yo, Po, whazzup, brother? You didn't forget ol' Dante, did you?' And Mo Crespo, he gives me that smile, the one that used to get him the girls."

The car now fills with phantom women, none of them Crisp's mother. *Philandering asshole. Narcissistic jerk.*

"Oh yeah, he had him *a few*." Dante nods. "He thought he was *the man*. Then one day he just up and falls off the map."

Mo Crespo falling backward off a map—Crisp sees it, the women evaporating and the car plunging off the urban grid as a young Mo Crespo materializes in Brighton Beach, where he spends nearly two years falling in love with Katya Spielman and getting married and having a baby and disappearing, but apparently not back into his old life. *Traitor. Deadbeat dad.*

"Finally, he says, 'Yo, Dante, what you been up to?' And I tell him, 'Same old, only better.' And before I know it I ask him, 'What you making hauling this rig 'round the streets?' 'Cause I know it can't be much. He tells me, 'Enough to pay my rent.' And I tell him, 'You can do better, my man, and I mean starting today. I got me a crew doing real business now. I'll bring you in. What do you say?'" Dante leans back and opens his arms to punctuate the grandiosity of his gesture toward his long-lost compatriot.

A chill runs through Crisp as he waits for the answer. He doesn't have to ask; he knows Dante will tell him.

"He says, 'Thanks, man, but I'm good. I got me another gig. Can't fit any more hours into the day.' 'What other gig you got, bro? 'Cause my eyes are telling me it ain't paying you squat.' 'I make stuff,' he says. 'Driving, it's a day job keeps me fed.' *Day job* my fuckin' ass: *loser* job. And he's turning down a real opportunity to make him some real scratch with me. I ask him, 'What stuff you make?,' but Po, he don't answer, just keeps driving."

Crisp takes that in: his father drives an Uber. His father *makes stuff*. His father has the sense to distance himself from Dante. Mo Crespo starts to take shape as someone with *discipline*, someone with *outside interests*, someone who's a *maker*, and this confuses Crisp. The anger doesn't work if his father isn't unfaithful to every habit of his son's life and mind.

"So me, I'm sitting there." Dante scratches his head to illustrate himself sitting in the back of the car, trying to make sense of what he's hearing. "And I say to myself, I say, *This fucking guy thinks he's better than me*. Huh. *He thinks he's better than all of us*." Dante's gaze settles heavily on Crisp. "Chip off the old block. Now that I think of it, last time I saw Po before the other day was right after he got hisself a white girlfriend too."

"If you mean Glynnie, she's not my girlfriend."

"Yup. That's just about what he said back then. He never was one of us, just like you ain't. You nothing but a suckass little prince, Princeton. Too good for us. Oh yeah, you a Crespo through and through. 'Let me go. I won't tell anyone.' Well fuck you—like father like son. I always wondered if Po was the one snitched that first time I got sent upstate."

The hairs on the back of Crisp's neck prick up, hearing that.

Why, then, did Dante offer him work?

And why did his father respond to Dante's ride request? With their history. Especially if he once informed on this goon.

A crash from the bathroom and Dante flinches as if suddenly remembering the body in the tub, Glynnie on the loose, how she won't fear him or cops or Big Man the way JJ does. He orders Crisp, "In the bedroom, big-ass suitcase in the closet—get it." Then heads to the bathroom to speed things up.

Dante's bedroom is a drab, undecorated square except for a floor-to-ceiling gilt-framed mirror propped against the wall beside a row of extravagant sneakers. Inside the closet a giant black suitcase takes up half the space, crowding out the hanging clothes. Crisp briefly wonders why Dante has such a huge suitcase before realizing that it would be useful for hauling bulk firearms. He pulls it out, shuts the closet door, and starts to wheel it across the room when he spots the dealer's Galaxy on the nightstand and, beside it, the silver bag.

Crisp opens the bag and takes out *his* Galaxy. Then, unable to resist, he puts his phone down and picks up Dante's and taps it awake, itchy with the knowledge that his father's alias is likely to still be on the Uber app: name, phone number, license plate—windows into the cipher whose absence has defined Crisp's life.

Dante shouts, "Yo Po, what the fuck taking you so long?"

Crisp impulsively jams the phone down the front of his jeans, then immediately regrets it as an idiot move.

Another crash from the bathroom, this one worse. Voices shout. Footsteps pound. Leaving his own phone on the table, he grabs the suitcase and hurries out of the bedroom.

Dante meets him at the bathroom door and grabs the suitcase handle.

Jerome's body is half in and half out of the tub, all four of his limbs turned in wrong directions. A sharp smell hits Crisp and he gags.

Dante turns, blood streaked across his forehead, and orders, "Stay where I can see you."

Crisp positions himself beside the bathroom door, back turned, but what he hears is almost as bad as seeing it.

"If we want to bag him," Rodrigo tells Dante, "we gotta cut him up first."

"Too messy," Dante decides. "Wait, I got an idea. See if you can get his arm behind his back, farther, all the way."

A loud crack tells Crisp that Rodrigo has broken Jerome's arm. His stomach bucks again.

"Awright, that'll work," Dante says. "Now do the other arm and both legs so we can truss him up like a Sunday chicken, and hurry it the fuck up."

Another crack. Another surge of bile. Another swallow.

16

Friday

Glynnie sits in the backseat of the unmarked car, holding the small purse she grabbed from home. The redheaded cop drives and the other one, the man, sits beside her in the passenger seat. Glynnie stares numbly out the window as the neighborhoods evolve from *nice* to *less nice* to *not nice at all* to *worn* to *broken* to *in the process of being rediscovered* to *the high-low mixed-use industrial residential mash-up* that is Red Hook.

Driving along Van Brunt Street, it all comes flooding in. Last night. One bad decision after another. She flinches at a visceral memory of the gun going off, the vibration burning through her hand to her arm to her brain, the weird lapse in time before she realized what she'd done.

She has no memory of deciding to pull the trigger, or of pulling the trigger, but obviously she pulled it.

She pulled it.

Jerome's bleeding forehead.

And the hungry look in his eyes when he hit the floor, like he still might come after her.

She knows she should tell that part of last night to the detectives—that she killed someone—but how can she? Until they talk to Crisp, there won't be any witnesses to the fact that she did it in self-defense. And what if they don't get there in time? What if Crisp...? She slams shut her eyes, refusing any thought that real harm will come to him. When she opens them, the car is in front of the housing authority sign, which in daylight she can see is shabby and horrible, the sign announcing WELCOME To RED HOOK HOUSES.

"Glynnie, you okay?" the man cop asks her. Detective Cole. Lex.

"Yeah. I was just thinking."

He twists around, elbow crooked over the back of his seat. "Don't do *that*." He has a nice smile, even with the space between his front teeth. His kindness in noticing that she's freaking out, trying to help her calm down, only makes her feel worse for lying about why they were really here last night. And about JJ, leaving him out of the story so she can keep her promise.

The lady detective, Saki Finley, pulls the car up to the curb. They wait for a couple of minutes, until half a dozen squad cars arrive. Every resident in the vicinity, young and old, scatters at the first sight of cops.

Lex tells Glynnie, "The three of us are going into the complex, along with some backup, and you'll lead the way to Dante's building. Okay?"

She nods.

"And then," he adds, "Saki is going to take you home."

"But how will you know which apartment is his?"

"Once we have the building we'll go to the fourth floor and we'll find it. Do you remember if it's to the right or left of the stairwell once you come out?"

"Right." She scoots across the seat to exit the car on the curb side.

A dozen officers in blue uniforms gather around them, their belts strung with billy clubs, holstered guns, walkie-talkies, keys, handcuffs, flashlights.

Glynnie lifts her chin and walks into the hive of buildings. The detectives and officers follow. A handful of small kids playing together stop upon sight of the white girl and her multiracial band of cops, and the hatred in their young eyes is razor-sharp. The benched grandmothers in attendance purse their lips and narrow their eyes. A pregnant girl who looks twelve but hopefully isn't stares as they all walk by, and Glynnie hears the unmistakable hiss "Snitch." She almost turns to the girl to ask for an account of what exactly she knows about this, but she doesn't, just keeps walking, because whatever the pregnant kid knows, it's enough to understand the essential situation. Anyone could.

Glynnie doesn't belong here.

Last night…Last night…She has never been a bigger fool.

The web of paths swallows them.

She stops walking—she can't do it.

She can't.

But she has to.

She starts walking again.

They come to a place where the path forks, one building one way, another the other way. To the left, where last night there was shadow, she sees a paint-chipped dark green bench with one slat missing and another slat broken in place.

"That's it." She points to Building 8.

Saki asks, "Are you sure?"

"Yes. Go to the fourth floor. Turn right. It's partway down the hall on the left—the door with seven locks."

"Good work," Lex tells her, and she feels a swell of pride. No one has said that to her since elementary school. He adds, "Thanks."

"Tell Crisp I brought you here, okay? I want him to know it was me."

"Sure thing."

Impulsively, she says, "Let me come in with you. I can find the apartment faster than you can."

"No," Lex says. "We'll take it from here."

"Please." She needs Crisp to see her. To acknowledge that she tried to reverse her fuckup. That she cares.

Saki is reaching an arm behind Glynnie as if to steer her back the way they came when another impulse takes hold, an unlatching of her voice. She screams, "Crisp! Crisp! I came back for you!"

Saki's hand claps over Glynnie's mouth while two of the larger male officers practically lift her off her feet, and together the trio whisks her away. After a brief struggle she gives in and uses her feet not to kick but to walk in the direction they're taking her. When they realize that she's no longer fighting them, they ease up.

At the car, the officers shove her into the backseat. Saki gets in the front and revs the engine, but before driving away she turns around to face Glynnie with those weird blue eyes of hers.

"What was that back there?" the detective asks. "I thought we were all on the same page."

"We are."

"So why did you want to tip off the whole place that something was about to go down?"

"You don't think they already figured that out?"

"I asked you why."

"I didn't want that."

"Then why did you do it?" Saki waits for an answer, which is just as well since Glynnie doesn't have a good one; she has never been able to explain her recklessness even to herself in calmer moments. "Who was the other boy last night? The younger one, at the bank."

"I don't know what you're talking about." Aware of the lump in her throat, Glynnie avoids swallowing it down; she assumes the detective knows how to read a person for lies. *How do they even know about JJ?* She promised she'd protect him. She *promised*.

"Yes, you do."

"Can I go home now, please? It's kind of been a long night."

"I'm not going to stop asking." The detective jerks the car into the street and navigates them in the direction of Boerum Hill.

Sitting in the backseat, Glynnie twists her purse strap around and around her fingers and wonders how long she can keep this up.

She killed someone last night.

They know about JJ and they won't stop asking.

They pull up in front of her house. Her parents are in there, waiting for her—undoubtedly with more questions. Later, her little brother will be home from school and he'll hear all about her "adventure." Her fuckup. Her latest self-created crisis. And the gap between the good Dreyfus kid and the bad Dreyfus kid will grow even wider.

17

Last Night

Crisp turns at the sound of a zipper: in the bathroom, Dante presses down on the top of the suitcase while Rodrigo, dripping sweat, forces the zipper all the way closed.

"All righty now," Dante says, emerging from the bathroom. "Let's get this show on the road." He looks at Crisp and gestures toward the suitcase. "How about Princeton does a little bit of work?"

Crisp takes the extension handle, tilts the heavy case onto its pair of rear wheels, and drags it toward the apartment door. It has to weigh over two hundred pounds, maybe two fifty, with Jerome crammed inside. He tries not to think of that, tries not to think at all.

Dante detours into his bedroom and emerges moments later with his hair neatened, his hat in place, and Crisp's Galaxy, which the dealer clearly thinks is his own, in one hand and the gun in the other. He drops the phone into his jacket pocket and shoves the gun into the back waist-band of his pants. He tells Crisp, "You go first, and no funny moves. We got our eyes on you."

Rodrigo flips the seven locks.

The door sways open, its squeal obscured by the pounding in Crisp's ears.

What if, he begins to think, then forces himself to stop.

Don't think. He pulls the suitcase.

Four flights feel like forty as he struggles to hang on to the handle while Rodrigo holds the bottom of the suitcase and they slide it down the crest of each step, trying not to let it jam on a stair. Dante follows, doling out advice about using the weight to "build up speed but not too much." Crisp ignores him and wills himself not to drop his end of the heavy case.

Keep going, get outside, find a way to escape.

Only when they step into the rising sunlight do other people start to appear. A nurse in a lavender pantsuit decorated with repetitions of Dora the Explorer and her monkey. A middle-aged man in a shiny ill-fitting suit and Payless business shoes. A younger man walking bowleg-ged and pretending his sagging pants aren't making his morning commute almost impossible. A harried mother carrying a baby, and her teenage daughter, who is clearly less than thrilled to be pushing a double stroller contain-ing a pair of toddlers. Crisp and the girl flash looks of mutual irritation as they pass each other, she pushing a load, he pulling one. What does she think: That he's on his way to school with a giant case of books accompanied by his two dads? He feels profoundly misunderstood, *unseen—forgotten*—and doesn't respond. The way people avoid looking at Dante and Rodrigo as they strut along confirms his sense from earlier in the hall that no one would help him escape. They might even help his captors get him back.

Fuck you, New York City Housing Authority, for building apartments like living tombs that segregate a whole race of human beings.

And you too, America, for slavery and its cotton-picking aftermath. For the fibers that never leave your lungs when you breathe the free air that isn't so free when your skin is black or half black or even just one drop black.

And you, NRA and Congress, for keeping the killing machine going with your lust for money and guns. For all this havoc down on the streets where you never, ever go.

And you, Mo Crespo, you, for … for breaking his mother's heart … for not sticking around to show him how to do this … for making him swallow anger that erupts at the wrong times … for this … for everything.

Don't think. Just pull.

Once they're at the edge of the projects, Dante takes the lead and Rodrigo the rear, with Crisp walking between them rolling the suitcase. Anyone who is out at this hour is engaged in the industrious pursuit of trying to get somewhere, which works in their favor. Time for work, school, day care, the parole office, dumping bodies. Crisp's stomach heaves bile into his throat. He swallows. Keeps pulling.

Twenty minutes into Dante's chosen route the streets

grow bleak and bleaker until they're the only people in sight. Once they clear a decimated ball field they enter an end-of-the-world scene of tow pounds and dump sites and parking lots for shipping containers. When a rat zags across Crisp's path he stops looking down and instead looks up: seagulls gliding in a blue sky. It's shaping up to be a clear morning.

If he could only get home and tell his mother and grandparents how sorry he is for all the trouble he's caused since Wednesday. Really, deeply sorry. If she still wants him to call Princeton, he'll call Princeton. If that's now off the table, he'll find another way to live his life.

Don't think. Just pull.

They turn off Columbia Street onto an unmarked road separating the Gowanus Bay from the Erie Basin.

"Hurry up," Dante commands. He points to a rocky spot at the edge of the water. "There. Set it down."

Crisp brings the suitcase to a rest.

"Unzip it."

Rodrigo falls into a crouch and pulls the zipper until it yanks to a stop. He announces, "Stuck."

Crisp can see that a slip of fabric from Jerome's shirt is caught in the teeth of the zipper, but he doesn't say anything, he stands back and watches Rodrigo struggle.

"Maybe we should push the whole thing in," Rodrigo suggests.

Dante answers, "No." Because the suitcase could lead back to Dante, which Crisp implicitly understands. Dante takes a switchblade from his jacket pocket and bends down to cut at the stuck fabric, pushing the knife in, sawing. When the zipper comes loose and he pulls out the knife, the blade is coated in blood.

"Look: Jerome got blood on my knife," Dante says. *"Fuck him."* He hands it to Rodrigo, who cleans the blade at the edge of the water and returns the knife spotless.

With the suitcase now open, Crisp glances at Jerome, a bruised and bloodied contortionist in death. Vomit bucks again and Crisp begins to gag.

"Put some rocks in his pockets and get him into the water, Rod," Dante orders.

Rodrigo drags Jerome as far as he can before dropping him under the surface, and emerges soaking wet. He zips up the suitcase and this time drags it himself as the three make their way back into the neighborhood.

They turn off Columbia Street onto Lorraine, where stores are beginning to open. A semitoothless man at the newsstand waves to Dante and he waves back. At Golden Fingers Dominican Hairstyles, a bulky Latina in a minidress a size too small spots Dante through the window and rushes out the door.

"Alva, baby." Dante opens his arms and offers his cheek for a kiss. Instead, she slaps him.

"Where you been?"

"Just flew in from Paris, France." Glancing at the suitcase, trying to make her laugh, but she won't have it. "What you doing open so early?"

"Nunna your goddamn business."

"What'd I do?"

"Shana got a fever—me and her up *all night long*."

Dante's expression sobers. "What's wrong with her?"

"I ain't no doctor! My mama got her now, says her fever comin' down. You gonna check in on her?"

"You know I am."

"You bring her some ice cream."

"I will."

"Chocolate chocolate chip."

Dante nods.

"Why Rodrigo's all wet?"

"Dude pissed his pants."

"My ass." Alva cracks a smile. She studies his hair and reaches to nudge an errant strand back into place. He runs a palm over her rear and Crisp thinks, *This is it, this is when I should bolt,* knowing that he's running out of time. "Chocolate chocolate chip," she reminds Dante.

"Rod!" he shouts. "You go in there and see if they got any!"

Rodrigo makes a show of entering the grocery store. Alva goes back inside, igniting a series of bells as the salon door falls shut. As soon as she's out of sight, Rodrigo returns to the sidewalk.

Dante starts walking again and Rodrigo and Crisp follow.

As far as Crisp can tell, no one seems to notice him; it's as if he's just another loser in training. His blood starts to boil, anger on top of fear now. He has got to get away.

I shall either find a way or make one.

He scans the surroundings and there is no place to go, mostly closed shops and boarded up storefronts, another housing project across the street. They walk under a dilapidated scaffold and emerge in front of a brick building with a colorful sign: BUMBLEBEE DAY CARE.

A small school bus grinds to a halt and two red stop signs flap out from either side. The bus door folds open. Tiny voices spill out before a potbellied matron steps off the bus. A dozen tiny children emerge onto the sidewalk carrying lunch boxes. The front door of the day care swings open and a tall man steps out, another man who knows Dante. They wave at each other and Crisp sees his chance. The eye in his needle. Passage back to a world where...

Don't think. Just go.

He leaps into the moment of sweet chaos.

18

Friday

The first thing Lex notices in Dante Green's apartment is a haze of something, maybe blood, on the floor in the main room. The officers step around it as they check everywhere: the living room with a strip kitchen and a padlocked refrigerator, a bedroom with a giant mirror leaning against one wall, a bathroom with a torn shower curtain and a jumble of towels, garbage bags, tools. More blood.

An officer emerges from the bedroom with a silver Faraday bag. She holds open the top to show Lex two phones: one a flip, the other an iPhone in a glittery case.

"What about that?" another officer asks of the refrigerator.

"Open it."

One of the officers produces a bolt cutter and severs the padlock. The door swings wide. Inside the dark fridge is a long black case.

"Lay it down right there." Lex indicates a spot on the cracked linoleum floor, away from the blood. The way the officer's neck tendons strain, Lex can tell the case is heavy. He hunches down to unzip it.

Pistols. Rifles. Machine guns. Service weapons with their serial numbers filed off. An arsenal of presumably illegal firearms ready to make their way onto the streets.

Lex and a few of the officers gather to take a look, shaking heads, mumbling curses. One asks, "Why do we even bother?"

"Close it back up," Lex instructs. "Drop it at the lab. I'll alert ATF." Disappointment simmers, because the girl was right, this guy Dante is selling guns, and because this kind of firepower has no place on the streets.

While he waits for the forensic techs to arrive, Lex calls Saki to check in. "Glynnie's tucked away at home now?"

"I dropped her off ten minutes ago," she tells him. "Just got back to the station house. Your boy's mother is here— she's downstairs with Gus."

Lex is pleased to hear that the public information officer is still with the 8-4. Gus has a soft touch and Katya needs that right now. Lex tells Saki, "I'll be over soon."

"What happened at the Houses after I left?"

"So far everything Glynnie said checked out except for one thing: Crisp isn't here." He adds, "No, two things: She didn't say anything about the blood on the floor in the main room, unless that happened after she was gone."

"Blood," Saki echoes. And then corrects him: "*Three*

things don't check out. The second boy. I tried, and the girl still won't talk about him."

"Let's pick up Green." Lex decides on the spot. "Your precinct—you want to do the warrant?"

"Done," she says. "What about an APB for Crisp?"

"I'm on it. And I'll put eyes on his building so we'll know right away if he comes home."

"When you're finished there—"

"Yeah." He already knows what she's thinking. "I'll make my way to you."

He catches a ride in one of the squad cars returning to the station house—sitting in the backseat like a perp, staring through scratched Plexiglas at the back of a pair of cops' heads. The image of all that weaponry locked in Dante Green's refrigerator returns to him with a visceral jolt at the thought of the immensity of damage you can do with a single gun. How did Crisp, Glynnie, and the mystery boy step into that quicksand—or maybe the question is, how can you not step in it, sooner or later, when it's all around you?

They park on Gold Street. Lex gets out in front of the station house where he was once briefly posted and realizes just how adapted he's gotten to the other end of Brooklyn, with its wraparound sky and crosshatch of fresh breezes. At the Coney Island station house, just half a block from the ocean, you open a couple of windows and in whips the salty air. Here, the air feels stagnant and it smells of something unpleasant. Gas, maybe. Garbage from the dumpster across the street. Barbecue from the housing projects on the other side of Gold. Coffee from the new Starbucks on the corner where they finally finished that flashy high-rise.

He remembers the weak brew from the old squad's Mr. Coffee and suddenly craves something much stronger to tackle whatever it is they're facing now. Two nights with almost no sleep is starting to creep up on him from behind with gnarly fingers and a stranglehold; as always, he has trouble breathing when he's sleep-deprived.

Adam calls these bouts of suffocation "anxiety" but Lex thinks that's bullshit: we aren't built to function without sleep—it's just the lungs protesting. Adam thinks a lot of things are anxiety when it comes to Lex. The "hyper-vigilant work ethic." The "stoic self-denying" reactions that Lex thinks of as *patience* or, better yet, *fortitude*. Their disagreements over semantics are always friendly, but with a bite. Thinking of Adam, Lex grinds his jaw to plug a surge of emotion.

At Starbucks, he orders a pair of cold double shots with whole milk. He has no idea how Saki drinks her coffee, or if she drinks coffee at all, but if she doesn't want it he'll have it himself.

As he passes through the station-house lobby, his brain pings before he even sees the sign directing visitors to the property clerk down a hall to the left. During the months he worked here, the awareness that this was where drugs were held before transfer to the evidence vault made his skin crawl with want. The mere knowledge of the treasures in there turned him into a creative genius figuring out how to crack the code to the electronic door lock without being noticed, and in his imagination he was always caught. Not responding to the urge took a lot of energy, and this was the real reason he put in for a transfer, with the official rationale that the 6-0 was closer to his new home.

Lex rides up in the dingy elevator to the second floor, emerges into the overlit hallway, listens to the dull clap of his boots on the linoleum—all of it so familiar it's almost as if he never left the 8-4. He stacks the two cups so he can ease open the squad room door. Looking around, he spots some familiar faces and some new ones. A former colleague nods, another waves, a third offers a vague headshake that could mean anything.

He finds Saki two desks over from his old spot near a painted-shut window. Her desk is very organized, a neat stack of papers weighted under a snow globe with all the fake snow settled at the bottom and the detached snowman free-floating in water.

"You solve that crime yet?" Lex uses one of the coffees to indicate the snow globe. "He doesn't look good."

She glances away from her monitor. "The glue wore out, I guess."

"Case solved, then." He offers her one of the cups. "It's cold."

"Is that whole milk or skim?"

"You didn't ask about two percent."

"I also didn't ask about one percent because the Starbucks down the street only serves whole or skim, and there isn't any condensation on the outside of the cups so I assume you got them at the closest one. Correct?"

"Correct. It's whole. That okay?"

"I usually drink skim." She reaches to take the cup from him anyway.

"You're welcome," he says.

"Oh. Thank you."

Lex smiles. Something about her no-nonsense attitude puts him at ease. "This case is turning into a real shitstorm. Wish I'd done the APB on Crisp sooner."

"Don't blame yourself—you couldn't have known."

"I thought we were looking for a couple of teenagers. Now I'm not sure what we're looking for."

He's reaching for a chair to pull up beside Saki's desk when she says, "If you want to set up shop here, Suarez is out this week." She points to an unoccupied desk amid the cluster of workstations.

"Probably a good idea."

"So, are you planning on talking to Mrs. Spielman?"

"Yes, but I should warn you," he tells her, "it's not *Mrs.* She doesn't like that, I found out. You want to be there?"

"Sure. Maybe she knows something about the other boy—I can't get him out of my mind. By the way, did you know Green's on parole for armed robbery?"

"I didn't."

"After you called me, I glanced over his record. He broke into an apartment when the owners were sleeping. That put him away for five years; he's been out for two. Before that, he did a couple two-year stints for possession of stolen property. He's also been tagged for domestic violence."

"How bad?"

"Beat up the mother of his daughter. Never happened

152

again, at least not on record. Social services has it that he moved out of the shared apartment eight years ago, before the longer sentence."

"Nothing on record about weapons?" Lex asks. "Besides the armed robbery."

"No, just that one time. Maybe he changed his game."

"Put away three times as a thief? I'd branch out too. Anything else of note?"

"Before the armed robbery there was a decade of petty charges, turnstile jumping and stuff like that, and later a couple of muggings."

"Started small and worked his way up," Lex says. "So he's ambitious."

"He's stupid," Saki corrects. She scoots her chair away from her desk and stands. "Ready?"

"Yeah. Thanks. And you're right: Dante Green is an idiot par excellence."

That gets a smile out of her. He smiles back. Together they take the stairs down to the public information office to temporarily relieve Gus of his guest.

They walk in to find Katya narrating the pages of an old-fashioned photo album she must have brought with her from home. Gus is sitting beside her and leaning over the pictures. At the crack of the door opening, the public information officer's bald pate rises, revealing his face: sagging jowls crusted with salty stubble.

"If it isn't Lex Cole!" Gus sits back with a broad smile.

Lex strides over and offers a handshake. "Couldn't keep away."

"Back for good?"

"Just coordinating on a case with Detective Finley."

Hearing that, Gus's expression shifts. He shoots a wary eye at Saki, who hangs back, looking annoyed by all the small talk.

"Thanks, Gus." Lex pats him on the back and he seems to relax.

Lex waves Saki over to meet the mother. While the women greet each other, he glances at the open album and sees a photo of Crisp Crespo as a little boy, cross-legged on the floor in front of an enormous Lego world that looks like the melding of several themed sets.

Tapping the photo of Crisp in his Lego kingdom, Lex says, "Quite a kid you've got there."

Katya closes the book. *"Where is my son?"*

"We don't know yet." Lex's tone is even as still milk, his policy being never to lie to a parent about a child, but at the same time to parse information judiciously. "We *do* know that he and his friend Glynnie Dreyfus, and apparently a younger boy, were together last night at an apartment in the Red Hook Houses."

Katya's lips pull apart but it's a moment before words emerge. "So much of what you just said doesn't make any sense to me at all."

Saki asks, "Have you met Glynnie Dreyfus?"

"I've never even heard of her. If she's a friend of Crisp's, it's news to me. Are you saying she lives at the housing project?"

"No—her family lives in a brownstone in Boerum Hill," Saki answers. "Apparently she's acquainted with your son through mutual friends. She observed him from her roof-deck last Wednesday playing basketball on top of the House of Detention."

"*Observed* him?" Katya says. "You know what's ironic? That all these places you're talking about are called 'House'—the projects, the jail. Even this police station—a station house. As in 'That's where people of color are at home.' My son was arrested on a stupid charge because he's black—he's *perceived* as black. That's what this is about. All of it."

Katya's outburst stuns Lex, who falls silent, off guard momentarily as the anger just below this mother's emotional skin finds its place in the nasty reality of American racism. This white woman from Brighton Beach knows bigotry as though she's lived it because she *has* lived it through her child; motherhood taught her the muddled pain of watching someone she loves turn racism inward. Katya Spielman's power is in seeing it, calling it, and shoving it back in your face.

"I apologize for the insensitive word choice," Saki says. "As for your son's arrest on Wednesday, I agree with you that it was—"

Katya supplies the word: "Bullshit."

"Yup," Lex agrees. "Perception becomes reality, and it isn't fair or right."

Katya says, "Did you know that his father grew up in the Red Hook Houses?"

Lex leans forward. "No, we didn't." He glances at Saki, realizing that he shouldn't second-guess her; maybe *she* knew. She shakes her head, *No*.

"He was still living there when we met—on a subway."

Half a smile leaks onto Katya's face before she kills it. "We hit it off right away, despite our completely different backgrounds. We were both looking for a change and I guess we found it in each other." She looks at Lex. "Do you think Crisp went back there because it's where his father grew up?"

"Could be. We don't know yet."

"What were they doing there last night?" Katya asks. "At the Houses."

Seeing that Saki is about to speak, concerned that she might blurt too much truth about the little they know about last night—about Green's criminal past, about the bloody floor—Lex jumps in. "Katya, what we know so far is that they were with a man named Dante Green. He appears to be trafficking in illicit firearms, but that still has to be confirmed."

"Firearms," Katya repeats, hard, like a curse. "Are you saying Crisp was trying to buy a gun? I don't believe that! That's another stereotype that—"

Saki interrupts her. "What kind of cell phone does Crisp use?"

Katya's eyes snap to Lex in response to the non sequitur of a question, as if Saki is his partner and he can somehow control her.

He explains, "We found two phones in the apartment that may not belong to Mr. Green." Glad to be off the quicksand of racism.

"How would you know that?" Katya asks.

Saki answers, "Because they'd been put into a Faraday bag, which is designed to block reception."

"Oh my Lord," Katya moans. "Crisp has a Samsung Galaxy. Was it there?"

Relieved to finally have some good news, Lex tells her, "No, it wasn't. We didn't find anything directly belonging to him in that apartment, Katya."

Saki adds, "But we'll know more when we hear back from the lab."

"The *lab*?"

"Routine," Lex obfuscates, wishing Saki hadn't mentioned that. "Glynnie's back at home and she's told us what she knows, which isn't much. She thinks the world of your son, by the way." A bit of an exaggeration, but Lex can tell how much it pleases the mother.

"He's never had a girlfriend before. Can I ask—what's her ethnicity?"

"She's Caucasian," Saki says. "My guess is she's of western European extraction—but again, it's just a guess."

"Glynnie says they're not dating," Lex clarifies. "She says they're friends, that they don't know each other well but that they were together last night."

"I see." Katya nods. "You said there was another boy. Younger. Who's he?"

"We're wondering that ourselves," Lex says. "Glynnie didn't mention him at all—we saw him with them on a piece of security footage."

"In Red Hook?"

"Yes," Lex says.

"This isn't good." Katya taps a finger on the tabletop, twice, then folds her hands together. "What now? Do you think this gun dealer has my son?"

"The truth is," Lex says, gently, "we just don't know. Listen, Katya, why don't you head home now? You'd be more comfortable."

"Not yet," the mother says.

Lex nods, stands. "Want some lunch? We'll put in an order."

"Sure. A sandwich. Tuna."

"Lettuce? Tomato?"

"Fine."

Lex calls out for lunch, then settles into Suarez's desk, turns on the desktop computer, and uses his password to log in to the central system. He and Saki fall silent, reviewing their case files. A new ballistics report catches his attention.

One of the guns in Green's collection, a Baby Browning .25, was loaded with a six-round mag—and one of the rounds was used up. None of the other guns were loaded.

Lex responds to the tech who uploaded the file and orders a rush on the Baby.

He turns to Saki and tells her his news.

"You're expecting to find blowback," she says.

"I expect nothing. I hope for everything." He smiles, but her pensive demeanor doesn't break. He asks, "What's up?"

"Just found out that Glynnie Dreyfus took off again. Seems when I dropped her at the house she never actually went in. Guess there's a reason teenagers treat adults like we're fools. She put her key in the lock and pushed open the door—I didn't think I had to wait to *see* her go inside."

"She got you good."

"I checked everything and she's completely off the grid."

"Sneaky kid," he says.

"Did you notice that she was wearing different clothes this morning? Last night, in the bank footage, she had on a striped T-shirt and ripped blue jeans. This morning, the T-shirt was white and the jeans weren't ripped. I got there five minutes after she did—she must have gone straight to her room to change."

Lex didn't think much of it at the time—after a long night out, anyone would want to strip down into something clean. But now he, too, wonders why she did it in such a hurry.

19

Hunkered deep in a shadow, Glynnie waits for JJ across the street from his school. Her thoughts twist and knot as she wonders how to tell him what he won't want to hear: that he was on the bank video with her and Crisp last night.

That the cops have been asking questions.

"Never miss a day of school," he said. "Can't draw attention or they'll put me back in foster." But he needs to keep his profile even lower than usual because this, school, *this* will be one of the first places they'll come poking around once they figure out who he is.

She needs him to know that she, Glynnie, will not be the one to tell them—just so he understands that. But as she's learned, the Authorities have their wily ways of knowing things, so he should be *very careful* and he should *hide* and he should do it *now* if he wants to stay off the radar and out of the foster system.

That she can and will help him.

That she isn't a total loser.

That even though she shot Jerome, even though she killed someone, it doesn't make her a bad person.

Do. Not. Think. About. That. Now.

The twist moves from her brain to her stomach.

She stands with her back to an ornate iron fence and watches as kids stream out of school. It's a half day early dismissal and the mood is buoyant—the way the little ones run to their mothers, fathers, babysitters, and the larger ones, the fourth and fifth graders, cluster within sight but not earshot of their parents in a perfect balance of protected independence. Innocence on the brink. Observing it from the distance of age and experience—she is a high-school graduate *and a murderer* now—Glynnie misses that precarious balance.

She waits another half an hour after the last student has emerged. Until the teachers have gone. Until a woman who must be the principal because she's wearing a dress and high heels comes out. Still no JJ. Maybe he had to stay after for some reason, or maybe he *likes* being the very last to leave—maybe that's another part of his plan to stay unnoticed.

Finally, when the janitor locks the front doors with a chunky padlock, she accepts that JJ isn't coming out. If he isn't at school, where is he? He isn't at the squat—she waited there all morning—and he wouldn't have risked being out and possibly catching the attention of one of the truant officers who lurk the streets between eight and three, salivating to catch you cutting school.

Keeping her head down, Glynnie walks away. She

spots a taxi, hails it, and tells the driver to take her to Fairway market in Red Hook. She crouches low in the backseat, trying not to be seen. And then, like a lightning strike, the twist in her stomach returns, too intense this time to breathe away. She closes her eyes and waits it out, willing herself to stay focused on what she needs to do…if only she knew what it was. Crisp would have an idea; he'd probably have a few ideas. She wonders if he got away from Dante and Rodrigo, maybe even got his phone back. It can't hurt to try.

Sitting forward, she asks the driver, "Actually, can we make one stop? Do you know if there's a phone store on the way?"

Minutes later they pull up in front of a sliver of a store nestled on a shabby commercial street at the edge of the Houses.

"Mind waiting?" she asks. "I'll be right out."

"It's your money."

The shop door opens with a clatter of bells. A man in a blue polo shirt with METRO PCS embroidered in the vicinity of his heart looks up from whatever it is he's doing behind the counter. Boredom flickers out of his eyes as he assesses her.

"*Good* afternoon," he greets her. Tight cornrows capping his skull. A diamond stud glistening in his left front tooth.

She approaches the counter. "I need a throwaway kind of phone."

"You want a burner?"

"Um, yes. One that has Bluetooth." So she can give

the phone to JJ and he can use the Beats—but first, she'll make her call. "I'm paying cash."

"What're you up to?"

"Just give me the phone, okay?"

"How you gonna activate it with cash? You need a number, buy some minutes—got to put a card on for that." He squints at her, then lowers his voice as if they're not alone. "What smart people do," he winks, "is they buy a debit Visa with cash. That way the burner don't trace."

"You sell those?"

"This look like a dollar store to you?"

"Fuck."

"How many minutes you looking for?"

"I don't know—five? Ten?"

"I'll tell you what. I have a cash debit in my pocket. I'll sell you ten minutes, for…thirty bucks? Plus you buy a phone from the store, make this visit official."

"Okay, I guess."

"New or reconditioned?"

"I seriously don't care at all."

He steps into a back room and reappears with a reconditioned Alcatel Fierce smartphone for forty-nine dollars plus the thirty dollars for a burner number and ten minutes of data and talk from his personal card. She probably won't need that much but it doesn't matter. He uses his card to load time onto the new phone. She zips open her purse and hands over a hundred dollars cash, then hurries out.

"Your change!" he calls after her.

"Keep it."

Riding in the taxi, Glynnie slouches in the backseat and hops online to search for Crisp's cell number. It doesn't take long to find it.

A gruff not-Crisp voice answers, "Yeah?"

Dante.

She hangs up.

Then she redials.

"Who the fuck is this?" Dante barks.

"I want to talk to Crisp."

"Princess!"

"Is he there? Why are you answering his phone?"

"Cause he got *my* phone, bitch."

"Put him on. Asshole."

"She got *bite*."

"Where's JJ?"

"Wouldn't you like to know."

"You're in big fucking trouble, Dante."

"Me? Wasn't me pulled the trigger on that pretty shooter."

"Give me Crisp!"

"You want him? Join the fucking club—took off with my phone *and I want it back*." He hangs up. As the taxi pulls up in front of Fairway, the phone rings and she ignores it.

The driver quips, "Good luck with your boyfriend troubles."

"He is *so* not my boyfriend." She pays in cash and slams the door to drown out the guy's laughter.

She's almost at the dead end of Van Brunt and the

broken gate, about to squeeze through, when it occurs to her that Dante could trace her location. She fingernails off the phone's plastic back, pries out the SIM card (she'll buy JJ another one), drops it onto the sidewalk, grinds it under her heel. With the brainless phone dropped into her purse, she slips through the gate and then the chain link and hurries to the squat.

She places the phone on top of the small bookcase, beside the St. Fleur family photo, so JJ will see it when he returns. Then she burrows into the corner where he's piled a dusty blanket and bare pillow, and waits. *What if he never comes back? What if she never leaves?* Her stomach hurts again, thinking that. She had no idea a person's life could unravel this fast.

The rhythmic crash of the tide outside the window seems to get louder. She covers her ears with her hands but it doesn't work. Then she spots the Beats lying on the floor and puts them on. Unconnected to a source of sound, they deliver an exquisite silence that blunts but doesn't stop her grinding thoughts:

Did Crisp survive the night?

What happened to JJ?

Is there any chance the police won't find out about Jerome?

Just how much trouble is she in now?

Searching her purse for the single-serve Advil she's carried around all year is useless with all the crap inside, so she upends the bag onto the floor. Everything tumbles out: tampon, hairbrush, Tic Tacs, bills, coins, MetroCard, paper-wrapped wads of gum, a spent pack of rolling papers, a crumpled napkin, and more stray beads than

165

she'd realized had escaped the tiny plastic Ziplocs she'd gathered on her forays to craft stores this past week. She locates the worn packet of ibuprofen and dry-swallows the pair of pills, then starts putting things back into her purse.

With pinched fingertips, she picks up one of the red skulls she bought at Beads of Paradise, sets it in the palm of her hand, looks at it. A flare of shame: *What an ugly, stupid gesture*. She feels like a different person than the girl who decided on such a mean-spirited gift for her mother.

One by one, she plucks every bead she can find off the floorboards and gathers them in her fist. Then she walks to the open window and rains the beads out into the universe. Standing there, watching them vanish into the bright sunlight, waiting for them to ping off the concrete below but hearing nothing, she remembers that she's still wearing the headphones.

She lies down in the middle of the floor and discovers that the Beats cancel more than noise; they also cancel time. She lets herself drift until she's in a field of wildflowers with a dry blue sky and a big yellow sun overhead, the warmth soaking into her skin, the air sweet.

20

Saki bends down and does her best friendly smile when the little boy, presumably Glynnie's brother, opens the front door. Straight brown hair with bangs fringing over his eyes. He takes a step backward, and blinks. She likes him.

"Are your parents home?" she asks.

The boy turns around and shouts, "Mom!" Then he resumes looking stonily at the detective.

"My name is Saki. What's your name?"

"I'm not supposed to talk to strangers," he says. "I'm Aidan, though."

"You shouldn't talk to strangers. That's absolutely right."

"Then why are you talking to me?"

A rustle of sound carries Mags into the foyer. She lays a hand on Aidan's shoulder and he presses close to her as a much younger child might. "Go finish your algebra," she instructs, and he spins away to dash up the stairs.

"Algebra?" Saki says. "Isn't that high-school work?"

"Aidan's advanced." The mother's matter-of-fact tone shifts to bitter. "Detective, how on earth did you lose track of my daughter?"

"I didn't lose track of her. I delivered her home. I saw her walk up your front stoop."

"And then you drove away." Mags folds her arms over her chest and looks at Saki as if daring the detective to admit she just ran over a favorite pet.

"Correct."

"Well that was a stupid thing to—"

A crashing noise draws both of their attention. Mags quickly steps away. Saki closes the front door behind her and follows the sound into the living room.

The glass coffee table is overturned, the objects that were on it scattered. Nik Dreyfus lies on his side, holding his right shin and wincing in pain. The room smells of alcohol and Saki sees that an amber liquid—whiskey, she guesses—has spilled onto the white rug. A toppled glass has come to rest in front of the sleek black face of a fireplace embedded into white stone. Mags hurries to right the table and replace everything.

"At least nothing broke," she says, ignoring her husband.

"Mags," Nik moans, "give me a hand."

She obliges, letting him use her as leverage to achieve something akin to a standing position.

Saki says, "Glynnie changed her clothes earlier when she was home."

Mags answers, "So?"

Nik tries to get to a chair and stumbles again, this time kicking the leg of the side table. The framed portrait of the happy family falls flat.

"Jesus, Nik!" Mags hurries across the room to right the frame.

He barks, "Why do you have all this crap on every table, Mags? Every single surface has something on it! And the pillows—everywhere." He swipes a pillow off the couch. "It's like a minefield. What are you trying to prove?"

"'Crap'?" Mags says. "'Prove'?"

Saki interrupts. "I'd like to take a look at what she had on last night. If you don't mind."

Mags wheels around to glare at the detective. "Why?"

"With the two investigations intersecting now, we're gathering anything we think might—"

"I just want my daughter," Mags snaps. "I want her home, *in the house,* not on the stoop. Go ahead—take her dirty clothes if you want them. Burn them, for all I care. Take whatever you want. Here: Do you want this?" She carries the framed photo over to Saki, an angry jitter in her step. "Go on, take it. Why not? It's all shot to hell anyway, isn't it? Isn't it?"

"Oh, Mags," Nik moans, finally settled safely into an armchair. "Leave the woman alone. Go ahead, Detective Finley," he slurs, "go on up to Glynnie's rooms, up on the third floor. Take whatever you need. Everything's replaceable except what really matters. Right, Mags? Right?"

"Are you blaming *me?*" Mags turns to him. "Is it *my* fault that Glynnie can't bear to be in this house? Is it *my* fault that she has the kinds of friends that know gun dealers? Are you *serious,* Nik?"

"She probably wanted a gun to kill you," Nik mutters.

Saki decides that this is a good moment to go upstairs and do her job. As she mounts the staircase, the couple's fight escalates.

"That's *insane!* Why would she want to kill *me*? She *loves* me. We're very close!"

"Oh, Mags, get off your horse."

"My horse?"

"Your high-and-mighty horse!"

The second-floor hallway is carpeted, with three doors, each closed. One door is decorated with decals of chess pieces—the son's door, Saki assumes. Poor kid.

She proceeds to the top of the house, where Glynnie has a suite of two rooms—a bedroom and a sitting room— joined by a spacious bathroom that's tiled floor to ceiling in dove-gray marble. An open tube of toothpaste oozes a blue-green snake over the edge of the sink. Wadded tissues on the floor surround an empty garbage can. A bad smell from the unflushed toilet propels Saki to hurry out and shut the door behind her.

The bedroom's red walls are plastered with photographs cut from magazines. Mags mentioned that the housekeeper was in yesterday, hence the perfectly made bed and overall sense of order. Otherwise, judging by the state of the bathroom after Glynnie's brief visit home, the bedroom would also be a wreck. Saki looks around for sloughed-off clothes but finds nothing.

A door with a hook from which several handbags and

scarves dangle suggests that it might be a closet. Saki opens it and finds herself face-to-face with a room sizable enough to be a bedroom in its own right, a walk-in closet so stuffed and piled with clothes that walking in isn't an option. Right there, at the edge of a heap of clothes, are the torn jeans and striped T-shirt Glynnie was wearing in the bank footage. Saki holds up the shirt to the ceiling LED and sees a reddish mist hazing the left shoulder that she didn't notice in the video. She checks the pockets, hoping to find something, anything, but comes up empty-handed. She unfolds one of the evidence bags she brought along and puts the clothes inside.

She glances around the bedroom—neat, clean, dusted—looking for something that might still have an intact fingerprint. On top of the dresser is a jewelry tree strung haphazardly with necklaces and dripping with unmatched earrings, a lone pearl that looks real, a ring with a stone dazzling enough to be an actual diamond tossed at the base of the tree. The gleaming dresser and nightstand smell like furniture polish, so they won't be any help; better, anyway, to find something she can take with her.

Holding her nose, Saki passes through the bathroom and into the sitting room, on her way plucking a nest-like hairbrush from the edge of the sink and dropping it into another evidence bag.

The sitting room must have been where Glynnie spent part of her brief visit home this morning, when she wasn't downstairs with her parents. A stylish couch and coffee table face a wall-hung television surrounded by built-in bookcases. The walnut floor and orange couch are the only swaths of deep color; everything else is white or beige, which reads more Mags than Glynnie. The shelves, though, are all unfinished girl: packed with a hodge-podge of stuffed animals, books, video game players, bottles of nail polish, a balled-up throw blanket. Maybe the cleaning woman doesn't bother trying to tame that wall; maybe she was forbidden to try.

On the low coffee table an iPad lies open beside a mug with a tea bag suspended in half a cup of murky liquid. Saki puts the iPad into a third evidence bag. After braving the bathroom again to pour the remaining tea into the sink and throw the tea bag into the garbage can, where it collapses alone and wet at the bottom, she also bags the mug.

On her way out, Saki pauses on the second floor to knock on the brother's door.

A small voice answers, "Come in."

She cracks open the door just enough to poke in her head and say, "Just wanted to make sure you're okay."

Aidan sits at a desk that floats in the middle of the room, facing the door, like an executive's situated in the power position. Sky blue walls and tidily hung posters of movies—*Star Wars, Back to the Future, The Truman Show*—create a sense of sanctuary. A chessboard is set up in the center of the desk, an algebra textbook pushed to the side. Aidan appears to be playing a game with himself.

"Who *are* you?" he asks.

"I told you. I'm Saki."

"I don't understand what's going on, and I don't know if I want to. I hate half days."

She closes the door softly behind her and makes her way downstairs.

Mags and Nik are now pressed together into the armchair, holding each other, weeping.

Saki detours to the kitchen, finds herself a large plastic garbage bag in which to carry her collection of evidence bags, and steals out the front door.

21

Sitting at his borrowed desk, Lex clicks Play and watches a jerky rendition of last night begin to unfold. The collation of public and private security footage, stitched together chronologically by a DAS tech, offers a visual quilt of unaligned sequences of varied quality—some color, some black-and-white, some grainy, some sharp.

Glynnie and Crisp walking into Red Hook via the Union Street bridge, she wearing a set of wireless Beats and he with earbuds and wires running to his back pocket. Turning south along Van Brunt until Fairway, then disappearing from view. Later, reappearing with the boy—the boy now wearing the Beats—and moving in a zigzag that leads them to IKEA. More shots of them along the route to Fairway when again they drop off for a while. Eventually, they reemerge to visit the bank and then make their way to the housing project.

Nearly an hour later, the boy emerges alone. The Beats

hang around his neck at a cockeyed angle. He hurries along the same Fairway-bound route to Van Brunt before disappearing.

At 5:56 a.m., Glynnie comes racing out of the projects as if she's on fire.

Crisp isn't seen again for nearly an hour, when he walks out of the central mall of the Houses, pulling a very large suitcase on wheels. From the way he's straining, the case looks heavy. A stone sinks in Lex's stomach—the loaded gun, the bloodied floor. But Crisp is not inside that suitcase; that's the good news. Two men appear, walking together at some distance behind him.

Lex freezes on a frame showing the two men relatively clearly: one in a red MAKE AMERICA GREAT AGAIN cap, the other in a leather jacket. Lex halves the screen and pulls up the most recent mug shot of Dante Green. The man in the red cap—that's Green.

Green and the other man follow Crisp all the way to Columbia Street. They continue straight along the mouth of the Gowanus Canal where it feeds into the bay. Like fraying fabric, the video clips are pulled apart by wider gaps of time and finally end near a fenced area packed with shipping containers.

Forty-seven minutes later, the three reemerge on Columbia Street and retrace their path in the direction of the Houses. This time, though, the unknown man is hauling the case and it appears to be less of a burden. And now, Crisp walks between them, shoulders drooping.

On Lorraine Street, a commercial strip with shops just opening for the day, the clips bind more closely together.

Green peels ahead to greet a woman who emerges from a hair salon; she slaps him, they talk briefly and appear to part amicably. She returns to the salon. The three continue walking and come to a stop at a nursery school where a bus is unloading small children. Then, quickly, things start to happen.

Crisp bolts.

In the chaos, Green and the man are unable to chase him.

Green shoots his gun at Crisp, and misses.

The children scramble into their school building.

The two men stand on the sidewalk in heated discussion. Then, in a deflation of energy, they turn in the opposite direction.

Here, the footage bifurcates into two tracks the tech has marked *A* and *B*. Lex watches *A* first.

Crisp runs through the streets, not slowing down until he reaches Conover Street. Then he vanishes.

Lex leans back in his chair and stares at the white ceiling, mapped with water marks he never noticed before, and thinks. Someone was either injured or, more likely, killed in the gun dealer's apartment. The body could have been packed into that suitcase and possibly disposed of somewhere along the bay shore, somewhere Green and the other man knew would be remote enough to avoid ready detection. Crisp might have been enlisted to help in the effort, and if he did so, it presumably wasn't voluntary; the footage demonstrates that in his impulsive escape. But who was in that suitcase? And who pulled the trigger on that Baby Browning, discharging a single bullet?

He glances at his barely eaten turkey sandwich, but hunger eludes him. His mind flits to Adam, *who still hasn't called or texted*. Lex shakes his head and rubs his eyes and feels his achy calf and craves relief and forces his attention back to the screen and the ballast of work.

The *B* footage shows Dante and the other man moving in the direction of the projects. They pause as Dante makes a call, or tries to; he becomes frustrated, waves the phone at his friend as if to show that something is wrong with it. They talk, continue walking, hail the first taxi that comes their way. Lex pauses the footage and tries to get a read on the license plate but it's obscured by a car driving close behind.

Thinking that he's now seen all the footage, Lex is surprised to discover two new tracks to watch: *C* and *D*.

The *C* footage shows Glynnie, at 6:09 a.m., running erratically, constantly checking behind her. Security cameras capture her through Hamilton Avenue, where she disappears in the direction of residential Carroll Gardens. Shortly thereafter, she's known to have arrived by taxi at her family's brownstone.

The *D* footage picks up the boy hurrying through the dark along Van Brunt, but only briefly. He passes Fairway and disappears. Hours later, at 7:25 a.m., he reappears with a backpack slung over his shoulders like any other kid on his way to school. He walks along Van Brunt until he turns onto Richards Street and disappears.

Lex looks back over the first run of footage to see if he can find any clear shots of the boy's face, but in every single frame in which he appears he's either turned or too blurry. Then Lex reviews the *D* tape and discovers one almost-clear shot of the boy just before he turns off Van Brunt Street, but it captures only a side angle, not enough to really show him.

Lex remembers something from a colleague's recent case in which a partial face was digitally enhanced to construct what the rest of the face would look like. That image was then run through a facial recognition database. No match was made, but the prospect was intriguing.

He gets on the phone with DAS and is forwarded twice before landing Carlotta Sanchez, a tech who specializes in facial recognition. She sounds busy, but after hearing him out she promises to kick his request to the top.

"I'll let you know if there's enough to work with," she tells Lex. "Don't get your hopes up."

He sends Carlotta a video still of the boy. In moments, he hears back via text: I'll give it a try.

When he looks up, Saki is returning with a large plastic bag full of something heaved over her shoulder.

"How'd it go?" he asks.

"The Dreyfus parents could use a marriage counselor. And the father was already blasted at, what, twelve thirty in the afternoon?"

Lex is aware of how shocking that would be to someone who's never lived with a full-on alcoholic, as he did as a young child. He asks, "Is Nik Dreyfus a nasty drunk?"

"Not to me. But to his wife, yes. And then she turned around and let it all out on *me*." She drops the bag beside her desk. "There might be blood spatter on the shirt Glynnie wore last night."

"I didn't notice it in the footage."

"It's a fine mist, just in one spot. I need to get this over to the lab but I thought I'd run in here for my salad. I'm so hungry I feel like I'm going to faint. It's in the fridge, right?"

"You could have picked up something else," he says, marveling at the odd choice to return to the station first. "Gone straight to the lab."

"But my lunch was already ordered. It would be a waste."

"True." He wonders how anyone could function with such rigidly systematic thinking—unless it's some kind of mysterious strength he can't yet fathom.

Saki retrieves her salad, picks up the heavy bag, and says, "Be back soon."

"Actually," he suggests, "since you're here, let's see if someone else can take it to the lab. I want to show you something."

"Who?" she asks. "Who would take it for me? Haven't you noticed the way people are with me here?"

He lets that slide because, yes, he has noticed the way her coworkers tend to avoid her and he doesn't want to rub it in. He glances around the squad room and spots the perfect candidate.

"Hey, Dinardo," he calls across the floor.

Jack Dinardo's head snaps up from its prone position gazing at his monitor. "Lex Cole—didn't see you here. You back?"

"Just for now. Got a minute?"

The habitually under-occupied detective has no choice

but to agree to run the errand. He even throws in a smile for Saki before lifting the bag and carrying it out the door.

Lex explains what he's going to show her, letting her know to expect several strands of video so that she won't interrupt with questions. He wants to get through it quickly so they can decide where to take this. The only thing that's clear right now is that these aren't just errant teenagers; those kids are on the run from something.

Saki pulls a chair up to his desk and uses her teeth to rip open the utensil packet the deli threw in with her salad. She pops open the plastic clamshell and digs in as the first section of video begins to play.

While she's on the *C* footage, Lex's phone vibrates with a case file alert: three new reports.

The first one tells him about the phones found in Dante Green's apartment: the iPhone is registered to a family plan under the name of Margaret O'Leary-Dreyfus; the LG flip is a prepaid burner. Throughout the night the signals for both phones pinged along a similar route followed by Crisp, Glynnie, and the boy on the security footage. Katya Spielman said that her son used a Galaxy, so the burner, presumably, belongs to the boy. Lex can think of several reasons, all disturbing, that a kid as young as that boy would want, or need, a disposable phone.

Lex is about to share that with Saki when she looks up from the monitor and preempts him: "Another thing I can't get off my mind, besides the boy, is that something looked crusted under Glynnie's fingernails. I noticed it at the house this morning. Did you see?"

"I noticed her nails looked dirty."

"Maybe, but it might have been thicker than regular dirt, more like something almost congealed."

"You're thinking blood?"

"I'm thinking maybe blood, could be blood. I'm thinking I'd like to find out."

He nods: *Yes, of course.* Peeved with himself for not thinking of that first.

Lex opens the second new file and reads the update aloud to Saki: "A signal from Crisp's phone is holding steady in Red Hook, somewhere on Lorraine Street— around where he was on the footage, with Green and the other man, right before he cut loose." Lex also fills her in on the phones belonging to Glynnie and, possibly, probably, the unidentified boy.

"And," he opens the third report, "it looks like Green's phone finally came alive…on Governors Island." He reads a string of screenshots of texts presumably directed at Crisp.

you got my phone motherfucker

give it back or u dead motherfucker

ima gonna find u motherfucker

yo po son u dead

motherfucker

answer motherfucker

we comin for u GUVNER

Lex stands abruptly. "Their phones got switched."

Think like a teenager.

If he was in Crisp's shoes, at that age, he would have done the same thing: get out of there as fast as he could; go anywhere, as long as he got away.

Half an hour later, Lex is bracing himself against the railing of a police response boat as it hurtles toward Governors Island. Standing on the bow, water spraying, a visceral memory of surfing two days earlier returns so unexpectedly he almost weeps.

His own mother leaving him through an apartment door. Three years later, dying.

His second mother also dying.

The certainty of loss.

Adam standing there, saying, "You got it—I'm out."

The words hit Lex now as if he's hearing them for the first time.

Wind pushes against him as he holds steady, facing shoreward, watching Governors Island grow closer as his heart hurls away.

PART FOUR

Invisible Boy

22

Crisp runs until he finds himself on Pioneer Street and keeps running until he turns into Clinton Wharf, where he spots a sign with an arrow pointing to the ferry.

He runs, and he runs, until he reaches the choppy azulene waters of the Buttermilk Channel. In the near distance one of the city ferries approaches, leaving two strands of froth in its wake. But there's another boat, some kind of maintenance vessel, preparing to depart *right now*.

He accelerates to give himself some lift and jumps from the dock onto the back of the boat. *The stern,* he thinks, *the back is the stern and the front is the bow*. Someone must be at the bow now captaining the thing because all of a sudden it jerks away from the dock and slides into the channel. He lands on his feet and falls to his knees and, in a surrender to gravity, buckles forward onto his elbows and lies there, just lies there, as the boat makes waves and distance.

When he finally lifts his head and looks behind him at a shrinking Red Hook, he knows he's made it. He rolls onto his back, faces the sky, breathes.

"You!"

Crisp jolts up to see a grizzle-faced white man in late middle age wearing a dark blue uniform with a name sewn onto the shoulder: SALVADOR. He struggles to stand on the swaying boat while Salvador stands firmly and watches.

"Good morning, sir," Crisp says.

"Another one of you damn kids." Shaking his head, Salvador spits over the side of the vessel into the water. "What, you lose your MetroCard? School doors don't open for another two hours. Eh, what do I care?" He waves a dismissive hand.

Crisp improvises, "My teacher wanted me to come in early."

"Don't tell me—Ed Sansone again. Tell him for me, Sal," he points to his embroidered name, "that he shouldn't make early appointments with kids from Brooklyn unless he plans to paddle his own damn canoe over here for the pickup."

He must be talking about the Harbor School over on Governors Island; Crisp remembers seeing it listed in the public-high-school directory, how they have designated ferries to take the students to and from the mainland.

Going with it, Crisp promises, "I will."

"And while you're at it, tell the school they need an earlier ferry. Eight thirty don't cut it—you're my second stowaway this month."

Sal opens a storage trunk bolted to the deck and throws Crisp a faded orange life vest.

"Thanks." Crisp snaps on the vest, its musty smell rising like a fog.

Sal disappears into the cabin.

Ten minutes later, they dock on Governors Island.

Crisp returns the life vest to the trunk and jumps onto a utility dock opposite the passenger ferry mooring at Soissons Landing. A feeling of early-morning abandonment permeates the place, a powerful sense of refuge— *Dante will never find me here*.

Crisp jogs along the dock, onto the island, and continues up the first path he comes to so that, if Sal happens to be watching, he'll see a boy hurrying to an early appointment on one of the last days of the school year—only seniors, graduates, are now free of the calendar.

A pair of cops roll by in a squad car and his first impulse is to hail them, ask for help, explain the situation. But then he pictures Officer Russo's dead eyes when he handed over that bike ticket. *No way*.

He comes to what looks like the back of a low, wide brick building surrounded by a grass-filled moat and remembers: Fort Jay. As he walks around to the main entrance of the old fort, all the research he did for an eighth-grade New York history project ("The Coast Guard and the City It Protects") comes flooding back.

Crisp at thirteen still hadn't hit his first growth spurt but he knew it was coming. His voice had already shifted and puberty was creeping up by way of lip fuzz and incipient acne. He remembers being uncomfortable in his body, almost afraid of what was happening to it, to him, and how when he worked and studied he could forget about all that. He remembers holing up in his room with library books and his laptop, reading every single thing he could find about the coast guard in New York City, and spending an entire night on its residency on Governors Island. He remembers building the poster board vista of Popsicle stick houses and trees of clay, and writing a lengthy history of the island's occupations over three hundred years. He remembers how reading about Governors Island marked the first time he ran across the name Robert Moses, who wanted to build a bridge between the city and the island. How this was Crisp's first taste of a man who, he would later learn, used eminent domain to mow down whole tracts of thriving neighborhoods in order to build a network of highways that only deepened the city's segregation. How this would eventually open his mind to a complex socioeconomic perspective on the city's evolution, urban planning, race, educational imbalance, and on and on. How he proceeded to read Jane Jacobs's *The Death and Life of Great American Cities* and fell in love with her ideas. How he came to view Moses as someone whose efforts encouraged the separation of races, even going so far as to consider the man a strategist in the demise of his own parents' relationship and thus a negative force in his, Crisp's own, childhood. (But there never was a bridge to Governors Island; the War Department objected on the grounds that it would pose a navigational threat to the Brooklyn Navy Yard. *Take that, Robert Moses.*)

Fort Jay's front gates haven't been opened yet for the day, but Crisp discovers enough give in the chain padlocking them together that he's able to slip through.

Two-story barracks fronted by Greek Revival pillars encircle a modest central yard. On the narrow verandas of the buildings are pairs of old white rocking chairs. Crisp settles himself into one of them to wait out the morning until ferry service back to the city starts up later. Then he'll catch a subway home, explain everything to his family, return Princeton's call, take what comes.

He holds Dante's phone in his hands and stares at the lock screen. He recalls the hack a friend once showed him for getting past a smartphone's pass code (that friend now on his way to study robotics at MIT), closes his eyes, and tries to summon the steps. After several attempts at the complex series of swipes, pauses, and taps, the lock screen vanishes and he finds himself looking at a photo of a woman—the hairdresser who slapped Dante earlier this morning—and a preteen girl wearing matching silver dresses. Crisp is so excited that he actually leaps out of the chair, sending the rocker into a violent backswing.

He starts to call his mother for help but decides, *No, she'll freak out and ask too many questions and the answers will only make it worse.* For all her fierce competence— this mother who can handle anything—he's come to understand that she raised him on a fuel of hypervigilance that can turn toxic on a dime. It will be better to tell her everything, truthfully, in person, when she can see with her own eyes that he's really okay. He opens a text and types a simple message: This is Crisp borrowing someone's phone. Home later. I love you. As far as she knows, he's still with his friends, and that's better for now.

Next, he opens the Uber app. A royal crest for Dante's icon. His handle: King of Kings. The gun dealer's last ride was two days ago, to an address in Sunset Park. And the ride before that was the one with Mo Crespo's face but not his name.

He recognizes the face instantly: an older version of the man in an old family photo holding baby Crisp in his arms—round and dark with a memorable half smile. There it is again, that almost smile on the mature face of a man with close-cropped hair slightly silver at the temples and the chin dimple he passed down to his son. A face that should have been accompanied by the name Mo Crespo but instead is called, here, Wilson Ramsey.

The name rings a bell, a whole orchestra of bells, but Crisp doesn't know why.

He copies the phone number into a text message that he sends to himself. Then he opens a search window on Dante's phone and types w i l s o before the battery dies and the phone powers off.

His mind whirs around the spiky stalk of *Wilson Ramsey Mo Crespo Wilson Ramsey Mo Crespo,* a dervish of possibility until suddenly the name lands with a jolt.

Wilson Ramsey is the graphic novelist whose series Crisp devoured when he was eight, nine, ten years old—*The Life of a Boy,* about an albino kid with invisibility powers. And then, when the character was twelve, the books stopped coming and Crisp moved on to other authors, other stories, other interests beyond cartoons.

The chance that his father could be *the* Wilson Ramsey rips at his inner lining, at his sense of the person he always thought he was, or wasn't. He imagined him many ways, but never like this. He learned early that his mother didn't like to talk about her ex-husband. Babu sometimes would, mostly describing him in innocuous terms like "not handsome but not not handsome," "not serious but not so funny," "not so good but not so bad." She never told Crisp anything he could get a handle on. But Dedu— Dedu was worse, trying to turn Crisp's questions away from the father he never knew, offering Russian proverbs to create the idea that if Mo would ever return to him it would happen passively, by accident. "A lucky man can stumble upon a treasure, while an unlucky one can't even find a mushroom." Meaning, if Crisp is lucky, if he really wants to know his father, the man will someday turn up. "If you were born lucky, even your rooster will lay eggs." And then there was the one that turned the good luck dictum on its head: "Bad luck is fertile."

Is this the day he'll be lucky, or unlucky, or both?

Tired, hungry, confused, Crisp stands and, the rocking chair swaying ghostlike in his wake, leaves the confines of Fort Jay.

In the quiet distance, a golf cart sprouting rakes and shovels rolls along a path like a piece on a board game, then disappears around a bend. Crisp turns in the opposite direction and after a few minutes wanders into Nolan Park. The collection of abandoned yellow houses encircling an old-fashioned green is densely peaceful at this hour of the morning.

Abundant trees shade the raw glare of a new sun as he walks across the dappled lawn. The houses, though worn at the paint, are evocative of a pretty way of life that Crisp has never known: a classic American village of front-porch neighbors, shared lemonade, a gazebo band on summer evenings. The way life used to be here, back when people lived on the island, before it was turned into a warm-weather playground for a restless city. He lies down on the grass to continue his wait.

He closes his eyes and tries not to think about his father. Instead, he time-travels back to the eighteen hundreds and pictures himself in a different life, his imagination first dressing himself in a hatted, booted uniform, an officer returning home, where a wife in an arsenic-green floor-length dress has dinner waiting on a polished table... until that image breaks apart. No. He wouldn't have been the master in this scenario; he would have been the slave. The picture inverts and the officer's skin lightens while Crisp fades into the background, servile against the wall, clothed in sagging burlap, awaiting orders.

Opening his eyes, it hits him how exposed he is, lying here in the open. That he might not be as safe as he thinks he is or wants to be. That he should find somewhere to wait out of sight.

He crosses the lawn and at the closest yellow house he jiggles the front doorknob, but it doesn't budge. All the wavy-glassed windows are also sealed, either locked or painted shut. It's the same at the second, third, fourth house he tries: front and back doors secured, windows immovable.

On the porch of the fifth house, he notices that one of the windows is cracked open. He slips both hands into the gap and is about to push up on the lower sash when he thinks he hears something—a surprise, as these houses have been unoccupied for years. He pulls out his hands and listens.

Footsteps, definitely footsteps, the old wood floor moaning with complaint.

He sprints across the porch, but a voice stops him.

"Are you early?" A woman, sleepy, unconcerned.

He turns and sees her in the doorway: mid-twenties, bed-tousled short brown hair, pajama pants falling below the hem of a paint-splattered bathrobe, bare feet.

"I thought you said eleven," she mumbles. "Come on in." Leaving the door wide open, she turns down a hallway and disappears.

Crisp steps into a spacious foyer, with a room opening to either side and a staircase rising straight ahead. The beautiful, balanced symmetry calms him. He takes a deep breath. Everything about the house looks worn down and half collapsed, the floors broom clean but the ceilings cobwebbed at the corners, marginally occupied yet unlived in. Who is she, if no one lives here? And why is she wearing pajamas?

At the smell of toast, his stomach bucks. He follows the delicious trail into a make-do cooking arrangement sprung from the relics of a nineteen fifties kitchen.

Cracked, speckled Formica counters. Rounded oven with crusted racks just visible through a porthole-size glass. Fridge with lever handle. A buzz of confused electrical charge in the air.

Crisp asks, "Who are you?"

Her shoulder blades draw together. Turning to him, she says, "Laura," her tone now pitched with incredulity. Backing against the edge of the counter, as if realizing she's made a mistake, she asks, "Didn't the Arts Center send you?"

"What?"

"Who are *you*?"

"Crisp."

"I thought you were...were the artist the Center assigned to work on the walls—Gary. Maybe you should—"

"It's okay." Crisp takes a step backward to reassure her that he means no harm. The irony of her having thought he was an artist hits him hard, as if there could be one iota of artistic talent in him. But what if Wilson Ramsey actually *is* his father and passed down some long-dormant genetic gift? "I'm an aspiring artist," he lies, hoping to put the woman at ease. Then, compounding the invention, he adds, "A graphic novelist."

"Ferry service doesn't even start until ten," she realizes suddenly.

"I got a ride from Sal."

"Oh," she says. "Sal," she says. "I'm confused, but..."

She puts two slices of buttered toast on the table and gestures for him to have one. The warmth and richness and perfect crunch of it unfurls on his tongue. He talks about his crazy night, leaving out the worst parts, and bacon sizzles, and the room fills with Laura's careful listening.

"Coffee?" she asks.

"Milk, no coffee." His stomach is too acid as it is. "If that's okay."

Smiling, she pours him a glass of cold milk.

Once they've eaten, she leans over the table and says, "Listen, Crisp, I'm okay with you hanging here until the ferries start running. But my supervisor's going to have a kitten if she finds out I hosted someone, because one of the rules is 'No hosting.' So would you help me out and do some work on the walls? Since you're here? So if she finds out and asks I can tell her it was an honest mistake on my part—I thought you were the Friday artist and you were early. Okay?"

"Sure."

She leads him to a slender pantry off the kitchen, deep with shelved art supplies. Someone has drawn an intricate pattern on the heavily dusted countertop.

"We're trying not to touch that," Laura tells him. "You know how they henna your hands when you get married and the test of an auspicious match is how little house-work you're made to do after the wedding—the longer the henna pattern lasts, the more hopeful your future?"

He resists the urge to dissect the clusters of generalities in her statement, or question, or whatever it is—the gross inaccuracies inevitable when you romanticize something you barely understand—and chooses instead to accept it

195

at its root intention of cultural inclusiveness. (Not that he's an expert in Hindu ritual; he isn't. But he'd have to be blind not to notice the glaring faults in her example.) He tells her, "Yes."

"We're thinking of it like Sanskrit," she elaborates. Jumping now from Ancient Indian body art to liturgical language. "It lasts as long as it lasts, and then it's gone, but in the meantime we don't mess with it."

"Who is 'we'?"

"The summer artists. It's a weeklong residency rotation. We overlap on Mondays. Plus a different day artist comes in every morning, so there are usually two of us here except at night."

"Cool."

"You can paint the walls before you start," she tells him. "If you don't like the base color that's there now, which is white."

"White's fine," he says. "Did you know that there are over four hundred shades of white?" Sensing she'd be interested in a detail like that.

"Actually, I *did* know that."

He scans the mysterious array of choices and, overwhelmed and uncertain, selects two paint markers: a black and a red.

"A minimalist," Laura observes. "Well, if you need anything else, you know where it is. Come on."

She leads him into the front room, on the left of the house, presumably once a place for receiving guests—*a drawing room*—empty save for a ladder folded against a wall. Another artist has already filled out the back wall with vivid bursts of color that suggest *but don't fulfill* (and there, Crisp assumes, is the concept) a floral motif.

"Start wherever you want," she tells him. "I'm going to get dressed, then I'll be on the back porch working on my installation."

With Laura gone, Crisp stands alone in the room and stares at the bland white wall. A bacon-y burp leaves a trace of bile on his tongue. He uncaps the black paint marker and approaches the wall. He has no idea where, or how, to begin.

He tells himself: *Start* anywhere. *Start at* right here. *Start at* maybe.

Finally he drags the ladder over and climbs it. In the wall's topmost left corner he spells out in crudely drawn balloon lettering *The Life of a Man*.

That is where he'll begin: with black outlines so thin you'd have to squint to read them from below. He climbs back down, returns the ladder to the opposite wall, crouches in the bottom left corner of the wall he's working on, and imagines his *maybe* father Wilson-Ramsey's mind-set from the beginning of a story Crisp has never understood: the place on the wall and in the personal narrative where a person can't get any lower.

Time passes without his notice as the wall fills with crude cartoon people and thought bubbles attached by spindly threads.

Depleted, he stands back and looks over his work. He's a terrible artist, without a single drop of talent, and his depictions are too obvious—he can't know what was going through his father's mind when he abandoned them, if

Mo ever felt remorse or guilt or sadness. If his father is *the* Wilson Ramsey, Crisp clearly didn't inherit the artist's gift any more than he understands the man's choices.

He wonders if the ferry back to the city has started running yet. About to pull the phone out of his pocket to check the clock, he remembers that the battery is dead. He finds the back porch and there is Laura, wearing overalls and leather gardening gloves, twisting wire into the shape of a gnarled tree limb. She seems to be building a kind of forest. A skein of Christmas tree lights drape over a shabby wicker chair in the corner.

"Hey," he says, "do you happen to have a phone charger?" Wishing he'd thought to ask this earlier.

"Yup—but it's an iPhone 5. That work for yours?"

"No."

"Check one of the drawers in the pantry. I saw a bunch of chargers in there—maybe something'd fit. And remember not to touch the—"

"—counter," he finishes for her. "I won't. Thanks."

"By the way, Gary—the *real* Gary—canceled. So this works out great."

"Oh. Good."

"I'm gonna break for lunch soon," she says. "You hungry?"

"Lunch?" Didn't they just have breakfast?

Laura smiles. "You're one of *those*. Not me. I never forget a meal."

She has to be kidding—it can't be lunchtime already. His stomach *is* growling but he always gets hungry when he hasn't slept. And he *was* surprised at how much he drew and wrote when he stepped back to survey his (awful, sophomoric) mural. But lunchtime?

Several different kinds of chargers are jumbled together in a drawer along with random other household things you'd find in or near a kitchen: tape, screwdriver, twine, mangled twisty ties. The charger wires are hopelessly tangled, so once Crisp finds the one that fits the Galaxy, he has to try a variety of plugs before one works. An image of a battery containing a white lightning bolt appears on Dante's phone. Crisp taps the screen but it's too soon.

Blue, he thinks out of nowhere, *instead of red;* the slash of occasional color in his mural should be *blue.* Seized by his first-ever artistic inspiration, he leaves the phone, returns to the supply cabinet, and selects a new paint marker, realizing, as he takes it in his hand, that he'll now have the option of purple if he mixes the red and blue, intentionally or accidentally—this could be interesting. And if he adds black to the blue, the black-purple could achieve his conception of blauvet (blauvé)—the exact shade a bruised night sky is, or should be or could be. So much to think about, so many combinations to try.

When he hears a series of bleeps emanating from the phone, he puts down the marker and returns to the pantry.

Each missive in the flood of delayed texts shows a round icon of Rodrigo's face contrived with menace, posing his hand like a gun. There are seven messages in all, each one nastier, more threatening, than the next—from Dante, obviously, having borrowed his lackey's phone.

Crisp drops the phone onto the dust mandala, smearing the intricate design. "Sorry," he mutters to Laura (who can't hear him), to the pantry counter (which doesn't care), to his abandoned mural (under-realized), to himself (for slacking). He untethers the charger, jams the Galaxy into his back pocket, and runs out of the house as fast as his feet can carry him.

He abandons Nolan Park and runs up Andes Road, Dante's pugnacious threats ringing loud and clear.

In the distance, a ferry like a small white toy moves away from the Manhattan skyline in the direction of Governors Island. He runs past low-slung brick barracks with white-painted doors. Past a flank of parked blue Citi Bikes. Past chain-link fences protecting newly seeded lawn.

As soon as Soissons Landing comes into view, he sees a Manhattan-bound ferry just then pulling out. In the distance, another ferry chugs closer, a spattering of ant-like figures growing human as the vessel nears. He hurries, hoping to meet it before it docks and disembarks again in the constant back-and-forth of arrivals and departures.

The road curves and a flare of red hat and jaunty walk comes into view and—Crisp would swear it—a sun-touched glint of gold teeth.

There's no time to make sure it's Dante, not if he wants to get away.

He sprints in the opposite direction.

23

The police boat pulls to a stop at a pier alongside the capacious ferry docked at Soissons Landing. Inbound passengers funnel down a gangway toward shore, where a line has formed for the reverse journey.

Lex jumps off the boat and sprints forward, gaze raking both queues for Crisp, Dante, Rodrigo. Nothing, no one. Is he too early or too late? Is this the right place or the wrong place? The ring of menace in Dante's threats shrinks time mercilessly, and now, now Lex can't get his body or his brain to move fast enough or steer him in the right direction.

He turns and hurries up the road that leads into the heart of the island, scanning every face as he passes Fort Jay and comes up on Nolan Park. He's so prepared for disappointment that the red MAKE AMERICA GREAT AGAIN hat seems to reach him in a time delay.

And then, all at once, Dante Green comes into sharp focus. The gun dealer is on his way from the inner island toward the ferry landing, radiating purpose as a group of camera-lashed tourists make room for him to pass. He looks like a man on a mission, on his way to do something—or having just done it.

Lex pauses to issue an alert that the target of his arrest warrant is within his sights and to request backup. In moments, a squad car appears and discharges a pair of uniforms.

Onlookers slow their pace, checking to see if what's happening is worth sticking around for.

Dante turns in the opposite direction, back toward the island's center, but he doesn't get far before a second squad car blocks the way.

Bolting forward, Lex reaches for his ID. "Dante Green, I'm Detective Lex Cole, and you're under arrest for the sale and distribution of illegal firearms."

"Say what?" Dante smoothly regroups as if he could trick a seasoned cop. Beneath the man's white jacket sprinkled with crowns and diamonds, Lex perceives a shift of muscle, a new readiness to spring.

Lex steps closer as a quartet of uniforms surround them. The tallest officer, a woman with broad cheekbones and a grimly set mouth, moves in to clap on the first cuff. Another cop, male, muscular, shaved head, grips Dante's arm to stop him from pulling away. Cuffs secured, wrists cinched behind his back, Dante levers forward from the pressure. Lex feels a ripple of satisfaction—they've got him.

The crowd has grown and clumped around them, phones aimed in a fusillade of camera flashes as the vigilante press corps begins its work of gathering and spreading the news before any of them has a chance to understand what it is.

"This ain't nothing but a misunderstanding." Dante makes his pitch directly to a smartphone lens. "They got the wrong guy."

"Tone it down," Lex hisses. "Unless you want to add kidnapping to the charges. How about murder?"

Dante's eyes narrow, and he's sweating; Lex can smell it coming off him in waves. "What did you do with Crisp Crespo?" he demands. Fearing now that he's too late.

"I did nothing to that fucker—it's what he did to *me*."

"Where is he?"

Dante faces a camera lens and inflects his tone with outrage. "I want a lawyer! Don't I have rights?"

* * *

A clock ticks against the wall of the 8-4's small interrogation room, windowless except for a panel of one-way glass behind which no one is watching. Dante Green sits with his knees spread wide and his now front-cuffed hands tucked into his lap. Lex sits across from him and waits a minute for Green to notice that he isn't taking notes or recording the conversation, though he might.

Green asks, "You gonna tell me why you picked me up?"

"Technically, parole violation."

"What you mean 'technically'? And what violation?"

"The twenty-seven firearms in your refrigerator."

"You been in my house?"

"Yup."

Green contemplates, apparently deciding that the search was warranted, because he asks, "What you on me for? It ain't guns."

"You tell me."

"Like hell if—"

"What else did we find at your place?"

"My clothes. My bed."

"What else?"

"I might've left a mess."

"Go on."

Green's eyes grow hard.

"Whose blood is on your floor, Dante?"

The dealer lifts his shoulders to his ears and lets them fall heavily in a mocking shrug.

"Where is he?" Lex asks.

"Who?"

"Crisp Crespo."

"Hell if I know."

"You see him on Governors Island?"

"Wish I did."

"So that's a *no*."

"You asking or telling?"

"You were looking for him—that's why you were there."

"I got a right to a lawyer."

"You haven't been processed yet," Lex reminds him. "Technically."

"Fuck you. *Sir*."

"You want your lawyer? Sure. I'll call the officer, get you processed, send you over to booking."

"Wait."

"Talk to me, Dante. Whose blood did we find on your floor? Who was in that suitcase? Where's the body?"

Green nods, understanding the offer: Talk, and measure the charge to fit the level of cooperation. "You after the boy—well, you got good reason. Crisp, he shows up at my crib with his girl, and then," he pauses, appears to calculate something, says, "*he* plugs my man Jerome. Kills him. I lost a friend to that trigger-happy kid."

"What did they want from you?" Lex asks. "Why did they show up?"

"Take one guess."

"You're saying Crisp shot Jerome."

Green hesitates, nods.

"Why?" Lex probes.

"How the hell do I know? Kid picks up the gun and pulls the trigger—*bam*. Jerome down. Made that kid clean up his own mess."

Lex says, "Tell me about the girl."

"Some white bitch. A real princess."

"I've met her. She ran home to her parents this morning. She had a lot to say."

"Oh?"

"Why'd you bring them up to your place? What was the plan?"

"She didn't tell you?" Green shakes his head. "I believe *that*. She doing some shopping, that's what."

"You're saying *she* wanted to buy a gun?"

Green keeps his mouth shut, maybe wondering if the interview is being recorded after all. It isn't. Until he's processed, Lex can talk to him all he wants without a lawyer. After, he's required to record the conversation, which wouldn't be long enough to tape once a lawyer's in the picture.

Lex asks, "How'd she know to go to you?"

"I got no idea." The gun dealer breaks eye contact. Fusses with his bracelets.

"Tell the truth—who wanted to buy? Crisp, the girl, or the boy? Which one?"

Green's head tilts from left to right. "What boy?"

"The smaller boy who was with them."

"Yeah, well, he must've been pretty damn small 'cause I didn't even see him."

Why is everyone pretending this boy doesn't exist?

Lex's phone vibrates. "Excuse me a minute."

"Bring me a soda?" Green asks.

"I'll think about it."

Standing in the hall beside the officer guarding the door, Lex checks his phone and finds alerts for two different lab reports that came in while he was busy with Green.

He reads the blood report first.

Most of the DNA on Dante's floor matches in the system to Jerome Bailey, an ex-con with a long record. So Green told the truth about who got killed.

And the blood on Glynnie's shirt also belongs to Jerome, the pattern suggesting blowback from someone shot at close range but from an awkward angle. Blood spatter found on the Baby Browning also IDs to Jerome.

Lex opens the ballistics report.

A single partial fingerprint on the handle of the gun aligns *closely enough with the right thumb posterior looping pattern found on prints taken from the home of Glynneth Dreyfus to make a 95 percent assertion of compatibility*. In other words, the gun that killed Jerome was in Glynnie's hand at some point, something Green left out of his story. No other prints were found on the gun.

Lex detours to the soda machine and chooses a Welch's grape soda for Dante because it looks disgusting and the man just lied to him. In the hall, before going in to Dante, he tells the officer, "I'll need you to take him over to booking in a minute."

"Will do."

"Thanks."

Clenching the cold can in one hand, Lex waits until the door clicks locked behind him before putting the drink down on the table.

"This shit ain't no *soda*."

"It's got bubbles so it's soda." Lex pops open the can and pushes it forward.

Dante lifts it with both hands, takes a thirsty swig, grimaces. "Too *sweet*."

Lex says, "Now that that's done, let's get you processed."

"I *talked* to you," Green argues.

"You lied about who shot the gun, Dante. Why?"

Green picks up the can and drains it. Drops it down so it bounces off the table and clatters along the floor.

Lex gets up, knocks twice on the door, and stands back while the officer leads Green from the room. When Lex is almost at the stairwell door, intending to head back upstairs, his phone vibrates with an incoming call.

"Elsa!" he answers.

"Your boy come back?" she asks.

For a moment he thinks she means Adam, *his boy,* then realizes she wouldn't refer to him that way. She means Crisp. "Nope. And the girl took off again, so now we're back to looking for both of them." He crosses the lobby, past the sign for the property clerk, and stands in the empty hall, where he can talk without bothering anyone or being bothered.

"You're kidding me."

"They were into something messy last night. Looks like someone got killed—guy who worked with the two she mentioned."

"Glynnie didn't say anything about that," Elsa notes.

"No she didn't. It's getting interesting. Just picked up the gun dealer."

"You're busy. I'll let you go."

Exhaustion overtakes him and he leans against the wall. "No, let's chat a minute."

"You sound wiped out, Lex. When did you last sleep?"

"I can handle it."

"How can I help?" she asks.

"Thanks, Elsa."

"No—seriously. Talk to me."

The door to the property room swings open and the clerk steps out. Lex remembers him from before: Marty, with that same bored look in his young eyes. Lex nods hello. Marty returns the greeting, pulls the door locked behind him, and punches in a code: 4291. He moves a cigarette from behind his ear to between his lips and heads for the station house door.

He tells Elsa, "My boy, Crisp, has an AWOL dad who might be part of this. I need to find him."

"You think Crisp is with him?"

"Who knows? I've been doing my best to think like a teenager—my brain feels like scrambled eggs, so maybe I'm succeeding." He can't, won't, tell her that this kind of enervation is exactly what scared him away from Vice, when, faced with a fat Ziploc of confiscated heroin, he knew he'd succumb if he didn't get out. That moment of surrender when you realize you're losing the fight, and it's step back now or you never will.

"Lex, go home and catch a few hours. You can't think straight; I can hear it in your voice. You're probably not doing anyone any good."

"Maybe." His eyes rest on the property room door.

"Promise me you'll go home and hit the sack for a bit."

"Thanks for calling, Elsa. I mean to have you out for that drink soon. I'll get in touch." As he slips his phone into his pocket, a powerful feeling takes hold.

He glances around; no one's there. Just out of curiosity, he tells himself, he approaches the door and keys in Marty's code. A metallic pop tells him that the same one is used to both lock and unlock. He opens the door, prepared to greet whoever's in there. *"Someone needs to tell Marty he should set different codes to get in and out. I mean look how easy it was for me just now."* But the excuse is unnecessary because he's alone.

He steps up to the counter and pretends to wait for Marty. Then, just to test how easy it might be, he steps around the counter and into the stacks of shelves. If Marty returns now, Lex will say the door was unlocked, apologize for not following protocol, and explain that he's in a rush to get something that belongs to his perp who was just booked—a gun he wants to drop at ATF for testing.

Lex opens three boxes before he finds some loser's confiscated stash: five large Ziplocs filled with tiny packets ready for sale on the street. He takes just one. Slips it into his pocket, returns the box to the shelf, and is out the door before Marty returns or anyone notices.

* * *

The pitched voice wrenches Lex's focus off the monitor. He looks up: one of the detectives across the room is getting loud with someone on the other end of his call. Lex rubs his eyes, brain fuzzy. He wonders if he dozed a moment. He doesn't need to check to know the packet's there; slight as it is, it weighs inside his pocket like a boulder.

While Saki, nearby at her desk, rewatches the collated security footage with intense concentration, Lex continues his review of Green's parole reports since his latest release. The names of the gun dealer's current sidekicks pop up regularly: Jerome Bailey, another parolee out after a twelve-year prison stint for aggravated rape, a middle-aged grizzled white guy with a necklace of blue tattoos;

and Rodrigo Rivera, with a long history of petty crimes but only one arrest and less than a year inside, younger and brawnier, midnight dark, wide-faced, deadpan gaze.

Thinking he recognizes Rivera, Lex pulls up the security footage and fast-forwards to a clip showing Dante and the unidentified man walking the streets of Red Hook several paces behind Crisp as the boy pulls the suitcase. Lex freezes the frame and compares the second man with the two mug shots. It's definitely him.

Lex moves on, farther down and backward into the criminal record. Guns most recently, drugs farther in the past, stolen goods peppered throughout. A headache comes on suddenly; he grinds his jaw, forces himself to stay awake.

His eyes stop on a name.

He rereads it, and it doesn't change.

The record details an arrest and dismissal on a charge of narcotics trafficking. Green's partner in crime on that caper: a juvenile with a sealed record who turned state's evidence in exchange for having the charges against him dropped.

Amos Crespo.

There it is: a buried connection, and possibly a lasting grudge, between the ex-con stalking Crisp on the footage and another teenager nearly twenty years ago. Is *that* why Green tried to push Jerome's murder off on Crisp, when all the evidence points against it? To deliver a sideways payback for an old grievance by fingering a snitch's son? Lex screenshots the page and saves it to a new file on the desktop labeled AMOS CRESPO.

He splits the screen again and plugs Amos Crespo's name into the system, initiating a global search through the national law enforcement databases, a collation of criminal and government agencies on every level. Usually what happens next is the screen fills with information ranging from arrest records to driver's license to voter registration to residence history to IRS alerts, the bureaucratic trail of modern existence that maps every life. Almost always, results populate like rabbits…unless the name hasn't been used in a very long time. According to this, Mo Crespo's official life ended seventeen years ago. Two years after his son was born. About a year after he walked out on his family.

Lex sits back and tries to take that in. When Katya Spielman said her ex-husband disappeared, she meant it literally.

The only information connected with Mo's identity is three employment records from his late teens, from working a variety of lowly restaurant jobs, busboy and the like; he never made it to waiter, at least not on the books. After that, he must have found a cash source of income, and if it was illegal he was very good at not getting caught. No driver's license. The second to last official record for Crespo is the family court approval for a garnishment of his wages by his former wife. The last record is an address on Staten Island where he lived for one year.

Lex sits back and mutters, "Huh."

"What?" Saki asks.

"Crisp's dad knew Dante Green in the bad old days, but then went his own way. How's yours going?"

"Trying to figure out what's happening behind Fairway when the cameras stop. I have a feeling that if I can find the boy, I'll find Glynnie."

"Sounds right."

"Funny about those headphones," she says.

"The Beats? Yeah, I noticed. First she's got them, then the boy does."

"They shared them, like friends. But then no one has them. They vanish."

"The boy lost them," Lex ventures, "or left them behind somewhere. Aren't those things expensive?"

"Yup. The Dreyfuses are obviously rich."

"Maybe Glynnie doesn't care."

Saki nods, but doesn't look convinced. "So, Crisp's father—where is he now?"

"Looks to me like Mo Crespo went underground as soon as his ex put a garnish on his paycheck."

"Typical deadbeat," Saki says, then rephrases: "Not typical—I shouldn't have said that. No one is typical. But irresponsible, for sure."

The words ring: *No one is typical.* Lex has seen investigators lose their way by thinking small and shallow, caricaturing being one of the best ways to misunderstand someone you want to know better...or someone you might want to find.

"I wonder," he thinks aloud, "if Crisp going over there, to the Houses, had something to do with his father's past association with Green. Or if maybe Green sought Crisp out for some reason."

"Could be."

Lex glances at the monitor, the dead end where Mo Crespo falls off the face of the earth and out of the Internet—it's as if he never even went on the Internet after it was unleashed to the general public, not for anything, not even once.

"Probably took an alias," Saki says. "I had that on a case one time. Located him by matching addresses with any personal detail I could find about the real name."

"Details?" Lex mumbles. What does he really know about Mo Crespo? As a kid, he ran with a bad crowd, then turned against one of his own. He was married young to a girl he met on the subway. Moved to the other side of Brooklyn and became a father. Had some shitty jobs. Abandoned his family.

"The mother still waiting downstairs?" Saki asks.

"As far as I know."

"Must be torture."

"Think I'll check in with her," Lex says.

He finds Katya alone in the public information office, sitting in a chair with her hands folded on her lap and her eyes closed, like a statue that almost looks human but can't be, it's just too still. He feels cold with recognition: that stony, helpless reserve; that tenuous plug on a simmering explosion.

Lex sits down beside her. "How're you holding up?"

Her eyes flutter open, bloodshot with worry. "I didn't hear you come in."

"Do you have any pictures of your ex-husband in that album?"

"Mo? Why?"

"He used to know Dante Green, the man Crisp was with last night."

"At the Houses?" Her jaw drops. "I don't understand."

"Neither do I. That's why I'd like to track down Mo, see if he can shed some light. But it looks like he fell off the radar seventeen years ago."

"Maybe he's dead," she says, bitterly. "That would explain *a lot*."

She leafs through the album until she comes to a snapshot of a young couple, slips it out of its plastic sheath, and hands it to Lex.

He studies it: Katya with long hair, visibly pregnant, a broad smile, looking right into the camera. Beside her, a young black man in soft profile, also smiling, his arm draped around her shoulders, gazing at his bride.

Katya shrugs. "He loved me, I guess. Back then."

"Can I borrow this?"

She nods. "How much longer?" A crimp in her voice. "Will Crisp—" But she doesn't finish. Lex understands how badly she needs to know that her son is safe; he also understands that what she needs may not be forthcoming.

He assures her, gently, "We'll find him." Hoping that's true. "Hang in there."

On his way back upstairs, Lex calls Carlotta, the tech.

She answers right away. "Detective! I'm almost done with your face."

"Excellent. Listen, can you do up another one? I have a profile it would help to see straight on, and twenty years older."

"Zap it over and I'll look at it right now. If it's doable, I'll send you both together."

"Thanks." He stops in the hallway, holds the photo up against the wall, and takes a picture of it with his phone, wondering why things went sour between Mo and Katya. The image is on its way to Carlotta by the time he reaches the squad room.

When he drops the photograph on Saki's desk, she looks up, hits Pause, asks, "What's that?"

"Crisp's parents before he was born."

She picks up the photo to look at it more closely, then puts it back down and yawns.

"How many times have you watched that?" he asks her.

"Twice all the way through. Now I'm jumping around, looking for a pattern in their movements. I think the boy is living somewhere near Fairway but it's frustrating without an ID on him."

"Just heard we're about to get the full face," Lex tells her. "Hopefully that'll help. Getting one on Mo Crespo too."

After a visit to the men's room, Lex checks his phone and is pleased to see two new case files just added by Carlotta Sanchez.

He opens the first one and the face that scrolls onto the screen is the one he wants most: Mo Crespo, staring right at him, contoured to evoke a man of about forty. A round face with slightly close-set eyes. Short salty hair and a widow's peak.

You're a wizard, he messages Carlotta. Thanks for the quick turnaround.

"Our faces are in," he calls over to Saki's desk. "Forwarding yours now."

"Thanks."

Working at the desktop, Lex feeds Mo's image into a program that compares faces with ID photos from all city-run agencies, and presto. Face after face, name after name, it's the same thing over and over for the past seventeen years.

Mo Crespo's image now belongs to a different name: Wilson Ramsey.

He's still in New York City.

But every one of his records lists his address as a PO box at the central post office near Penn Station in Manhattan. No phone numbers come up anywhere.

Lex pounds the desk and a stapler jumps.

Saki looks over at him but says nothing; preoccupied, she returns to her own search, face-to-face now with the boy.

Lex returns to the face of Mo Crespo/Wilson Ramsey. On the split side of the screen he runs a search for just the alias, which instantly produces nearly two million links. Seems the guy's some kind of cartoonist, a graphic novelist with several books to his name and enough of a following to own a corner of the Internet. Lex clicks the first link, WILSON RAMSEY | AMERICAN AUTHOR AND ILLUSTRATOR | OFFICIAL PAGE, and starts reading.

24

A tenderness in the boy's eyes unnerves Saki. He seems to be looking right at her. She runs the face through the system and suddenly, just like that, he has a name: Janjak "JJ" St. Fleur.

The information filling the screen tells his story, up to a point: undocumented except for school records, over a year ago his parents are deported and he turns up in the foster system—a first placement that doesn't take followed by a second listed as his current address.

Saki notices that, though his foster parents, Dov and Shoshi Nachman, live in Midwood, JJ continues to attend school close to the St. Fleur family's last address in Red Hook. This in itself isn't that unusual in a city where local schools are mostly a thing of the past—except that his school MetroCard history shows him commuting out of Red Hook, near Fairway, as recently as yesterday morning. And yesterday afternoon he rode the same bus back in the opposite direction. Interesting, she thinks: interesting and strange. Why didn't someone, anyone, notice the discrepancy between the boy's address and his daily route? Maybe not interesting *or* strange but just unfortunate—another example of a kid falling through the proverbial cracks of a broken system.

She dials the number listed for the Nachmans. A woman answers with a harried-sounding "What?" A background cacophony of children's voices, crying, whining, shouting, makes it difficult to hear.

Saki introduces herself as "working for the city," a basic truth, and says, "I'm calling to check in on JJ St. Fleur." She waits for the answer, which seems to take too long.

"JJ's doing good," the woman says.

"Health okay?"

"Perfect."

"Getting all his schoolwork done on time?"

"Oh yeah, he's good with all that."

"Any issues?"

"None."

"Stay out too late? Give you any lip?"

"This child's a bookworm. He never goes anywhere. And he's very…quiet."

"Gets to school on time every day? He's got a long commute."

"Every day. He takes the bus down the street. JJ's like clockwork."

"Your foster payments coming through on schedule?"

"Yeah, no problem. Listen, sorry, my kids need me and I gotta go."

Karen Ellis

"Thanks for your time."

Saki is amazed at how flagrantly the woman lied—a mother, surrounded by children who depend on her. She makes a mental note to contact Social Services.

She writes down JJ's regular bus stop, sticks the Post-it in her pocket, and stands up.

"Found my boy," she tells Lex. "Who he is, I mean."

"Oh?"

"Janjak St. Fleur. Goes by JJ. He's in the foster system."

"How old?"

"Twelve." She straps her fanny pack around her waist. "I'm heading back to Red Hook."

"Looking for him the old-fashioned way?"

"Sometimes feet on the ground work best."

"Before you go," Lex says, "check this out."

She stops to look over his shoulder at a split screen showing, on one side, the facial reconstruction image for Crisp's father, Mo, and, on the other side, a long list of links for someone called Wilson Ramsey. She says, "You found his alias."

"The guy is kind of famous. He has this huge following, all these fans, there's a lot written about him but he never personally puts anything online. He hides behind a PO box at the main post office. Can't find a phone number anywhere."

"Maybe he doesn't have one," Saki suggests.

"It's possible."

"Well, call me if anything happens or if you need me."

"Ditto."

"And get some rest," she tells Lex.

"I'll be fine." He stifles a yawn, unable to resist even the suggestion of fatigue.

"Your brain will function better after even one sleep cycle, four hours. That's a fact."

"I don't doubt it." But still, he turns back to his screen.

Saki heads out, knowing there's no point trying to convince someone as stubborn as Lex.

Fifteen minutes later, she's in Red Hook, driving down Van Brunt Street. She turns onto Van Dyke and pulls to a stop near the end of the desolate block where JJ St. Fleur meets his daily bus. Other than a bike store, there's just about nothing here. There are better bus stops nearby: one on Van Brunt, with all the stores and people, and one by IKEA, with all the employees and shoppers. But this lonely place is better if you're trying to hide.

She drives over to Fairway and parks in the lot. On the sidewalk, she pulls up the facial reconstruction she downloaded to her phone.

She looks at his eyes, those dark wells, and is taken aback by the visceral need she feels, a hunger, almost, to find this boy. To find him for his own sake, with or without Glynnie. She won't take her focus off the girl, of course, but now—now she wants them both.

25

C risp jumps from thought to thought, from the prospect of Dante appearing again and then back to his father, always his father, a yearning stuck on repeat. Anxiety mounts as the ferry queue inches forward following the long hour he spent barricaded in a bathroom stall hiding from Dante.

Giving in, he taps out a message to the car-hailing service, claiming to have left something important in car number 223, and would that driver please meet him at the Manhattan battery ferry landing in twenty minutes or as soon as he can get there. Wondering if, as the message will come from the King of Kings' phone, Wilson Ramsey will even consider showing up.

The Send whoosh rattles Crisp, and his ruthless thoughts loop in on themselves. *He shouldn't have sent it.* But it's too late to stop it now.

He walks up the gangway onto the ferry. Climbs the stairs to the deck and sits on one of the white benches. Holds his breath while the vessel disengages from the dock and heads into New York Harbor, sun warm on his face. After a few minutes, he stands and walks over to the starboard railing, where he watches the ferry kick up foam en route to the southern end of Manhattan...and begins to breathe.

He pulls out the phone to check the time, but the Galaxy has died again. He never should have held on to it this long anyway, knowing that Dante is after him. Crisp pulls back his arm and pitches the phone into the harbor. The water takes it with a gulp and a swallow, and then it's gone.

Behind him someone gasps. Someone else applauds. A child laughs.

He stands there for the rest of the brief trip, watching the water churn around the boat.

Crisp has never seen the Battery Maritime Building from this angle and its beauty takes him by surprise—the trio of moss green and pink arches restored to a nineteenth-century splendor. Gentle and welcoming. But still, his brain grinds: *Will my father be waiting? Will Dante find me before I have a chance to find out? Should I ask for help—can I trust a cop? Or should I just make my way home?* He tries to force his thoughts to settle somewhere, anywhere, but they won't. Every decision now feels ripe with error.

The ferry docks at the lip of the center arch and creaks to a halt.

The passengers from the Governors Island side begin to file off. Crisp tries to hide himself in the middle of the group in case Dante or Rodrigo or both of them are out there watching, waiting. Across, at the entry dock, people are lined up to make the reverse journey—tourists, mostly, he guesses. People visiting a different New York, *not his*.

His New York is what lies behind the restored facades and culinary gems, the gleaming skyscrapers and limousines.

His New York is the one with rats on the sidewalk and old ladies haggling in broken English for a better price, where fitting yourself into a rush hour subway is an art and finding an apartment you can afford is a blood sport.

His New York is the one you struggle to live in, not aspire to visit. The one where a father leaves a son and a mother fights to survive simultaneously in black and white and living color, where life can feel both unreal and too real. It's a city where everything collides into a giant mess. Where avarice is celebrated and poverty is abided like a bad cold.

His New York is a city where you can reinvent yourself if you're willing to be ruthless. Where doors don't swing open so much as get kicked down.

He proceeds cautiously through an underpass that lands him on the sidewalk in front of the terminal.

Yellow cabs, along with Ubers and Lyfts, snake along the curb. Across the street, a looming window-checkered monolith of an office building makes Crisp want to never grow up. A loud buzz of traffic makes him long to cover his ears. But he will grow up and he doesn't cover his ears. He has learned by now that head-on is the only direction.

Standing in front of the building is a trio of beat cops,

all staring at their phones, and he feels a wave of relief. *Help at last.* But then one of them looks over at him with an excited glint, as if she's spotted a criminal, and he goes cold.

Of course—his mother would be frantic by now, ringing alarms. Dante might not be the only one looking for him: the cops might be too—but maybe not to help him.

Has Jerome been found?

Did anyone see Crisp coming and going from Dante's apartment?

Did Glynnie run to her parents and the police and blame *him* for the murder?

No, the cops are not your friends, never have been, never will be.

Just get home.

The cop detaches her gaze and turns her attention elsewhere, maybe deciding that he isn't who she's looking for, maybe for some other reason. He can't wait around to find out.

Crisp hurries to the curb and glances into the driver's window of every car that could be an Uber, piercing the bright reflections to ascertain a face. He searches the eyes of man after man after man, men of every race and age and size and color, none of them his father.

A scuffed taxi pulls up at the end of the line behind the last car. Anger rises in his chest and he welcomes the familiar spiky feeling. The way it rattles and bursts into his brain like fireworks, its pure energy intoxicating. Anger is better than wishful thinking—he's known that his whole life. He knew deep down that he'd be disappointed; it was a mistake to entertain any other possibility. This is what his mother and grandparents tried so hard to inoculate him against: this unrequited wanting of his father.

The taxi driver scrolls down the passenger window, leans over, and asks, "You getting in, or what?"

Crisp feels a scowl gather and a sharp rejoinder, another insane overreaction, seek form in words…

What's your problem?

Leave me alone.

Who do you think you are, Travis Bickle?

He speaks none of it aloud, recognizing in the nick of time that the driver asked him a simple question.

"Make up your mind," the driver demands.

"No, thanks." Crisp turns and loses himself in the sidewalk crowd and hurries forward.

At Stone Street, he veers into the first subway entrance he sees, tucked into the side of an old limestone edifice. Plunging downward two steps at a time, he's thankful that it's the R train. The R to the B…and he'll be home.

* * *

"Last stop, Brighton Beach," a metallic voice intones. And again: "Last stop, Brighton Beach."

Crisp's eyes open—brain fogged, head tilted back against something hard and cold, face covered by a newspaper. Disoriented, he lets the paper fall to his lap and suddenly remembers using it to hide behind in case a cop got on the subway. He looks around, wonders how long he's been sleeping with his head against the window. The

B train has come to a rest, the doors are open, people are getting off. He staggers onto the platform and down a long stair that deposits him onto Brighton Beach Avenue, the commercial spine of his neighborhood.

A uniform at the far end of the block stops walking and seems to look at him, and Crisp's alarm bells go off again. In the moment the cop pauses to consult his phone, Crisp backtracks to Sixth Street, walking as fast as he can without running, trying not to attract attention.

He turns the corner from Brightwater Court onto Fourth Street, his block, and sees a lanky man leaning against a light post, checking his phone, glancing up the street as if waiting for someone, checking his phone again. A plainclothes cop this time? He can't take any chances.

He pulls back behind the corner and waits it out, until the man reaches both hands into his front pockets, adjusts his pants as if to relieve pressure on his bladder, hunches his shoulders, and walks quickly in the direction of Brighton Beach Avenue.

Crisp hurries into his building, where, in the lobby, Mr. Biederman is waiting for the elevator as though it's any other day. Shirtless and potbellied, the old man has started his warm-weather sunbathing right on schedule and will be brown by August. Not as brown as Crisp, of course.

"Hi, Mr. B." Crisp wills calm into his voice.

The elevator arrives and they get in together.

"How's school?" Mr. Biederman asks in the heavy Russian accent that dominates the neighborhood. "You getting good grades?"

"I graduated yesterday."

"Mazel tov."

Biederman gets off on the third floor. Crisp rides all the way up to six.

The apartment door is double-locked, which typically means his grandparents are out.

"Hello?" Crisp calls. "I'm home!"

He's answered by total quiet, by undisturbed dust floating in a slant of sunlight, by a familiar mustiness he never thought he'd be so happy to smell. At this time of day, his mother would be at work in the city, Babu and Dedu somewhere in the neighborhood—errands and a stroll on the boardwalk ending with a sit-down on a bench to take in the view.

Crisp's footsteps clap across the parquet floor to the galley kitchen. On the counter, the old landline his grandparents refuse to part with.

He knows he should call his mother now, at work, and tell her everything, *everything*. He could ask for her help and she'd give it in a nanosecond. His mother would know what to do. His grandparents would come home. They would all band together to take care of him just as they always have.

He could call his mother right now and destroy whatever might be left of her faith in him. Make her feel that all her efforts have come to nothing. That she made bad choices early on, a heritable defect that's now derailing her only child.

His stomach curdles, then a stab of hunger.

Inside the fridge he discovers the remainder of a

roasted chicken and potato dinner in a plastic container. He takes a fork and knife from the drawer and devours the leftovers standing over the counter, then drops the empty container into the sink.

His bedroom door is closed, the way he likes it, his neatly made bed the way he left it Wednesday morning before heading out for the long trek to school on his now forsaken bike—two days ago. Two whole days since he's rested on his own bed. He lies down and exhales. Allows his eyes to close. Waits for sleep, and waits, but nothing happens; the subway nap must have ruined him for the kind of heavy slumber he is hoping for.

Finally he sits up and goes to his desk. His computer monitor awakens at the first touch of his keyboard.

He types WILSON RAMSEY and links stack up for the graphic novelist mixed in with random links for other Wilson Ramseys, none with a photo that matches his father. WILSON RAMSEY + MO CRESPO brings up a bunch of nonsense. "WILSON RAMSEY + MO CRESPO" yields nothing at all.

For a moment he wonders if he dreamed the whole thing—Glynnie, JJ, Dante, Rodrigo, Jerome, Red Hook, Governors Island, Laura, the mural—wonders if everything about last night was some strange journey of his imagination arcing toward his father. He's had dreams like that before, bizarre happenings that end with Mo's discovery and a reconciliation. Last night's dream merged his father with an icon...no, not a dream...more like a nightmare...*a man was killed*.

It occurs to him to plug his own name into a search; assuming his mom *did* declare him missing, it might have been reported somewhere. He clicks the news heading and his latest school photo appears with—there it is—a missing persons report from early this morning. Shame curdles through him for what he's put her through. He'll call her, right now, *he will*.

But then a second link catches his eye, a link joining his name to Dante Green's.

He clicks.

A YouTube video unfurls—posted just hours ago, it's already been viewed more than nine thousand times.

A white guy in jeans and cowboy boots, with brown hair tucked behind his ears, approaches Dante, introduces himself, and informs the dealer that he's under arrest. A bunch of uniformed cops close in and Dante is restrained, handcuffed, and led away under the scrutiny of an energized crowd. The photographer's jittery lens also captures a yellow house in the distance, half a sign announcing Fort Jay, a cartoon ferry above an arrow pointing to Soissons Landing.

A sharp exhale as Crisp realizes what this means: Dante is in custody.

But what about Rodrigo?

And what about Glynnie and JJ? Where are they? Are they safe?

No.

Stop.

They'll have to take care of themselves now.

In the bathroom, in full fluorescent light, Crisp sees himself in the mirror: filthy and red-eyed. He smells himself when he takes off his clothes: sour and rotten.

A hot shower melts off the dirt and the sweat and even a layer or two of the exhaustion and doubt. He's home, *home*. Closing his eyes, he lifts his face into the rushing water. Turns to douse and lather his hair. Then, as he shuts off the faucets and goes to step out of the tub, he notices a stream of red racing away with the water, a pink froth swirling into the drain.

Out of the tub now he twists in front of the mirror to inspect his back, shoulders, neck, looking for the source of the blood. No cuts. And he doesn't recall being injured.

He remembers Glynnie coming away from scrubbing the bloody floor and sitting beside him and the plaintive look in her eyes before she settled her head on his shoulder. Skin on skin, hair mingling.

He leans over the tub and touches the drain but the blood has washed away.

Jerome's blood.

The blood of the man Glynnie killed.

His mind lurches back to her. If she did make it home, did she tell the truth or any version of it?

Is that why the cops are looking for him now? Not because he's missing, but because he's become a person of interest…*a suspect? Did* she tell them something about him, and about Jerome, that isn't true?

And what about JJ? Where did *he* go? What did *he* do? Wondering why he trusted the boy and his story when for all Crisp knows he could be a sociopathic liar.

The more he thinks about it, the more he realizes how easy it would be to turn the narrative around and pin Jerome's murder on *him*. How staying home could make him a sitting duck, passive, ripe for more plucking by a justice system prone to working against him. *Black teenager shoots gun dealer in housing project.* It wouldn't even merit a headline.

He opens drawers until he finds a pair of scissors. He leans over the sink and grabs a clump of fro and cuts as close to his scalp as he can, handful after handful until his head is choppily shorn. In his bedroom, he quickly dresses in clean clothes. Takes a garbage bag from under the kitchen sink and returns to the bathroom to jam in his jeans and T-shirt and underwear and socks, all of it. Scoops the puffs of his hair out of the sink and into the bag. Double knots the bag with shaking hands.

He cleans the tub with spray bleach and paper towels, then rinses the sink until every snip of hair is washed away.

He needs to buy some time, to figure this out.

Sitting at his bedroom desk, he writes his mother a note.

Hey Mom,

Been having postgraduation fun with friends and everything's okay so don't worry. Had a bite and a shower and now I'm off to hang again. Promise I'll touch base later. I love you.

Your son,
the one and only
T.C. Crespo
x o x o x o

He's thinking that the light tone and witty flourish at the end might make her smile, and it's better, anyway, than telling her the truth: *Last night, my so-called friend Glynnie Dreyfus lured me and a homeless kid into a terrible situation and now I'm an accomplice to a murder. Oh, and Glynnie's insane and perfectly capable of pinning the murder on me.*

He tri-folds the note, scripts *Mom* on its front, then magnets it to the front of the refrigerator.

He looks at the landline. Picks up the phone. Dials the number he memorized that morning on Governors Island—the one that won't stop looping through his brain.

It rings and rings and rings and rings and then, after the fourth ring, instead of a click into voice mail the call is answered.

A man with a reedy voice says, "Hello?"

So that is what his father sounds like.

Crisp doesn't speak. He can't. He doesn't know what to say.

And then the call is suddenly ended on the other side.

A wave of emotion pushes Crisp backward onto one of the kitchen stools. The repetitive tone of a dead line natters at the quiet kitchen, and he lets it, lets it hammer at the pulp of his hopefulness in making that call. He replaces the receiver, ending and ending and ending any intention ever to try again, his attention fastened now to who he has to be, what he has to do if he's going to be better than his father.

26

L ex walks into the public information office just as
Gus is packing up for the day. Lex's head is swimming with Wilson Ramsey and *The Life of a Boy*—the
invisible boy the artist chronicled through a series of
graphic novels before stopping when the kid was twelve.
The more Lex saw, the more he understood that Mo
Crespo's secret life as Wilson Ramsey has been a journey
both toward and away from his son. He wonders what
Mo found, if anything.

"Where's Katya?" Lex asks.

"Gone," Gus tells him. "She called her folks and they
said her son came home and ate something, left her a
note, went out again."

"What did the note say?"

"Something about sorry and been with friends and
going out again and yada yada yada. You know how they
are, teenagers. I got three." Gus rolls his eyes.

"When?" Lex asks. "When did this happen?"

"Just now—she bolted out of here. Asked me to let you know. I was about to stop upstairs before I left."

"Thanks, Gus."

"No problem."

Gus slaps Lex's back on his way to the door, just a tap, really, nothing too hard, but it nearly knocks the wind out of him. He feels dizzy. Breath seems to stall in his lungs. He thinks of the packet. Tells himself *no*.

Hoping to catch Katya before she descends into the subway, he dials. Her phone rings several times and she answers abruptly: "Lex, sorry I—" The call drops out. She must be in the tunnels already, possibly between stations. A mother, questing.

He tries again and gets her voice mail. "Katya, I heard Crisp stopped in at home. That's good news. Give me a call, though, okay? I have a few questions." Questions he won't bombard her with on a message, understanding this mother to be a hair-trigger worrier. Her son isn't home by two a.m.: she jumps to the police. Her son sends texts from a stranger's phone: she camps out at the station house. Her son dips in for a quick visit and leaves behind a handwritten note: she runs back home.

Outside the station house, Lex takes a deep breath of the cooling air, hungry for the release you feel at the end of a day, except for him the long sleepless day has gone on since Wednesday and now it's Friday night. He thinks about the note Crisp left his mother, and despite its promise, he feels a rattle of discomfort but doesn't know why. Something about this just doesn't sit right. Unless it's his delirium playing with him, trying to drive him crazy, to make him invent reasons to stay away from home—to avoid Adam, or the absence of Adam, a little longer.

The door swings open and Dinardo steps out, bumping a pack of cigarettes on the heel of his hand to slide one up. In one smooth movement he catches the filter with his lips and flicks his lighter and sucks so hard the end glows orange, followed by a melodramatic first exhale in the way of die-hard smokers.

Lex greets the older detective. "Bad habit."

"Old dog." Dinardo shrugs. "He's gone."

"Who?"

"Black dude standing across the street. This is my third smoke in two hours and now he's gone." The detective flicks his burning ember into the street.

"No one you know, I take it." This close to the Walt Whitman Houses, it could have been anyone.

"Nope."

Lex's phone vibrates—Katya Spielman calling him back. He turns away from Dinardo and answers: "Where are you?"

"Lex, I'm sorry. I shouldn't have taken off like that without talking to you first, but my parents told me he was home, or had been home, that he'd left a note and—"

"Katya, is he back now?"

"No. But the note—"

"Your parents saw him?"

"They were out."

Surprised that they hadn't stayed in the apartment in case their grandson returned, Lex asks, "You still haven't told them what's been going on?"

"I just did." Katya sighs. "They took it hard."

"The note—it's his handwriting, for sure?"

"What do you mean, 'for sure'? Of course it's his handwriting. Who else's would it be?"

"I have to ask."

"All right. Yes, it's his. For sure. Lex, what's happening on your end? With all that other stuff."

All that other stuff. A missing girl. A gun dealer. One dead man.

"Well, we've arrested the gun dealer."

"Thank *God*."

"Detective Finley's out looking for Glynnie. Personally, I'd love a word with Crisp if he comes home again. Will you let me know?"

"Right away."

A word. He wants a paragraph—a chapter, *a book*—with Crisp.

Back in the squad room, Lex refreshes the monitor and reviews each page he left open—page after page filled with Wilson Ramsey's art, just his art, since it appears the man never invented a life to go along with the pseudonym. Lex doesn't understand why an artist would want to bury himself underground like that, unless he's hiding. Mo Crespo *is* hiding behind Wilson Ramsey. Lex's thoughts jig to Adam—why is *he* hiding? *What* is he hiding? Why not talk about whatever's going on? What's the point if keeping the secret could itself be potent enough to destroy them?

Why do people hide?

Why do they leave?

Why can't they just stay with you and face you and love you?

His exhausted mind conjures a two-headed beast gnawing him from either side: his first mother, Nina, on the left and Adam on the right, with Lex, pulpy, dissolving between them. He takes out his phone and scrolls through his personal cloud until he finds her, the young mother holding her smiling son. *What if,* that craving for answers flaring even now, *what if she* is *still alive?*

Now, he thinks without thinking. *Now.* He reaches into his pocket and pushes at the zipped seal of that tiny packet. He could go to the bathroom and snort it. No one would know.

Dinardo returns holding an interoffice manila envelope and heads for Lex. "Just came in—front desk asked me to bring it up."

Lex puts down his phone, pulls his hand out of his pocket, straightens out his face, takes the envelope. "Thanks."

Det Cole is scrawled in an unfamiliar hand on the line beneath the crossed-out names of all the previous recipients. Inside is a black smartphone—a Samsung Galaxy—along with a note saying it was found in a trash can on Lorraine Street in Red Hook.

Lex powers it up and after a moment an orange screen saver with a big leopard print *P* materializes—the Princeton logo. To confirm that it's Crisp's phone, he dials the teenager's number on his own phone and almost immediately the Galaxy rings with a jazzy syncopation.

He stares at the pass code screen. Stares at it some more. Then his weary brain generates the useful thought to call Carlotta, the tech whiz over at DAS.

"Hey, Lex," she greets him. "Need another face?"

"Actually," deciding on the spot, "yes."

"Pop it over."

"Will do—thanks. And there's something else. I need to hack into a cell phone. You know how?"

"Hold on." She muffles the call with something, maybe her hand, and speaks to someone in the room with her. "Not my wheelhouse, but I'll put you through to Ajay and he'll help you out."

While Lex waits for the call to transfer, he returns to the family photo, pinches out the image to take a screenshot of just Nina's face, and sends it to Carlotta. He's put his mother's name through databases before, but not in a very long time, and as he's just learned from Mo Crespo, these days a picture really is worth a thousand words.

Ajay comes on the line and breezily instructs Lex through the steps of unlocking Crisp's phone. A text alert appears center screen:

9174892752

The message was sent at 8:06 a.m., when Dante's phone was in Crisp's possession. He must have sent it to himself as a reminder of something. Lex wonders why it didn't come up on the trap and trace; he's never understood how so-called topflight technology can have fault lines that things vanish into, but they do. Just like people.

He dials the number into his own phone.

A man with a flinty voice answers, "Uber."

"Who is this?"

"You called *me*."

"I need a ride."

"Who are you? Why didn't you use the app?" The driver abruptly hangs up.

Lex starts dialing his way through the Uber maze before reaching a supervisor and being told that if he wants personal information on one of its drivers he'll have to provide a warrant. So he plows through the bureaucratic paces until he scores a home address for a driver calling himself Wilson Ramsey at the number Crisp sent through to himself.

Lex borrows a precinct car and starts driving. Out of Brooklyn. Into Queens. All the way to the far end of College Point, where he pulls up in front of a row of two-story brick houses. The lights are off in the second-floor apartment that Mo Crespo aka Wilson Ramsey calls home. He gets out, rings Crespo's bell several times, then returns to the car to wait.

He tunes the radio to a pop rock station with music so annoying he's sure it will force him to stay awake. Watching, waiting, a crackle of heat up his spine gives him the eerie feeling of being observed. He untucks his Glock from behind his belt and puts it on the passenger seat in quick reach.

He leans back against the headrest and is about to drift off when his phone vibrates in his pocket. A new file has arrived in his case file.

He taps open the DAS app and there, *there is Nina* as she'd presumably look now: more than twenty years older, with a rounder face and the start of jowls and deeper lines around those loving eyes. Carlotta has given his mother a slightly receded hairline and a touch of gray. She looks so real that Lex can't help greeting her, *"Zdravstvuy Mama."* He uploads the image to Interpol and stares at the spinny wheel that freezes his screen while the system searches the world for any trace of Antonina Fedorova Chkalov.

Finally the wheel vanishes and four definitive words appear.

Subject cannot be found.

He sends the image to his personal e-mail and deletes it from the case files, but the memory of this new face, this now face—it lingers.

27

Crisp squeezes through the tear in the chain-link fence and the Yankees cap he took from home pops off. He jams it back on and tugs the bill low over his sunglasses—a meager disguise that has gotten him this far. Hatted, hidden, sans his signature fro, he slipped past the surveillance cop returning from his pee break, continued unseen along Brighton Beach Avenue, and made it back into the subway. Then he rode the train south to north and north to south, thinking, until he forced himself to decide.

He promised JJ he'd come back so he's doing it: coming back.

His mind bends around the darkness, the moonlight, the water's surface undulating in expanding circles as if reacting to a sudden movement with no obvious source. He glances back through the chain link and sees a couple in the distance, walking along Van Brunt, but they don't appear to have noticed him.

Inside the musty building, the fibrous history returns

but he won't breathe it in this time…and he won't think about Officer Russo or Robert Moses or the NRA or anyone who raises up his or her hand to squash down others who look weaker. You look weak and then they *make* you weak, that's how it works…his mind bouncing light off that idea as it crystallizes…

Stop.

He holds his breath and takes the stairs. Steps into JJ's squat. Slung with shadows, its emptiness hits him hard.

"JJ?" His voice bounces from wall to ceiling to floor and back to him. "Are you here?"

"*Crisp.*" In one quick movement Glynnie is on her feet and there he is, looking almost like someone else in that cap and with those dark glasses. She feels like hugging him but something, a stiffness, tells her that he wouldn't welcome it so she holds back. "What happened to your hair?"

Surprised to see her standing there, the Beats slung around her neck, he asks, "Have you been here the whole time?" But then he notices the white T-shirt she wasn't wearing yesterday glowing in a shaft of light slanting in from the window.

"I'm *so glad* you're okay," she says. "I'm *so sorry* about last night."

He resists the drama in her tone that yesterday felt compelling but now grates. "It's a little late for that. Where's JJ?"

She doesn't want to tell him, but she has to. She takes a breath. "This morning, when I was home, the cops were there."

243

Cops. "Is that why they're looking for me?" A whiplash of anger fades when he realizes that that's also probably how the cops knew to pick up Dante on Governors Island, why Crisp was able to get off the island without the gun dealer intercepting him. Glynnie, in her priceless way, hurting and helping all at once. "What did you tell them?"

"Not much. But Crisp, they know about JJ."

"We promised to help him—not give him away."

"I did not tell them." Firmly. Because she needs him to know that.

"Then how did they find out?" But before she can even try to answer, the realization hits him. As soon as their parents started to worry, as soon as they called the cops, the surveillance state would have kicked into action; all those hidden camera eyes you never really think about would have opened at once. The three of them walking around Red Hook last night, around IKEA, in and out of the projects.

"I waited at his school but he wasn't there," Glynnie says. "And I sat here all afternoon but he didn't come back. Look." She gestures toward the small bookcase, at the fixed-in-time image of a once-happy family. "That's the phone I bought him. I did it. I kept my promise." She needs Crisp to know this too.

He wants to trust her, he does, but how can he? He watches her face crumple and it's as if she's a different girl, or at least could be someday, and the feeling slips past his defenses and into his mind. He lets out a breath. She takes a step closer and he doesn't move away.

"I screwed everything up," she says.

You kind of did. But, even now, he can't say that to her face.

"Listen," she says, "this might sound crazy, but I have an idea about JJ. About where he might be." There are so many places a placeless person can go, but she's had so much time to think about it and it won't stop flickering through her mind: a vision of JJ not just hiding, but resting. Crisp, with his excellent bullshit detector, will let her know if it's a decent idea. "Last night..." she begins, picturing JJ serene on that bed at IKEA, looking as though he remembered what it felt like to be home.

* * *

Without the buzz of fast friendship and strong weed, IKEA's charms of last night are gone. Instead, Crisp feels a vulnerability he can't shake as, the cap's bill pulled low to hide his face, he follows arrows through the labyrinth of displays. Living room after living room. Kitchen after kitchen. He pauses to rip a paper measuring tape off an inch-thick sheaf and continues until he reaches the bedrooms.

At the threshold of the orange and mahogany display, he glances around to make sure no one's watching him. His breathing grows shallow as he enters the life-size diorama, pulls out the desk chair and glances underneath, pretends to inspect the dresser, runs his hand along the smoothed-out duvet—no sign now that JJ ever lay down here last night. Recalling how delicious it felt, this afternoon, to lie on his own bed after just two nights away, Crisp is filled with sadness at the thought of JJ's year without a bed. He falls to his knees onto the fake bearskin and pretends to measure the clearance between floor and bed frame.

Ten inches.

His eyes roam the empty under-bed space where he hoped to find the boy. Instead, he takes in a clear view of moving pant hems, calves, ankles, sneakers, sandals, boots walking both ways over the showroom's floor arrows. He wonders why he thought this was a good idea; no one could hide under here—you'd be spotted too easily. He backs out and, kneeling, telescopes his disappointment onto the measuring tape, as if he's just a random shopper and whatever he hoped to stash under this bed would never fit.

"Crisp."

The faintest whisper. His own wishful thinking, he decides.

But then he hears it again, and freezes.

He ducks back under the bed and it's still a void.

The whisper repeats: "Crisp."

He turns to the dark edge where floor meets wall, beneath the top of the headboard, *and sees him*. Or *it*: a long boy-like shape pressed into a deep shadow.

JJ whispers, "What are you doing here?"

"Looking for you," Crisp whispers back. "What are *you* doing here?"

"Waiting. Soon as it closes, I can come out."

Crisp reaches a hand across the floor into the shadow. "Come out now."

"*Can't.* Dante had me—he was looking for you but I didn't know where you lived so he grabbed *me.* I *told* him I don't have your address. He didn't *believe* me."

"When?"

"On my way to school. Took me to his baby mama's place, and me and Rodrigo, we waited."

"For what?"

"I don't know. But Dante got picked up. Rodrigo, he saw it on his phone, some video. Then he took off. So I took off. Saw someone in my window at my crib so..."

So he came back here. "Have you been here all day?"

"Most of it."

"JJ, *please.*"

JJ backs deeper into his shadow.

Crisp stretches, manages to touch the boy's pant leg, pulls against his resistance. He wonders if it would help or hurt for JJ to know that the cops are looking for him and decides that for right now less fear could mean more courage. "Last night, when I said I'd help you, didn't you believe me?"

A pause, and JJ admits, "Yeah, I did."

"I came to find you, didn't I?"

Another pause. Another "Yeah."

"I was just at your place, looking for you. Glynnie's been waiting all afternoon. She got you that phone she promised."

"Really?"

"Come out."

JJ hesitates, then rolls away from the wall. His eyes appear bright in the under-bed dark. A whole highway

of tear tracks glisten down his cheeks. He squirms closer
and the cracked lips and snot dried under his nose finish
the job of breaking Crisp's heart.

"What time is it?" JJ asks.

"Not sure, but it isn't nine yet or they'd be closing."

"It's night already?"

"We're getting out of here." Crisp pulls him all the way
out from under the bed. "Act as natural as you can, don't
run but keep moving. Can you be cool?"

"I'm as cool as they come," says the tear-streaked boy,
attempting a smile, shifting to his feet, standing for the
first time, Crisp would guess, in hours. "Hey, why'd you
cut your hair?"

"Tell you later." Crisp removes the Yankees cap and
snugs it low over JJ's eyes. "Keep the visor down. Don't
look at anyone. If we get separated, plan A is to meet
me downstairs in the parking garage. Plan B is to go
to the IKEA dock, jump on whatever comes first. We'll
reconnect on the other side."

"Why would we get separated?"

"I'll explain that later too."

28

Lying on the floor of the squat in the charcoal darkness, Glynnie wonders if she should have gone with Crisp to look for JJ, but something was nagging at her and still is. A feeling. A need to understand what happened last night, what really happened—how and why that man died. Obviously she killed him, but why can't she remember pulling the trigger?

She covers her ears with the Beats, canceling out the scant ambient noise, and tries to think. But she can hardly hear herself even in the absence of sound. She takes off the headphones and puts them on the floor and waits with all her might.

Minutes pass in the effort. Hours. Years. Centuries. The world outside the windows gets darker, the quiet heavier. She has to pee but it's too late now; if she leaves to find a bathroom, she'll lose all her nerve and she may never come back but there's something she needs here. Something she needs to learn about herself.

* * *

Saki walks the length of Van Brunt, passes Fairway on the right and shuttered artisanal storefronts in the rehabbed Beard warehouse on the left, and reaches the end of the street, where it meets the bay.

Each time she walks this path, her search ends right here.

Where does JJ go when he vanishes from sight?

But this time something different happens: a raft of clouds shifts northward, the night sky brightens, and lucid moonlight washes over the end of Van Brunt. Things veiled in darkness turn silvery bright: the slick black paint on the building's huge arched shutters shines with a gloss unexpressed even in day, the diamond-shaped END sign on the iron fence splashes its yellow color into the dark, and she sees an opening in the fence that wasn't there earlier, where a vertical bar angles out at the bottom like a loose tooth. Big enough for a kid to get through.

Or a slight woman.

Saki pushes through a foot, leg, hip, torso, which isn't easy but she manages—and then she's on the other side of the fence. Testing her hunch, she presses the iron post back into place. Whoever passed through last neglected to replace it.

She follows the oceanfront path that edges the old factory building all the way to its end, where water wraps around two sides. The wind whistling. Waves crashing against the embankments.

Here, at the blunt end of land, a warped and torn chain-link fence is all that separates you from easy access to the bay. And what else?

She shoulders through an opening in the chain link and observes that the far end of the old factory is untouched by renovation, its bricks crumbling, a pair of second-floor iron shutters wide open on a glassless window, taking in air.

The door is unlocked.

Inside a broad foyer, history appears to have frozen a century ago. Cobwebs hang from the ceiling. Yet in the thick layer of dust on the floor there is a heavy traffic of footsteps leading up a wide old staircase.

Saki follows them, her shoes squeaking, echoing, into the emptiness.

Halfway up the stairs she stops to listen. Hears nothing. Wonders if she should be afraid, here alone, if a "normal" person would feel afraid. She doesn't. Wonders if she's wasting her time and reminds herself that she won't know until she looks.

* * *

Glynnie feels the vibrations in the floorboards before she hears the squeak of footsteps coming closer. And then…

And then.

The redheaded detective appears at the door, wearing her all-black but not-cool clothes. Glynnie sits up, surprised by her own calm.

"Hello, Glynnie," the detective says.

"Hi, Detective Fin...Fin..."

"Finley."

"Right."

"You can call me Saki, if you want." Saki Finley glances around the moon-slashed dark. "Is JJ here too?"

"No," Glynnie answers—an easy truth.

"Where did he go?"

"I don't know." An uneasy lie. But she has to give Crisp a chance to find JJ and, if he does, get the kid somewhere safe. Somewhere as safe as this place used to be until Glynnie wrecked it for him. The twist of remorse in her gut returns, sharper than ever.

The detective stands there, looking down at Glynnie, and doesn't speak. She has pretty eyes, blue, though they don't really look at you. She seems to be looking more around Glynnie than at her. Strange. Reminds her of her brother, Aidan: super smart but somehow not totally connected. "A touch of Asperger's" is what their mother says he has, but only when he isn't listening. Saki blinks once, and Glynnie's sure that's what it is.

The detective spots the Beats lying on the floor, crouches to pick them up, and turns them over in her hands as if this, these headphones, is precisely what she's been looking for.

"They're wireless," Glynnie tells her. "My folks gave them to me for graduation. I gave them to JJ."

"That was nice of you." Saki looks at her now.

Glynnie says, "I killed somebody last night."

"Who?"

252

"Jerome. At the projects. Big white guy who wanted to rape me."

The detective freezes a moment. This time she blinks twice.

"I want to ask if I can go home now," Glynnie says. "But I have a feeling I know the answer."

Saki leans over with the offer of a hand to help pull Glynnie off the floor. She accepts it, surprised by how relieved she feels, though she isn't sure if this means she's safe or in deeper trouble.

"We'll need to go over to the station. I'll call your parents and ask them to meet us there. They might want to get you a lawyer."

"Okay."

The detective makes the call, then asks Glynnie, "Ready?"

29

Lex doesn't realize he's been sleeping until the car becomes something else and he's sucked into that middle passage between dream and reality. At first, the explosive crack makes no sense in the dream's already sketchily incoherent story in which he is himself but not *here,* somewhere else, Moscow, maybe—yes, Moscow… in a square surrounded by colorful onion-domed buildings…and his father…*no,* a man…*no,* a mob of men, *detectives,* are berating him in Russian but also pelleting him with hard sharp bits of…stoning him, punishing him, trying to kill him for…*for being gay,* and pain riddles his whole body before concentrating in his…in his ear. It's the stabbing sensation in his left eardrum that pulls him all the way out of the dream.

His eyes snap open in a panic of disorientation. Tinny music fills the car. His first thought, *It's a blessing I was sent out of gay-loathing Russia,* is subsumed by the realization that he can't hear out of his left ear. He jolts his head off the driver's-side window, covers his ear with his hand, sucks in a deep breath, gets his bearings.

He's in College Point. He fell asleep. *Shit.*

A chalky haze hangs just outside the car's window and he knows, even before grabbing his Glock and stepping into the street and being hit by the familiar acridity, *he knows* that a gun has just been fired. He slips a finger over his trigger and shouts, "Police! Drop your weapon!"

"Cole—stand down!" A familiar voice it takes a moment to identify.

Jack Dinardo stands there, bull-faced, sweating, gripping a gun pointed at a man on the ground. A heavyset black man in a leather jacket. Lex's brain stutters before it comes to him who it is: *Rodrigo Rivera*, on his back, wincing, leather ripped open at the shoulder, blood seeping onto the asphalt. The hand belonging to that shoulder rests palm up, fingers splayed. A Ruger lies to the side. Lex kicks it to the curb, far from Rivera, and looks at Dinardo.

"Lucky I pay attention," the older detective says.

"*This* was the guy standing outside the station house?"

"I had a gut feeling and I was right—he followed you here."

Sirens approach. Lex crosses over and pats his colleague on the back. Dinardo's shirt is drenched with sweat, his breathing labored.

"I waited till he had his weapon on the glass," Dinardo says, "right next to your head. There's no question he was going to shoot you."

Lex notices that his left ear still isn't picking up much sound. "I owe you one, Dinardo."

"You'll help the next guy."

Lex nods. He will.

"So, what'd he want with you?"

"I arrested his boss today. Seems he was pissed. This guy, he was the lackey." Lex recalled how, frame by frame, the video feeds revealed Rodrigo Rivera's subservience to Dante. "Loyalty's a funny thing."

"Stupidity, more like. Staking out an officer of the law at the station house?" Dinardo snorts. "I mean, who does that?"

Lex and Dinardo stand together and observe the transformation of a quiet street into a crime scene. The rotating pulse of blue and red lights. Yellow tape cordoning off the area. Techs hunched in floodlit darkness. Rivera being patched up and readied for the ambulance.

Lex looks up and notices a light in the second-floor window of Mo Crespo's building and realizes that he slept through the man's return.

"Well." Dinardo smiles. "Like I always said: When I retire I wanna go out with a bang."

Lex laughs. "And you did." Mo Crespo's window goes dark. "I need to get moving."

Dinardo claps him on the back. "Good seeing you again. Try and stay alive."

"You too."

Lex crosses the sidewalk onto a patchy lawn, climbs the short stoop to Crespo's building, and presses the buzzer for 2B. The second-floor window lights up again. After a moment, footsteps thump down the stairs and the front door creaks open.

Through the clear glass in the top half of an exterior storm door he finds himself staring at a face.

The face.

Carlotta *is* a wizard: her reconstruction nailed Mo Crespo right down to the wide mouth, the close-set eyes, the widow's peak. Though she missed the dimple punctuating his chin.

"I didn't see anything," Mo offers, glancing beyond Lex to the commotion in the street. He has a tired voice that sounds underwater until Lex shifts his right ear forward.

"I'm Detective Lex Cole—I'm looking for your son."

"My son." Spoken tentatively. "Does it have something to do with that?" He points at the street.

"It does, in a way. May I come in?"

"You called me before, didn't you?"

"Yes, I did."

Mo steps aside in the shabby common hall to make way for his visitor. The storm door clatters shut behind Lex. He follows the father upstairs.

Lex is surprised to discover that a person as successful as Wilson Ramsey, at least according to online sources, lives in a studio apartment at the far edge of an outer borough, but then again, the man drives an Uber so can't be flush from his creative work. A bed in one corner, drawing table in another corner, strip kitchen against a wall, stained armchair facing a television perched atop a dresser. It's exactly the life Lex feared for himself before he met Adam. He feels a tug of compassion for this lonely man: a man who once had a wife and child, who left them. Lex reels in his sympathy.

Mo offers his visitor the padded chair at the drawing table, takes a folding chair from against the wall, and sets it up for himself. Before sitting, he asks, "Can I get you something? Tea, water, juice?"

"No, thanks."

Mo sits. "Was someone killed outside tonight?"

"Not killed. Shot. If anyone was getting killed it was going to be me, but my colleague stopped that from happening."

"You must be shaken."

Was he? Mostly, Lex was upset about his ear. He'd try to see a doctor in the next day or two, find out how bad the damage is. He says, "I'm fine."

"You said you're looking for Titus."

"That's right: you don't know that he calls himself Crisp."

"Crisp," Mo repeats with a slight smile. "Crisp Crespo. He must have a sense of humor."

"He had quite a night last night. Quite a few days, for that matter. A lot has happened and I'm trying to under-stand your son's role. He may still be in some trouble."

"But he wasn't hurt?"

"We've had indications that he's okay, but afraid. Mo, you once knew a man named Dante Green."

Mo's hands tighten over his knees. "What about him?"

"The guy lying on the street outside? He works for Dante."

A twitch of alarm across Mo's face. "Tell me what's going on, Detective. Please."

"Dante's accusing Crisp of shooting, and killing, a man named Jerome Bailey. You know him?"

"Is Titus the kind of boy who would do something like that?"

"All the evidence so far says no."

"I don't know any Jerome Bailey."

"Rodrigo Rivera?" Thumbing in the direction of the window.

Mo shakes his head. "Dante Green, though—he's bad news. Mean *and* stupid, the worst combination."

"We're trying to figure out how and why he got to Crisp. Do you know anything about Dante's life since you left the Houses?"

"No." Mo pauses, then adds, "Last week, I picked him up in my Uber. I didn't know it was him—his picture was a crown, he didn't use his real name. He got into my car and—" Mo shakes his head.

"You turned state's evidence on him back in the day."

Mo nods. "Yes, I did."

"So he's got a beef with you."

There's a flash in Mo's eyes when he asks, "Did he go after my son?"

"We still don't know if Dante looked for Crisp, or if they crossed paths and he figured it out."

"Last week in my car? He asked me to join his crew. I should have done it; I should have said yes. Maybe he would have left Titus alone."

"Well, twenty-twenty hindsight is an excellent thing," Lex says. "Unfortunately, no one has it."

"Twenty years ago...*twenty years ago, I got out*."

"By marrying Katya."

He nods. "I fell in love. Moved out of the Houses. Had a kid. Then I fucked it all up. I wasn't there when they needed me. I'm not there now."

Lex waits out a pause.

"I had to go," Mo says. "They needed more than I could handle, and I was in a downward spiral. I was chasing the dragon—you feel me?"

So that was it: Mo was a heroin addict, he'd fallen into that tempting abyss, let his life go to ruin. "Yeah," Lex says. "More than you know." The mere thought of it triggers a shiver of craving mixed with dread. A sharp memory of heavenly release and its hellish aftermath. Gratitude that, so far, he's won against the packet in his pocket—though it calls him still, he can't deny it. "What about Katya? Was she aware?"

"No, I don't think so. She just thought I was an asshole, which I was."

They share the uneasy laugh of a discomfiting truth.

"I'm clean now, if you're wondering," Mo says. "But the shame doesn't go away."

"She thinks you went underground to avoid paying child support."

"Nah." Mo starts to tear up and squeezes his eyes to stop it. "I did my best work when I was high, that's the ugly fact. Published a lot in those days. When I cleaned up, the work stopped. Everything stopped. I stopped. I couldn't bring myself to tell her any of it, couldn't bring myself to face the kid." He pauses, then says, "This explains something: she tried calling me today. It was the same home

260

number from always. I recognized it. I answered, but no one said anything."

Lex tells Mo, "Katya was at the station house all day. If someone called you from the home landline, it was probably Crisp. What time was it?"

Mo crosses the room to pick up his cell phone, Wilson Ramsey's cell phone, from the kitchen counter. "Six eleven."

"Yup, that's about the time he dropped in at home before taking off again. Left his mother a note—they're tight, you know. She did a good job with him."

"He called me?" Mo tears up again. "He called me and I hung up the phone."

Lex feels the pull of compassion, and tries, really tries, to push it away. Then he thinks of how he might have felt if his mother *had* still been alive after all these years. The answer comes to him easily: scared, but also grateful. And if someone intervened to bring them back together, he'd have been grateful for that too.

30

Crisp can tell from the pungent aroma of spicy ground meat and peppers that their sixth-floor neighbor made *galumpkis* for dinner tonight. His stomach flips with sudden hunger, despite the earlier meal.

JJ hangs back when they approach the apartment door.

"It's okay," Crisp assures the younger boy. "My mom and grandparents are always getting on me for never bringing home any friends. They'll be happy to meet you."

"Why don't you bring friends home?"

Crisp shrugs. "I just live so far out. Most of the kids I know from school don't want the schlep." *Knew* from school, that part of his life now officially over, the next part still undetermined, as far as he knows.

"This feels funny," JJ says. "Maybe I should head back."

To where? "Smell that?"

JJ closes his eyes. Inhales.

"Mrs. Napora's famous stuffed peppers. I have an in with her. If she's got any leftovers I could get her to give us some later."

Crisp keys open the front door and, together, the boys step inside.

"And who is *this?*" Babu appears at the first sound of visitors.

"Hi, Babu." Crisp throws his arms around his substantial, impossibly soft grandmother. Squat, floral, gray, beloved.

"The stories I've been hearing—we thought we'd never see you again." She gently lays a palm on his cheek and he feels balanced, grounded, *home*. "You brought a friend?"

JJ squeezes out a smile, a kind-of smile, more a sucking in of his lips. "Hi, ma'am." He juts out a hand for Babu to shake.

But Babu doesn't shake JJ's hand so much as possess it, sandwiching it between both of hers. She crooks her ironic half smile that promises you she's thinking something but you'll never guess what.

"Do you have a name?" she asks.

"Janjak St. Fleur. People call me JJ."

"Welcome to our home, JJ."

Dedu appears and, right behind him, taking Crisp off guard, is a man who looks vaguely familiar: tallish and thinnish, with longish brown hair tucked behind his ears. Blue jeans. Cowboy boots. He looks a little too hipsterish to be hanging out with this family or in this building or, for that matter, in this neighborhood. Then Crisp realizes where he's seen him before: he's the cop from the video, the one who arrested Dante.

A cop, in their house.

His mind cartwheels through possible escapes, as if he could reverse time or un-bring JJ into what suddenly feels like a trap. After everything, will *he* be the reason JJ didn't get away?

JJ makes a quiet move for the door. Crisp reaches out to grab his arm and hold him back. There's no point now; it's too late.

The cop surprises Crisp by laughing at something Dedu mutters half in Russian: "If it isn't the *bludnyy syn*." Laughing and listening with his head angled to favor his right ear, an old-person habit that strikes Crisp as strange for this not-old man.

"Detective Lex Cole." The cop puts out a hand, introducing himself with an inexplicable friendliness that only pulls at Crisp's nerves. "*Really* glad to meet you. You had your mother plenty worried last night."

"Like his grandparents would have been," Babu's tone melodramatic with half-meant rebuke, "if our daughter hadn't treated us like children and kept us in the dark."

"She saved you the worry," the detective responds, though he didn't have to. Crisp knows from long experience that his grandmother enjoys throwing verbal bombshells but never really expects anyone to take a whack at them.

"So, Crisp." Dedu comes up close so he can look directly into his grandson's eyes, the thick folds of the old man's face gray and soft, familiar, treasured. "What's this about a gun dealer?"

Just being asked that by his grandpa fills Crisp with shame. "I was *not* trying to buy a gun, Dedu. I swear."

"I believe you, of course." Dedu smiles. "But I had to ask."

Detective Cole turns to JJ, the boy struck dumb in the presence of a cop, and looks at him with withering recognition. "Really glad to meet you too, JJ."

JJ manages a stiff nod, his cheeks trembling, eyes blinking back fear. Crisp wants to take this boy into his arms and hide him, in full view of everyone, hide and save and protect him from what's now inevitable. But he doesn't; he can't.

A rapid clip of footsteps announces Crisp's mother's presence in the apartment, and mortification paralyzes him.

Why didn't he just go home last night instead of following Glynnie?

How could he have brought this on his family? Left them alone to fear for his safety, only to return as an accessory to murder.

Is that why the detective is here—to arrest him?

What are the chances that Glynnie really will admit what she did without trying to shift the blame?

What about Dante? Crisp can only imagine the lies the dealer will tell to save himself.

Stop.

Like a ray of sun in a storm of worry, his mother appears. The sight of her floods Crisp with relief; his smile comes on so abruptly he feels it could break his face. He raises his arms for the embrace he knows is imminent and she comes through, nearly gripping the breath out of him.

"Where have you been?" Her voice hot on his neck. "I've been going out of my mind!"

"I'm sorry, Mom." He rubs her back in firm circles,

the way she used to comfort him when he was little. *"I'm sorry."*

And then he sees, standing behind her, another stranger, another man, this one painfully familiar though in Crisp's conscious recollection they've never met. A man who almost matches Wilson Ramsey's Uber photo but in person is something else: fleshy, worn, real.

The man smiles at Crisp and it's a genuine smile but complicated with woe, regret, hope, yearning, so much emotion it almost rends his heart. Almost. Because *fuck it,* no way will he let this person, this father, waltz in and stand there with those furrows across his forehead and that dimple in his chin *just like Crisp's* and that fizz of gray at his temples—stand there with that look in his brown eyes as if he's been as *fucking terrified* as Crisp has been all these years, as if he's been imagining and strenuously *not* imagining this homecoming for an entire lifetime.

Crisp looks away. Closes his eyes. Holds his mother tight, burrowing into her, yearning to flee the confusion but unable to locate an inner exit door. Eyes sealed: he will not look at the man again. But he can feel his father drinking him in and it disturbs him and he wants it to stop but he also wants it to continue forever.

He doesn't know what he wants.

"Please leave," Crisp hears himself saying. "I can't do this right now."

The same thin voice from the phone answers, simply, "Okay." Then adds, "You can call me whenever you're ready. Any time of the day or night. This time, I won't hang up."

Crisp listens until the front door closes.

He opens his eyes and his father is gone, just like that.

"Why was *he* here?" he asks his mother.

"Detective Cole tracked him down. He thought if we put our heads together we might be able to piece together what's been going on—that it might help us find you. But here you are!" He's never seen her face this red or her eyes this wet without actually crying—this woman who rarely cries in front of him if she can help it.

"What were you doing just now? You and *him*?"

"He wanted to see your room."

"What for?"

"I think he wants to know you, Crisp."

After that, no one says a word. Not Babu, who usually can't stop commenting; not Dedu, who is a font of wisdom; not Mom, who rarely wastes an opportunity to defend her son against perceived trouble. They all stand there waiting to see what he'll say, what he'll do. His reaction, though, is inchoate, inexpressible.

Crisp leaves the foyer for the living room and sits alone on the couch. Just sits there and tries to think, but nothing comes. After a minute, Lex Cole joins him with the kind of placid smile meant to calm you in advance of something difficult. Crisp braces.

"How are you?" the detective asks.

"Fine," Crisp tries. Then, "I don't really know."

"What happened?"

Words swirl without gathering into a simple, coherent explanation. "I'm not sure where to begin."

"You know what they say."

Crisp nods. "'Begin at the beginning.'"

"It's always a good place to start."

"Is this the part where I'm supposed to ask for a lawyer?"

"If you want one, sure."

"Yeah," Crisp says. "I think I want one."

Lex stands. "You'll need to meet me at the station and I'll get things started."

"Thanks," Crisp says. And then, "I didn't shoot anyone."

The detective nods. "See you in a bit."

When Lex is back in the front hall, Crisp hears him say, "He wants a lawyer—smart kid. If you don't have someone, I can get you in touch with legal aid."

"That would be good," Katya says. "Thank you."

"Will you make sure he's at the Eighty-Fourth Precinct within an hour?"

"Tonight?"

"Hopefully it won't take too long."

"Fine," she says. "Thank you, Lex."

The front door opens and closes and Lex Cole, too, is gone.

"Look at you," Crisp hears Babu say. "So thin. How old are you?"

JJ answers, "Twelve."

"You're hungry," Babu informs him.

Dedu says, "Of course he's hungry!"

"Do your parents know you're here?" Mom asks.

Crisp doesn't hear JJ say anything but presumably the boy shakes his head *no* because Babu's reaction is so strong.

"You need to tell them. Do you have a phone to call?"

Another pause.

"Use mine," Katya offers.

Quietly, JJ says, "My parents are in Haiti."

"For vacation?" Katya asks.

"No."

"You're living where?"

Nothing. No answer. Not the slightest sound.

Katya says, "Oh. Okay. I see."

"Feed him!" Dedu orders.

Babu barks, "Like you need to tell us that?"

In a warm but unmistakably insistent tone, Katya assures JJ, "Don't worry about them, it's all in fun. Go ahead to the kitchen and eat what you want. If you need a place to stay, you'll stay with us for now. We've got a comfy fold-up mattress that fits on Crisp's floor."

JJ's silence at the invitation, the directive, is deep and broad as an ocean, his acquiescence inevitable.

Crisp inhales and holds it and exhales and his mind clears.

He's home.

31

Lex stands on the boardwalk listening with half-cocked hearing to the steady beat of the tide against the shore. He allows a gust of wind to push hard against him and he doesn't push back. He gives way to it, steps backward to make room, but it pursues him.

Walking along the Spielman-Crespo block toward the avenue, he pauses to glance up at the row of sixth-floor windows and pinpoint theirs at the far right of the building: two perfect rectangles of blazing yellow light. He wonders what's going on in there now. He wonders how Crisp is doing with his mother and grandparents, if he's telling them everything, if he's realized yet that they forgave him before he even walked through the front door. Lex wonders, again, about the boy, Janjak, JJ, and hopes he'll be all right when all this settles down. Lex doesn't like to hold bets on how a case will come out, but he finds himself hoping that JJ won't turn up anywhere in the realm of culpability for the gun dealer's alleged murder. Or Crisp. Or even Glynnie, though that's doubt-ful. Regardless of where the courts throw them down on the legal yardstick, or how many reckless choices they made last night, they're basically still *kids*.

But murder is murder, and that's a problem. And if the body is found, things could get worse for one of them or all of them. Glynnie, he guesses, all that evidence against her piling up.

At the corner, Lex raises his hand to a passing taxi. It swerves to a stop and he gets into the back. "You know where the Sixtieth Precinct station house is?"

The driver nods, turns on the meter, pulls into a lane.

The moment the car is in motion, the mere presence of the muted backseat TV starts to make Lex queasy. He reaches to turn it off as a news zipper moves across the bottom of the screen: MIDEAST TALKS TO RESUME . . . SHOOTING AT MALL IN LITTLE ROCK . . . FIRST LADY ISSUES RARE TWEET ON RUSSIA PROBE . . . BANKSY STRIKES AGAIN . . .

32

The elevator in the lobby of the police station seems to take forever. Walking to the second floor would be faster, and the stairwell door is just over there. But Crisp knows better than to suggest it, not at this time of night and not with his grandparents and their crinky feet, knees, hips, lungs, hearts, and overall belief that since they've made it this far in life they "deserve a few extra sweets," as Babu likes to say. And they do. And this, going through *all this* with their grandson, was never supposed to be on their menu.

JJ stands farthest from the elevator doors, as if an opportunity to slip away might present itself. Crisp veers from his family to herd the boy back into their fold. Looking into JJ's terrified eyes, Crisp whispers, "It's going to be okay, no matter what." Almost believing it himself.

"No," JJ whispers back. "It probably isn't."

The elevator rattles down to a stop. The dented metal doors scrape open.

Dedu steps aside as though he's the doorman, the conductor of this off-tune chamber piece. ("Time to face the music," he said as they gathered themselves to head over here, the family unwilling to let Crisp out of their sight.) Dedu waits until everyone is inside the elevator, then he joins them. Babu waves a hand at the doors as if using her special magic to will them closed, and they do, they close, drawing together in a tight seam.

Detective Cole is waiting for them in the second-floor hall just outside the elevator, having been given a heads-up by the front desk. With him is a waistless young woman in a wrinkled blue dress, her messy hair balled into a topknot secured by a chopstick. Chipped polish on her fingernails. Battered sneakers. She smiles when she sees them and Crisp thinks, *Don't let this be my legal aid lawyer*.

"Hiii." She reaches a hand to Crisp, directly to Crisp, and *Yes it is* and *Please no* and *How can this mess of a person help me?* "I'm Marylouuu. I'm so happy to meet you, Janjaaak." A drawl at the end of every phrase.

Realizing that this woman is not here for him, Crisp reflexively steps up beside JJ and slings a protective arm around the boy.

"No," Lex corrects Marylou. "That's Janjak." Pointing now at JJ.

"Oooh, sorry. Hi, Janjak, I'm Marylouuu. With Social Serviceees. I'm your new caseworker, okaaay?" Her smile is flecked with bits of lettuce.

The elevator emits a cranking sound and the doors close; with a squeal, it begins a new descent.

273

Crisp glances at his mother, in whose eyes he recognizes a gleam of apprehension that always means she's engaged in a difficult calculation. The tight face, burning focus, fixed mouth of an executioner before pushing the button, plunging the needle, flipping the switch. On the way over she leaned in and whispered, "What if JJ stays with us for a while?," and he answered, "Great! How long?," but she didn't have a chance to go into her thinking before they arrived at the station.

His mother steps forward. "Marylou, I'm Katya Spielman and these are my parents, Joe and Galya Spielman. This is our son, Titus, who we call Crisp. We raised him all together, and now that he's on his way to college, his bedroom will be empty. I would like to foster JJ in our home."

"Oooh!" Marylou says. "Are you liceeensed?"

"Not yet. How long does it take?"

"There's an application, a course, a whole proceeess. But let's face it, we can use all the help we can get, so how about we talk about it and see how we can make this wooork? That is, if it's okay with Janjaaak."

JJ nods decisively.

"Okaaay," Marylou says. "Detective, is there somewhere the family and I can go to taaalk?"

Lex, smiling, says, "Follow me."

Just then, the elevator pulls in, the doors open, and a white cane taps a pattern on the floor, testing the perimeter of a safe exit. A tall black man wearing large sunglasses in round white plastic frames appears. He wears a white three-piece suit with a red tie and red pocket handkerchief. A red feather slants from the band of a white fedora. Carrying a briefcase in his free hand, he follows the tapping cane into the hall. An undercover investigator, Crisp assumes, posing as a pimp.

Lex steps forward to greet him. "Hi, Harry. Good to see you."

"Good to see you too, Lex," the blind man says without irony.

"Mind waiting here just a minute? I'll be right back."

"Will do." Harry aligns his back with the wall, sets his briefcase on the floor, and rests both hands atop his cane.

Lex leads Crisp and his family around the corner to a door marked WAITING, behind which is a small windowless room furnished with worn couches and chairs. Again, Dedu holds open the door and is the last to file in.

Before Crisp has a chance to sit, Lex looks at him and asks, "Come with me, okay?" Except it isn't a question.

He glances at his mother, positioned stiffly on the couch. She nods, telling him to go. Crisp has a cold, sinking feeling and doesn't like this at all. He accompanies Lex back into the hallway and asks, "Harry's not an undercover pimp, is he?"

Lex chuckles. "He's your lawyer. Crisp, he may be blind, and maybe he's not the greatest dresser, but he's a good attorney. Give him a chance."

Crisp follows the detective down the hall but a thought nags and he stops walking. "Why did you bring my father to our apartment?"

Two steps ahead now, Lex turns. "He has roots with

the people you got mixed up with, Crisp. We didn't know where you were or if you were safe. I wanted him and your mother to brainstorm."

"Brainstorm?" A bitter, unintended tone, but it fits; Crisp lifts his chin to own it. How could Mo Crespo possibly know anything about the life the Crespo-Spielmans built without him? How could he even begin to *brainstorm* with someone as smart and capable and loving and reliable as Crisp's mother?

"Give him a chance."

"Why?"

"He's your father."

"It's none of your business. My mother never wanted to see him again, and neither did I."

"Are you sure?"

No, Crisp isn't, he isn't sure of anything. For all he knows his mother is glad for the chance to have learned the truth about why Mo left them. Everything's happened so fast and they haven't talked about it yet.

Lex says, "He might have been a terrible father but he's a really good artist—you have to admit that, at least."

"Actually, I don't." When Crisp learned that Mo Crespo is in fact *the* Wilson Ramsey, his brain immediately tangled around the problem of what that means. For him. As that complicated man's biological son. All it does is confuse things, as far as he can tell.

"Well, let's not keep the lawyer waiting." Lex starts walking again.

Crisp follows, mind spinning—*the* lawyer, *the* father, *the* artist—the ultimate roles of these men left up to him as if he knows anything about anything when now more than ever he feels he knows nothing at all.

Harry's face turns at the first sound of their approach, the round glasses like portholes reflecting the overhead fluorescent glare.

"Crisp," Lex says, "this is your attorney, Harry Johnson."

Smiling in Crisp's general direction, Harry says, "What do you say we get you out of trouble, son?"

Crisp shakes the lawyer's hand, soft, firm, and hopes this man can help him.

"I understand there's another team on this too," Harry says. "So let's head downstairs to confer. Tomorrow we'll meet separately at my office and go over a battle plan."

* * *

Glynnie looks up at the first crack of the conference room door opening. She can't help staring at the big pimp guy who follows Lex Cole into the room. Two days ago she probably would have burst out laughing, but not now. At the sight of Crisp, her pulse gallops. She wishes she could talk to him alone, let him know that she plans to tell them everything. The actual truth.

Crisp looks around the long table at Glynnie and her crew: two men, both white with salty hair and business suits, one dark gray, one dark blue; and two women, the white one blonde and dressed in a silk blouse and pearl choker, the Asian one red-haired and wearing all black. Clearly the woman in pearls, the bony one, is Glynnie's mother. He wonders which of the two men is her father.

Sandwiched within the austere quartet, Glynnie looks washed out and, somehow, slighter than before. A new gravitas weighs around her eyes. They look at each other, just look, the way you'd take in someone you know too well and wish you'd never met.

But *does* he wish that? Is it *her* fault that last night happened? Or did he abandon his free will out of…what? Self-doubt. He doubted his perceptions and his instincts, overthought his way through the disastrously stacking hours. He has only himself to blame.

Glynnie wonders if maybe last night wouldn't have happened if Crisp hadn't shown up outside her house. If she hadn't felt bad for him, the way he got arrested for diddly-squat on Wednesday. But as soon as she thinks that she knows it isn't true, knows it was her own choices that hit the flipper every time they spun off in a wrong direction. *Her* insistence that they get high. *Her* insistence that they go find JJ. *Her* insistence that they buy a gun. And *she* pulled the trigger, no one else.

Glynnie offers Crisp what looks to him like a genuine smile.

Crisp offers one back, a small gesture that Glynnie appreciates immensely.

As if upset by how they smiled at each other, the mother looks sharply at the man seated immediately to her left, the one in the blue suit. Crisp notices their matching wedding rings. Then he realizes that the other man, in the gray suit, looks familiar but he doesn't know why.

Harry finds the edge of the table, drops his briefcase onto it, scrapes out a chair, and arranges himself. Lex sits beside the lawyer. Crisp sits beside Lex, directly across from Glynnie's lawyer—and then the gray suit, receding hairline, and hangdog face strike a chord and Crisp remembers seeing him on one of the TV news stations Dedu likes to watch.

"That you, Ben?" Harry asks.

Ben Brafman, the celebrity lawyer, answers, "Harry, how'd you know?"

"Your cologne." The attorneys share a laugh.

Glynnie's lawyer looks at his clients with a stiff smile that appears to warn them against reacting to the blind pimp's appearance—at least that's how Crisp reads it, like a secret code between rich people to always pretend you're okay with whatever when really you almost never are.

Glynnie pretty much knows what her parents are thinking now. Her dad is figuring out how much it would cost to pay her lawyer to represent Crisp too, so as not to weaken *her* case; "The cost of doing business" is how he'd sum up the loss. Her mom is wishing she knew Harry when she cast *The Deuce* because sometimes hiring a nonactor who doesn't fully understand his own gifts of authenticity can be a stroke of genius on the part of the casting director. Or maybe not—maybe they're not thinking either of those things right now. Maybe her parents are just scared, like she is, and worried, like she is, that this time she might have pushed things too far. Maybe her parents just love her. Maybe if she could try not being such a prick to them all the time they could relax a little; maybe her dad would cut down on his drinking; maybe her mom would put on some weight. Maybe that's why they signed her up for Outward Bound: because *she's* the asshole, not them.

Saki says, "For the record, each person will need to identify him- or herself. I'll begin. My name is Detective Saki Finley, Eighty-Fourth Precinct, Brooklyn, New York."

Crisp glances up and around and locates the cameras installed in two corners of the room, filming them from opposite angles.

His brain lights up. Panic rises.

Don't.

He reminds himself of his intention to simply tell the truth, regardless of what Glynnie says or how her fancy lawyer might try to spin things in her favor. His own representation of what happened will stand as his own truth, the only truth he can carry all the way.

As the introductions continue, Crisp looks at Harry and it hits him that the blind lawyer doesn't see any of the surface details, not skin or clothes or whether someone chews her nails (the red-haired detective) or has an obvious eating disorder (Glynnie's mother) or the veiny nose of an alcoholic (her father) or that Crisp, though biracial, reads as black to the world. Crisp wonders if Harry was born without sight. He finds himself thinking about how that could be an asset, never being able to see yourself in a mirror or catch yourself reflected in someone else's eyes.

33

Walking along Newport Avenue through the quiet streets of Belle Harbor, toward home, Lex smells and hears and senses the restless lash of ocean two blocks in either direction—the long slip of the Rockaways traced by water from its beginning to its end. If he keeps moving in a straight line he'll simply plunge into the bay; then, if he lets himself drift, the ocean will have him. The thought of something so easy, so free of resistance, entices him for one flash of a moment. At first, what he loved about living here was this very sense of limitlessness. But now, tonight, perched on an edge all his own, the proximity to so much water and so much sky feels laced with threat.

He imagines various scenarios for what he might find at home, ranging from nothing (Adam gone, really gone) to everything (Adam waiting with one of the meals he sometimes makes with his signature flourishes of special oils and fresh herbs). In between, the possibilities are endless, and Lex settles on a compromise of Adam on the couch with a beer, absently watching the news while pretending not to wait for him to turn up. Exhausted, sad hellos. A takeout order placed. A glass of wine, two, and enough normalcy to allow them to slide into bed without stepping on each other's egos. In the morning, a civilized talk about how to repair things between them.

The white Victorian where they rent the second floor sits like a tatty but proud dowager that keeps the past alive in an otherwise changing world. So few of these old houses are left now amid the proliferation of brick apartment buildings and charmless single-family homes constructed more recently. The first-floor tenants appear to be home, the place lit up golden in the dark. No lights are on in the upstairs apartment.

Lex begins to cross the street when Adam appears on the path alongside the house, behind which their private entrance is accessed by an external rear stair.

So he didn't move out—unless that's what he's doing right now.

Dressed all in black, Adam is nearly swallowed by the darkness, but Lex knows that loping walk like he knows the rhythms of his own body. Feeling the tug of a cord of joy snarled by a filament of sadness, he backs into a shadow so he won't be seen.

Adam pauses to open his backpack. He takes out a knit cap and pulls it on. Swallowed up by some role he's playing, some secret he's convinced he can't divulge.

If you were working a case you'd follow him without question. As soon as Lex thinks this, he stops agonizing long enough to decide.

He silences his phone, slides it into his back pocket,

waits until Adam is a good way down the block. Stealthily, he trails him to a deli, where he emerges with a bag bulging with a purchase, then to the subway.

They arrive at the Prospect Park station at the edge of Prospect-Lefferts Gardens. Lincoln Road is populated with a mix of everyone at this hour—that last-chance margin of time between dinner and bed, a free-floating dance of coming home and going out. Lex yearns for that kind of normalcy, to reclaim the prosaic rhythms of an average day.

He wants to tell Adam to be more careful, to look over his shoulder from time to time, to notice when the atmosphere shifts from bustling to remote, as it does now, entering the park. To notice, damn it, that he's being followed! Lex knows he's good at this, he's surveilled enough people to know how to simultaneously hold a lead and fall away. But Adam should be more alert if he's going to lurk around alone at night dressed like a burglar.

A nineteenth-century lamppost sluices light across a stretch of path. Adam wades into it with the confidence of someone who knows where he's going. Lex trails him along the edge of East Drive, the road open to car traffic for only two hours on weekday mornings. Cyclists and runners own it now, and they whiz through the dark, lit mostly by a strong moon and the occasional lamppost. Adam and Lex pass signs for the Boathouse. Then Adam veers onto a footpath that cuts through a wooded area.

The lush silence is full of warning to Lex's vigilant ears. Each crack of twig, swish of pine needles, rustle of breeze carries some unnamed potential. He steps only when Adam steps, pauses when he pauses. At one point he thinks Adam is going to turn around—he almost *wants* him to turn around, to pay attention. Oblivious, Adam continues on the path until he reaches a clearing beneath an old stone bridge. A parks department sign on a defunct lamppost identifies Eastwood Arch.

Lex hangs back and watches. A twinge in his right calf reminds him of yesterday's cramp, how he hasn't felt it all day until now. He flexes his foot and realizes that, at last, it's gone. But still, a pulse of craving echoes in his brain like a beacon searching, searching for a willing receptor. *Fool me once*. He shakes his head, shuts it down.

An upturned floodlight illuminates the curved underside of the bridge under which some kind of quiet but determined activity is taking place. Half a dozen men and women dressed in dark clothes, some on ladders propped against the curved inner walls, some crouched at the lower edges. One man, perched high on a ladder, clenches something slender, a paintbrush, between his teeth. They're painting...lace, Lex sees, as his eyes adjust. A giant's orange body parts emerge from behind the lace with quiet violence, protuberances of elbow, knee, nose, toe tearing through the filigree. The only other color is a splash of yellow—a monstrous head of cartoon hair.

Is Adam part of this art project? The idea strikes Lex first as ludicrous, then perfect. Adam's said occasionally that he'd like a creative outlet, something to distract him from the complexities of studying the human mind. But this? And why would it need to be a secret?

Adam stands at the lip of the arch, and one of the artists

turns and sees him there. She begins to smile, as if he's expected, but her reaction hardens as her eyes move from Adam to Lex, thirty feet behind him.

Adam turns around to see what the woman is looking at.

Lex ducks into a shadow and hangs back until he's confident he wasn't noticed, feeling like a dirty old man caught observing something not meant for him. His mind churns, trying to understand this…this…what?

Then he remembers one of the headlines that zippered across the taxi's screen: BANKSY STRIKES AGAIN. He always assumed the guerrilla artist was just one person, but maybe he has a crew, and maybe Adam, *Adam,* is on it. The way Banksy's trademark quick flashes of work appear out of nowhere—it makes sense.

"Sorry," Adam says. "I didn't mean to interrupt."

"Yeah." A woman's voice, the woman who almost spotted Lex just now. "Could you maybe not say anything about this, at least until we're done?"

"I won't. Okay if I pass through?"

"No problem."

Lex's heart races—*Wrong again*. He edges out of the shadows to see Adam walking under the arch as the artists get back to work. He waits until Adam is all the way through and then follows, extending his own apologies and promises to the artists.

He follows along an asphalt path and then over root-humped grass and into a dark thicket. He hears a rhythmic slurp of water—they must be near the ravine. As they approach a low stone wall, Adam slows nearly to a halt and looks around.

Lex hangs back behind a stand of trees whose trunks are webbed with enough overgrown vines to provide decent cover. He watches Adam place the deli bag atop the wall, climb over, take the bag…and then disappear from view.

Adam says something inaudible. Another voice answers—a man's. The second voice is vaguely familiar and then it lands hard. It's William's voice, *William,* who Lex hasn't seen or heard since the night of Diana's party, the night he met Adam.

With a surge of adrenaline, Lex abandons pretense and comes out from behind the trees. He climbs over the wall and there, *there is Adam,* sitting on the ground, sharing a blanket with William.

William.

William on his back, bearded now, in filthy clothes, stinking of piss and booze. When Lex imagined Adam having a romantic rendezvous, it wasn't with *William* and it wasn't *like this.* An empty jug of water is over-turned beside the wall. Two cardboard cups lie scattered. A small plastic hairbrush, the kind a child might use, lies half inside one of the cups.

William rises onto his elbows at the sound of Lex's approach, then drops back onto the blanket, shaking his head.

Adam turns, freezes, stammers, "You—you followed me."

"What is this?" Lex stands at the edge of their blanket, feeling helpless as an eight-year-old.

"I've been trying to find the right time, the right way,

to tell you," Adam struggles to explain. "But I couldn't, and the longer I waited, the harder it got, and I knew you'd be angry."

"I'm not angry," Lex says. "I'm…I'm…" Enraged. Broken. A fat ant crawls along William's stomach and Lex can't find the right words for what he is.

"When I had lunch with Diana a couple weeks ago," Adam says, "she told me William was—"

But Lex doesn't want to hear it. He's seen enough. He suspected someone, anyone, but not William. William the thorn, the hopeless drunk, the giver of pain too tempting for Adam to resist. Adam the enabler, the fixer. Is that it? Has the power of their old dysfunction clawed them back together?

Appalled, Lex climbs back over the fence.

No. He won't let other people's failings weaken him.

He will not.

He digs into his pocket for the little packet of heaven and hell and tosses it into the darkness. *Never again.*

Adam jumps up to follow and keeps pace as Lex breaks into a jog. "I just wanted to help him," Adam says. "He's in trouble and—"

Lex's patience hardens, cracks. He stops. "When was he ever *not* in trouble?"

"This time's worse."

"*Right.*" Lex tries to hold back but emotion rises too quickly. "So now you're running back to him. No. Not running. Slow walking. Dragging it out to torture me. I'm going home. Don't come back. I never want to see you again."

"You've got this wrong."

"Go to hell, Adam—I'm not stupid and I'm not blind." Lex walks quickly in the direction of Eastwood Arch and the road out. Finally Adam's footsteps fall away and Lex is alone.

34

L ex lies on the couch at home, mired in a familiar heartbreak, exhausted beyond reason, mindlessly following a beam of light as it creeps across the ceiling.

He stiffens at the sound of footsteps coming up the outside stairs.

The apartment door rattles open and the quiet of Adam seeing him penetrates the living room. Adam asks, "Can I come in?"

"You here to get your things?"

"That's up to you." Adam turns on the overhead and the room pops into focus. He looks at Lex and says, "Please just hear me out."

Lex swings his legs to sitting. He can't feel anything, not even anger. He's too tired, too empty, too sad. Listening is something, maybe the only thing, he can manage right now.

"You followed me," Adam says.

"I shouldn't have. I didn't want to, but I couldn't resist."

"Then you *did* want to." Adam sits across from Lex.

Closer now, in full light, the dark rings beneath his eyes contrast vividly with his paler than usual skin. "Lex, what do you think you saw tonight?"

"To state the obvious, I saw you with William."

"What did you see that maybe wasn't so obvious?"

"Oh, *please*."

"Can I tell you?"

"I guess you're going to."

"You were right before—William's never not been in trouble. But now he's homeless, Lex—*homeless*. I've been trying to help get him off the street, that's all. Every night I call all the shelters and every night there's never a bed available. It's the least I can do—"

"Why do you have to do anything for that—" Lex holds his tongue. That what? Loser? Drunk? Shallow insults, like pebbles thrown at a storm, will only make him foolish. Now, in the calmer aftermath, Lex can recall that Adam and William had genuinely loved each other, they lived together a long time; what they had was real even if it rotted at the core.

"I don't *have* to do anything." Adam tones back his rising defensiveness. "I *choose* to. It's my...right."

"Are you going back to him?"

"He's a wreck."

"So you're not—"

"No fucking way."

"Adam." Lex inches forward on the couch. So the agony, this agony, won't come in the shape he expected days or even hours ago. It won't come shaped as abandonment, or reprieve. It will come as surrender. *"Adam."*

How long has Adam felt this troubled by guilt for leaving William last year? He's never talked about it. Another secret held tight to avoid upsetting Lex. And he realizes: *that* long.

Lex makes a call to HOME-STAT, the police department's partnership with Social Services, pulls a string or two, and by morning William's been picked up and installed in a bed at a shelter in the Bronx. As simple as that. Lex doesn't say it, but all Adam had to do was ask.

But it was never that simple, and it still won't be. In the morning, as they wake up in their bed and reach to hold hands, Lex grudgingly reminds himself that there's no such thing as simple when two adults with histories love each other. Adam may need to visit William (a self-destructive need, but a need still). Lex may need to let him (a need that will cross every boundary of his always-waiting-to-be-broken heart). Adam may need help coping with his codependency, which appears to be a more intractable problem than Lex realized. And Lex—Lex may need help staying strong. And if they make it, if they can stay together, this knowing of each other will only get deeper and harder and more surprising. And if they don't make it, it won't be for the reasons he guessed.

* * *

Early that evening, Lex feels something jabbing at him on the hammock's underside; someone is kicking him, not hard, but *kicking him*. He must have passed out, depleted after being on the water that afternoon, trying and failing to latch onto a decent wave.

He opens his eyes, raises his head from within the cocoon netting, and sees who it is. His brother, David, standing there with a raised foot.

"Wake up, loser."

"Who invited *you?*" Lex asks, as if he doesn't instinctively know the answer. He propels his legs around, pauses to still the chaotic rocking and to rub his deaf ear, then gets out of the hammock.

There, at one of the surf club's courtyard tables, Elsa sits with Adam under an open umbrella throwing its shade far afield. Adam in cutoffs, a *Yellow Submarine* T-shirt, and sunglasses. Elsa in her summertime white linen—long sleeves and long pants. Her hair falling around her shoulders in a pretty mess. Three open beers on the table.

Lex asks David, "How long have you been here?"

"You said five o'clock, so we were here at five."

"I told *Elsa* five o'clock." Lex grins, leans closer to his brother. "But I'm glad she brought you. I had a feeling she might. So where's the kid?"

"It's Saturday."

Right. Weekends, Ethan is with his mother.

Adam turns. "If it isn't Rip van Winkle."

"Sorry about that." He bends to kiss Adam's cheek.

"You needed it," Adam says. "How was the surf?"

"Ankle busters." Lex yawns. Stretches. "Hoping it'll pick up." He takes a seat at the table.

Adam asks, "Get you a beer?"

"Sure—unless Elsa really wants to see me on the board."

"You promised," she says.

"Seltzer," he tells Adam.

As soon as Adam disappears inside the club, leaving the beaded curtain shaking in his wake, Elsa leans forward and says, "Seems like things've settled down between you two."

"Last night," Lex says, "certain things came clear. I think we'll get it worked out."

"Hope so." She turns to smile at Adam as he appears through the shivering curtain with a cold bottle of seltzer.

Lex gulps down the water, bubbles sharp enough to sting going down. He tosses the empty bottle into the nearest recycling can. Smiles when it jumps off the rim of the can and lands inside. "Ready to hit the water?"

Elsa says, "Let's go."

Lex collects his board from his locker and they all walk the two blocks to the beach. The crowd has dispersed, leaving behind a handful of sunbathers and a stalwart few surfers.

Adam and David sit on the sand, facing the ocean. Elsa stands, her white linen snapping in the wind. Lex feels the plank of her gaze on his back, watching for clues that he'll be okay, that he knows what he's doing.

He wades into the froth, hoists the board above his head, immediately feels that the energy lacking earlier is here now. The water has come alive. He drops the board and hauls himself up and zags the surface until a wave appears that might pose an actual challenge. And then he rides it straight into its hollow heart.

PART FIVE

The View from Here

35

Sunday

A tiny child speeds past on a three-wheeled scooter and his mother chases, ponytail flying. Crisp watches until they vanish and Nolan Park is quiet again, just a couple picnicking on the grass and a lone woman reading on a bench.

Laura, the resident artist, comes out of the house with their tea, piping hot chamomile, and puts it down to cool on the front steps. She sits beside Crisp.

"Glad you decided to come back," she says.

"Yeah. Me too."

"That who you're waiting for?" Her gaze follows Crisp's to the man just then ambling into the park.

Crisp doesn't recall telling her he was waiting for anyone. It must be obvious. He says, "Yes."

She picks up one of the mugs, blows on it, stands. "Catch you later. Don't leave without saying good-bye this time."

"I won't."

Crisp studies everything about his father: the quick rhythm of his stride, the dark hue of his skin, the tight cut of his short hair, the deep set of his eyes, the breadth of his smile when he notices his grown son paying such close attention. Crisp's brain toggles between Crespo and Ramsey, Crespo and Ramsey, unable to settle on which one he most needs this man to be: the miserable father or the inspired artist. Right now, there is no both.

Mo raises a fist to bump hello but Crisp won't go for it. *Really?* They aren't a couple of dudes hanging out. He isn't sure exactly what this is. Finally, Mo lowers his hand and asks, "How'd it go? At the police station."

"How'd you know about that?"

"Called your mom. We talked."

"You *talked?*" Crisp can hardly imagine that conversation.

Mo nods soberly. "I hurt her very badly."

"Did you now?"

"I hurt you too. And I'm sorry."

But the words are ineffectual pellets against the hardness of this man's actions. Crisp asks, "Who the fuck are you, anyway?"

"I'm still your father."

"You were never my father."

"Okay. Well. I get it. Can I sit down?"

"Not yet."

"You tell me when."

Feeling patronized, Crisp doesn't respond to that. Confusion rears. He shakes his head. "I don't know why I asked you to come here."

"I was wondering that myself."

"You know what?" Crisp realizing this as he speaks: "I didn't ask *you*. I asked *Wilson Ramsey*. I used to read *The Life of a Boy* comics, I was really into it for a while—I mean, an invisible boy with no parents, no skin color, *and* superpowers? This is so fucked up I can't even process it."

"Listen, man, I can't process this shit either."

Despite himself, Crisp laughs.

Mo's smile returns. "Can Wilson Ramsey sit down, then?"

"Answer me something."

"Sure."

"Am I the invisible boy?"

"You don't look invisible to me."

"I'm not, obviously. But was I? Back then? In your mind?"

Mo takes a breath, nods. "I was trying to find you without looking, but I, well, let's just say I was the worst mess you could imagine back when I was about your age and even older."

"'I,' 'I,' 'I,' 'I,'" Crisp echoes, delivering an unsubtle observation about his father's narcissism, about how any father who abandons his children really only cares about himself when you strip away all the excuses. If Mo wants back into Crisp's life now, and if Crisp agrees to take him, he will have to realize that no one's going to make it easy.

Mo's eyebrows jerk up. "Yeah," he says smoothly. "I do hear that."

"All right," Crisp allows. "Wilson can sit down."

Mo places himself beside Crisp. "Never been to this island before, believe it or not."

"I hid out here all Friday morning."

"In this house?"

Crisp reconsiders whether he really wants to show Mo, Wilson, whoever he is, the mural he started on Friday: how he tried to invent and define someone whose absence was a perpetual wound, how he tried and failed to turn a feeling into a person. He looks at Mo, loose skin on a round face, their matching chins, the sorry eyes, and returns to the decision he reached lying in bed last night. *This* is how he can take control of the situation, at least for now.

"I want you to see something," Crisp tells him.

He leads Mo through the front door of the house. A white-haired woman in overalls kneels in one corner as if she's trying to burrow into the wall. Without turning around, she says, "Laura?"

"No—it's Crisp," he answers.

"And Mo," the father adds.

"Don't mind me," she says. "If I take my eyes off this I'll lose my line."

Reviewing his drawings, Crisp can't tell if they're better than he thought or worse. He can't tell if the small figure in the various frames looks like a man or a woman or even a person or just a blob. He can't tell if the stories are capable of translating from his thoughts into the mind of someone looking. He can't tell if he even cares.

Mo is looking. Looking intently. Stepping closer to see with tight focus. He asks Crisp, "You did this?"

"Just to be clear, I'm not an artist of any kind and I have no intention of ever being one."

"Got that. This supposed to be me?"

"Maybe. Yes." Obviously.

Mo looks at Crisp. "Want me to show you a thing or two?"

Crisp hesitates, wondering if that's a bad idea or a good idea. Every gesture from Mo feels overloaded. He answers, "Yeah, okay."

On their way to the supply cabinet, Mo asks, "What's my superpower?"

"What do you mean?"

"If I'm the man, what's my superpower? You going to make me invisible too?"

"I was thinking about it."

Standing in front of the open cabinet now, Mo inspects the paint markers. "Kind of meta. I like it. Except it could be more like a negative superpower, you feel me?"

"Yeah." And Crisp does; he *does*.

Using varying shades of gray, Mo begins to teach Crisp about working with black on white, how to shadow and shade, to create suggestions of light and dark without forfeiting shape. How to nuance a simple line.

As they work, bent together over the same patch of wall, Mo says, "You never answered me before. How'd it go with the cops?"

Crisp's pulse jackhammers. "Not sure I want to talk about it right now."

"No problem."

"I told the truth," Crisp says anyway. The last time

he saw Glynnie, she was sitting at that table with her parents and her fancy lawyer and the detectives. The next day, Crisp and his family gathered in Harry Johnson's drab government-issue closet of a work space. The blind lawyer, who saw things more essential than what Crisp observed with his eyes, steered him smoothly through the process.

His father asked a simple question and it feels stupid not to say what's what. "I'm not the one in trouble. They're charging Dante with breach of parole, unlawful firearms possession, and also kidnapping—for taking our phones and locking us in, and for grabbing JJ on his way to school. And Glynnie, my friend, *she* might have some problems."

"Dante Green." Mo sucks in his lips, picks up a smoke-gray paint marker, and in a few deft strokes creates a comically malicious figure wearing a crown and a flowing cape.

"That is spot-*on*. What, he have a thing for crowns his whole life?"

Mo grins with what looks like satisfaction, hearing his son break free for a moment. "Used to wear a plastic crown on his head when he was a kid, till the guys told him he looked like a royal fool."

"His jacket has crowns all over it."

"Oh, my." Mo shakes his head.

"What were you thinking," Crisp asks, "when he stepped into your Uber?"

"I almost drove away, but he got in too fast."

"Should have run him over."

They share a laugh.

"Listen, there's another thing your mom told me about—this thing with school. College. You ever call them back? Find out what they wanted?"

Crisp notices that Mo didn't say Princeton, didn't or couldn't or wouldn't. "I'm not so sure that place is for me," he says.

"Why not?"

"I won't fit in."

"You think everybody there's gonna be white, don't you?"

"Mostly, yes."

"Well if you don't go, most everybody *will* be." Mo laughs, but Crisp doesn't, can't.

"I don't even know if I'm black or if I'm white or what I am or even exactly *who* I am."

"You ever hear of Barack Obama?" Mo asks. "What is he?"

"He's just...Barack Obama."

"That's right."

"I'm not him."

"He wasn't him either at the age of nineteen."

Mo has a point. Obama must have felt out of place in the Ivy League, at first, until he dominated with his brain and his talent and his decency and became just *himself*.

Crisp asks, "Did you go to college?"

"I got married and had a baby. I went to work. I junked it up. That's three *I*s in a row—yeah, I'm a narcissist, you nailed me there. But you, you don't have to be *that*. You go get yourself some real skills, turn things around, stop thinking so much about yourself. You go to that school. Unless…"

"Yeah, I called them," Crisp tells him. "I did. I don't think they even know about any of the shit that went down."

"What'd they want, then?"

"Somebody backed out of freshman year, some kid they gave a fellowship to. So they offered it to me, said I was second on the list."

"A fellowship." Mo nods. "At *Princeton*." Finally saying it, and with emphasis. "What kind?"

"The lady called it a CLS—Critical Language Scholarship. For next summer. Something about the Department of State. I guess they think I'm good with languages."

"Are you?"

"Yeah. I am."

"Then you go *be* that."

"Maybe."

"That what you told them? *Maybe*?"

"Stop trying to be my father, okay?"

They get back to work on the wall. Crisp thinking now about next summer, which critical language he might choose to learn, because of course he told them yes.

36

Monday

Flanked by her parents in the sedan's backseat, Glynnie can see enough through the tinted windows to be reminded that it's a bright June morning: people crossing streets with their takeout coffees en route to work, nannies pushing strollers. The car crosses Atlantic Avenue and leaves Boerum Hill behind for downtown, where a long line of people shuffle through a tall arched entry as the arraignment court opens for the day. Two news trucks are parked on Schermerhorn Street across from the court. Standing on the curb in front of it, reporters and cameramen wait together, chatting like old friends.

The sedan loops around the block to a driveway that leads to an underground entrance that Ben Brafman arranged for them to use. Glynnie's attorney waits inside the glass door, where, just as he promised, there isn't a reporter or photographer in sight.

He takes her elbow and draws her in front of her parents, who follow close behind. The lawyer's cologne is strong up close. Orange juice bubbles up from her stomach into her throat and she coughs. She shouldn't have eaten anything, but she wasn't nervous then. She's nervous now, though, being led through the corridors under the courthouse. Their footsteps sound like a cavalcade of horses. The smell of something fried lingers in the elevator. The air, when they step into another hallway, is too cold and the skin on her arms and neck prickles.

Brafman opens a door marked BOOKING. He tells Mags and Nik, "Wait here, shouldn't be too long."

Her mother tries to smile but Glynnie wishes she wouldn't. Mags looks terrible, wrinkled and dry and beyond unrested. Her father put too much product in his short gray hair this morning and it holds the runnels left by his comb. She figures her parents are functioning the best they can without sleep. It's been a long, long few days for all of them.

The other night, as soon as they got home from the police station, her father went straight to his computer to make a fifty-thousand-dollar wire transfer to Ben Brafman, half for her bail, half for his retainer. In exchange, he arranged every shortcut in his power. He promised that, once she turned herself in, he'd plea down the initial charge of felony involuntary manslaughter to a misdemeanor. That there was a good chance she wouldn't have to do any jail time. That she'd be in and out of booking so fast, with him at the helm, that she wouldn't need to be transferred to a women's holding facility somewhere else. *Women's,* he said, and she *knew* that no one would ever again try calling her a girl.

At the booking desk, a heavyset African American officer places each of Glynnie's fingertips on a scanner one by one and uploads the images into her file. The glass feels greasy, which surprises her because she thought that, without ink, it would feel clean. Nothing about any of this, from Thursday night until now, has been what she expected.

Next, she stands against a measurement chart and the officer snaps her photo, front and profile, both sides. Her face goes slack and heavy as a dead animal each time the shutter clicks. So this is what it feels like to be arrested when, in your mind, at least—*in the context of the story as you experienced it, which, by default, was through a wholly subjective lens*—you did the only thing you could have in the moment, made the only choices that seemed available to you, but at the end of the day it's just another crime. Her mug shots are saved in the computer and it's done: her identity is fixed in place.

Is this how Crisp felt getting arrested last Wednesday? Watching your life take on a brand-new shape, knowing that even if you tried to smile you'd end up looking like shit in the photos.

The booking officer tells Brafman, as if Glynnie isn't even here, "You got about an hour before she can see the judge."

An hour. How can she wait here a whole hour? Brafman told them the process would be quick. But he doesn't complain.

He fake smiles at the clerk. "Thanks. Is there somewhere we can wait?"

The officer's gaze lifts off the screen and lands on Glynnie. "Holding cell, just like everyone else."

"No," Brafman immediately argues. "She'll be the only woman. It isn't acceptable."

"We could get her transferred to Queens for the wait."

"Not for an hour. Let's be reasonable."

The officer's eyebrows lift like caterpillar humps. "Sir, I'll need to get to my next customer now." A little smirk when he says that: *customer*.

Brafman looks at Glynnie as if to assess how much she can tolerate. She leans in to whisper, "There's a basketball court on the roof. If it isn't being used right now, could I wait there?"

It takes several phone calls but the lawyer makes it clear that he's worth his hefty retainer by swiftly accomplishing this minor goal. He goes to wait with her parents in the public area while a guard handcuffs Glynnie and escorts her back into the elevator. They ride in silence and get off at the last floor. He leads her through a hallway and past two locked gates. A box filled with worn basketballs sits outside a third gate.

"Want one?" the guard asks.

She shakes her head.

He deposits her alone into the outdoor cage, clangs shut the gate, locks it, and posts himself outside.

Glynnie walks to the middle of the cage and recalls the *snap snap snap* of the basketball on Wednesday, how she looked up and saw Crisp. Now all she hears is the mixed rumble of traffic and restaurant generators from the streets below—the exact same urban cacophony you hear from the Dreyfus brownstone whenever you open a window.

The view from up here is summer sky and an endless checkerboard of buildings. But if you pull in your gaze and look right in front of you, you see individual roof-tops with trees and umbrellas and furniture. You see a cracked-spined sun-bleached book someone left on a table. You see a pair of sandals stashed in a corner by a door. You see the lazy snake of an uncoiled hose dangling off a spigot.

You see the Dreyfus house.

She stands at the fence and curls her fingers through the chain link and tries to see what Crisp saw when he spotted her on her roof the other day. She notices how nice her family's deck looks from up here, nicer than she ever realized. She notices that the slew of buds on her mother's rosebush are plumper than they were last week, almost ready to bloom. She tries to picture herself there last Thursday afternoon, smoking her dope, thinking her thoughts, feeling the sun on her skin, feeling so great because high school was finally over. But she can't see it; that girl is gone.

ACKNOWLEDGMENTS

Every idea that becomes a book is guided by silent partners who deserve distinction alongside the author. This book's invisible hero is Emily Giglierano, whose extraordinary editorial instincts shone a path through thickets of early drafts as together we discovered the shape of this novel. I'm deeply grateful for her willingness to read and reread, to think and rethink, to talk and talk some more as we found our way to the heart of this story. It's been a true pleasure to work with so many talented people at Mulholland Books and Little, Brown and Company: Josh Kendall, Reagan Arthur, Judy Clain, Maggie Southard Gladstone, Sabrina Callahan, Pamela Brown, Michael Noon, Nell Beram, Nicky Guerreiro, and Neil Heacox. At Mulholland UK, editor Ruth Tross continues to be a fantastic partner on every front. The other invisible hero standing behind this book is my agent and guiding force, Dan Conaway at Writers House, who, along with Andrea Vedder and Peggy Boulos Smith, keeps the channels open and the work flowing, always with heart. Last but certainly not least, thanks to my husband, Oliver, for all his love and support throughout our long shared journey.

ABOUT THE AUTHOR

Karen Ellis is the author of *A Map of the Dark* (book one in The Searchers series) as well as numerous other novels. She lives in Brooklyn, New York. Learn more at karenellisbooks.com.